THE ABDUCTION OF MARY ROSE

Joan Hall Hovey

ISBN: 978-1-77145-213-7

Published By:

Books We Love Ltd.
Chestermere, Alberta
Canada

http://bookswelove.net

Deep into the darkness peering long I stood there, wondering, fearing,

Doubting, dreaming dreams no mortal ever dared to dream before.

Edgar Allan Poe, The Raven

.

Chapter One
1982

The teenage girl hurried along the darkening street head down in a vain attempt to divert attention from herself as she headed for her bus stop, still over a block away. The car behind her was a soft growl in the still, warm air.

It was mid-June, only two weeks till school closed. The air was fragrant with the smell of lilacs that grew here and there along the street. She wore a jean skirt and white cotton shirt, and yet she felt as exposed and vulnerable as if she were naked. She was anticipating the freedom of summer and thinking about spending more time with her new friend Lisa when she became aware of the car following her. She had been thinking maybe she and Lisa would swim in the pond edged with the tall reeds near her house where she sometimes fished with her grandfather. She'd let grandfather meet Lisa. She knew he would like her. It would be impossible not to like Lisa, even though her grandfather didn't quite trust white people.

The growl of the motor grew louder, and she heard the

window whisper open on the passenger side, close to her. "Where you goin' in such a hurry, sweet thing?"

She didn't turn around, just kept on her way toward the bus stop, one foot in front of the other, as fast as she could go without running. Music thumped loudly from the car radio, pounding its beat into the night. It was not music she would have listened to, not like the music they'd played on Lisa's tape player tonight, and that she and Lisa had danced to in Lisa's room. Lisa had tried to teach her some new steps; it had been so much fun. They danced to songs by Ray Charles, Stevie Wonder, Diana Ross' Mirror, Mirror and a bunch more she couldn't even remember. Lisa had a lot of records.

The music that blasted from the car sounded angry and unpleasant. The car drew up so close to her she could smell the alcohol the men had been drinking, mixed in with the gas fumes.

The car edged even closer to the curb, and the man said something ugly and dirty out the window to her and his words made her face burn, made her feel ashamed as if she had done something wrong though she knew she hadn't. She pretended not to hear, made herself look straight ahead, her eyes riveted on the yellow band around the distant pole that was the bus stop, just up past the graveyard. She kept moving forward, one foot in front of the other, trying not to look scared, and prayed they would go away. Fear made her heart race.

The day was fast fading, the sky a light mauve, only a sprinkling of stars yet. Soon it would be dark. She was always home before dark. Grandfather would be worried.

A few more minutes and you'll be at the bus stop, she told herself. Ignore them. But it was impossible to do with the car following so close that the heat from the motor brushed her bare legs, like a monster's breath.

The car crawled along beside her. She moved as far away as she could get, but the pavement was next to none along here and broken. "Hey, sweet thing," the man said. "You trying to get away from us?" He laughed.

Despite herself, she turned her head and looked straight into the man's face. He was grinning out at her, showing his square, white teeth, causing her heart to pound even louder than the music. He made her think of the coyotes that sometimes came skulking around grandfather's house at night hunting for small cats and dogs. No. I am wrong. He is not like the coyotes. They are just being coyotes. It is a noble animal. An evil spirit dwells within this beast. One tied with the most fragile of chains. She could feel him straining toward her, teeth bared. She would not have been surprised to see foam coming from his mouth.

Softly, he said, "Hey, Pocahontas, want a ride?"

Feeling as if a hand were at her throat, she darted a look behind her, praying to see someone, anyone, who might help her, but the street was deserted. She'd left the row of wooden houses behind her a good ten minutes ago and was now at River's End Cemetery. There was no sidewalk at all here, just the dirt path, broken curb on her left and the empty field to her right, leading up into the graveyard. If a car comes along, she thought, I'll just run right out into the middle of the road and flag it down. But none did.

She visualized herself safely inside the bus and on her way home to Salmon Cove, to her grandfather's small blue house on the reservation. She would tell him all about Lisa, her new best friend from school. Her grandfather would smile at her, and be pleased for her and call her his little Sisup. She fingered the pendant around her neck that he had made for her, a kind of talisman. To keep evil spirits away.

Grandfather didn't always understand the white man's world though, and there would be worry on his weathered face because she was not home yet. But she would make them a pot of tea and they would talk, and he would forget his worry.

She was still focused on the bus stop, the utility pole marked by its wide yellow band. With the car so close, the thrum of the motor vibrating through her, the bus stop seemed a mile away. She walked faster, a chill sweeping through her body. She was forced now to walk on the slight incline that led up to the graveyard. Only the ruined curb separated her from her tormentors.

A taxi fled past, but she'd been so intent on getting to the bus stop she'd noticed it too late. It had been going so fast, out of sight already, just pinpoints of taillights in the distance, then nothing.

"Hey, what's your hurry, squawgirl?"

She gave no answer, swallowed, and kept going. When the man did not speak for several minutes, she became even more frightened by his silence than his talk. The boys at school sometimes called her Indian, and other dumb stuff like pretending to be beating on war drums, or doing a rain dance, and though it hurt her feelings and sometimes even made her cry, this was different. The boys thought they were being funny. Not so with this man. She could feel his contempt, even hatred for her, and something else, something that made her mouth and throat dry and her blood race faster. As she continued to put one foot in front of the other on the worn, rocky path edging the graveyard, she was very careful not to stumble and become like the wounded deer under the hungry eye of the wolf. She kept her eyes on the pole with its yellow band. In the darkening sky, a high white moon floated.

Everything in her wanted to break into a run, but a small voice warned her that it would not be a wise thing to do. Anyway, no way could she outrun a car. Why did the bus stop seem so far away? It was like a bad dream, where no matter how fast you run you don't go anywhere, and whatever is behind you ... draws closer and closer.

She shouldn't have stayed so long at Lisa's. But they'd been having such fun, just talking and listening to music, sharing secrets. It was nice to have a best friend, to feel like any other teenager. *But you're not like any other teenager. You're an Indian.* She should have listened to her grandfather.

The man spoke again. "C'mon, get in, Pocahontas," he said, his tone quiet, chilling her. "We'll have us a little party." He reached a hand out the open window and she shrank from his touch, stumbled, nearly fell, tears blinding her. She heard the driver laugh, a nervous laugh and she knew he was a follower of the other man. There was an exchanged murmur of words she couldn't make out, then, the car angled ever closer to her, wheels scraping the curb, making her jump back.

"Got something for you, sweetheart," the grinning man said. "You'll like it."

More laughter, but only from him now. Adrenaline rushed through her and she started to run, ignoring the warning voice. But it was too late. The car shrieked to a stop and instantly the door flew open and the man burst from the car and grabbed her. She screamed and fought to free herself from the steel arm clamped around her waist, but it was no use. She kicked and clawed at him, but he lifted her off her feet as if she were a rag doll and threw her into the back seat, and scrambled in after her. He shut the door and hit the lock. "Go," he yelled at the driver but the car remained idling. The man looked over his shoulder, started to say something but the man holding her down yelled at him a second time to go, louder, furious, and they took off on squealing tires.

"Please let me out," she begged. "Please…" Her pleas were cut off by a powerful back-hand across the mouth, filling it with the warm, coppery taste of blood. "Gisoolg, help me," she cried out, calling on the spiritual god of her grandfather, and of his grandfather before him. But no answer came.

Up in the graveyard, an owl screeched as it too swooped down on its night prey. And all fell silent.

Chapter Two
Twenty-Eight Years Later

Naomi's mother lay motionless in her hospital bed, her cancer-ravaged body a small mound beneath the white sheet. A child's body rather than a woman's. She'd become so thin in the past weeks, as if she were slowly disappearing before Naomi's eyes, which was, in essence, true.

Naomi glanced up at the now familiar footsteps out in the corridor and gave a brief, sad smile of acknowledgement to the tall, slightly stooped man walking past the door, nodding in at her. They were unwilling members of the same club. Mr. Howell's wife had been admitted two weeks earlier with terminal cancer, the same cruel disease that was killing her mother.

Muffled conversation drifted to her from the kitchen across the hall, along with the aroma of freshly perked coffee. Someone laughed. Life defiant, even in the midst of death and dying. This was the Palliative Care unit of River's End General Hospital. No one got better in here. Only made as comfortable as possible in whatever time was left.

This was Naomi's first intimate experience with death and dying. Her mother was the most important person in her life, and it was hard to think about her not being here. They'd never experienced the mother/daughter conflicts she'd heard and read so much about, and witnessed between Aunt Edna and Charlotte, and she knew how blessed she was. They were best friends as well as mother and daughter. Her mother was her cheering section, and always the first to hear the latest book Naomi had narrated.

Though she had little heart for work lately, she did manage to finish narrating the last two chapters of the new children's book her publisher had sent, before leaving tonight for the hospital. Deadlines couldn't be put off, and she hoped it was good enough. If not, they could assign another voice talent to redo it and she would forgo her fee.

It was so hard to focus, to shut out the horror that was happening to her mother. She's given so much of herself to others. To me. It wasn't fair.

Naomi saw herself as if in a movie, shutting down the computer, showering, giving her long, dark hair a quick brush into a chignon of sorts because it was easiest, then driving here to the hospital. Sometimes she'd grab a sandwich in the cafeteria, and often spent the night on the cot they'd brought in for her, her routine for the past three months. A routine that would soon be broken.

"A matter of hours," the nurse had whispered when Naomi arrived tonight. "I've already called her sister."

At the ping of the elevator down the hall, Naomi glanced at her watch. 7:00 p.m. Her stomach clenched involuntarily. Aunt Edna. Her aunt's presence was further announced by the aggressive click of Italian leather boots on the highly polished floor. The fragrance of the L'Eau d'Issey perfume she always wore preceded her into the room.

Edna strode in with barely a nod at her. Her hair is different, Naomi thought. It was a lighter shade of blond, cut shorter, youthful. She wore a dove grey suit and a silk royal blue print scarf.

Edna always looked so nice, so perfectly put together. If she would just smile once in a while. But then, she rarely smiled at her niece. Her mother's younger sister had never liked her, in fact barely tolerated her, though she was always careful to hide it when Mom was around. But a look can speak volumes, especially to the shy, sensitive child she had been. She had tried so hard to please Aunt Edna, running to her with a poem she'd written, a drawing she'd done. But her aunt acted as if Naomi were a scraggly mutt wanting to jump up on her with muddy paws. Naomi had stopped trying a long time ago. But the hurt was still there. And Aunt Edna never failed to stir a vague sense of inadequacy in Naomi.

Standing at the foot of sister's bed, Edna said, "How is she?"

How do you think she is? She's dying. She didn't say that of course. What she said was, "Sleeping quietly."

Edna gave a sigh of impatience, of resignation, as though her niece was quite incapable of intelligent thought or comment. "I can see that, Naomi. You should go home and get some sleep yourself. You look like hell. Almost as bad as Lili."

"I'm okay. But...thanks."

Edna wasn't there five minutes before she began her predictable fidgeting, Now restlessly turning pages in a *People* magazine someone had left. Why did it seem so loud? She tossed it on the chair and wandered to the window.

Not much to see out there, Naomi thought, following her gaze. Through the opening in the heavy oatmeal drapes, only the lower half of the steeple of St. Luke's church was visible, its top erased by the thick fog that so often shrouded River's End. Naomi was glad the sun wasn't shining. It would have seemed a further betrayal to her mother who would never feel the sun's warmth on her face again. The thought brought a lump to her throat. *Don't cry, dammit. Not in front of her.*

Edna abruptly turned away from the window and busied herself pouring more water into the aqua plastic glass with its L-shaped straw. An unspoken criticism of the nurses? Or me? Naomi thought. What else is new? No, I'm being unfair. She just feels a need to perform some small act of kindness for Mom while she still can.

Thinking Edna might like to spend some time alone with her sister, Naomi rose from her chair, "I'm going to get a coffee, Aunt Edna. I'll bring you a cup? How would you like ...?"

"No, no coffee for me." She glanced at her watch as if there were some important appointment she had to get to. "I can't stay."

Anger flashed hotly through Naomi, but she didn't give it voice. The last thing Mom needs is a scene between me and Edna. She motioned Edna out in the corridor. Maybe she didn't understand that the big sister she claimed to love so much, she might not see again.

"The nurse said it's just a matter of hours, Aunt Edna," she whispered. "You might want to..."

Edna had turned to the picture on the wall with its mirrored frame and began fussing with her scarf, fluffing it just so at her neck. "That's what they said last week, and the week before that. Not that it wouldn't be a blessing. Damn, I hate this place. It stinks of death. You can taste it."

She was right about that. There was an underlying smell of death on this floor that all the potpourri in the world couldn't mask. But at least you get to leave here, auntie, she thought. And was glad when she did.

Naomi couldn't see the vengeful bitter malice on her aunt's face as Edna headed for the elevators but she sensed it in the rigidness of her back, and it puzzled her, as she was always puzzled by Edna.

* * *

Edna was gone maybe a half hour when the night nurse popped her head in and said hi.

Carol Brannigan was an angel with red hair, a million freckles and kind brown eyes that had witnessed many such nights on this floor, with many families. Over the past weeks, a friendship of sorts had formed between them. She was a comforting presence.

"Anything you need, Naomi?" she half-whispered. "Can I get you a cup of tea?" "Just had coffee, thanks, Carol. I'm good. How about you? Busy night?"

She came further into the room, her shoes squeaking faintly on the tiled floor. "Not so bad." She checked her patient's pulse, a futile task, Naomi knew, performed mostly for her benefit. "She's so good," the nurse said softly. "If it's true what they say about nurses making the worse patients, then your mom is the exception."

It was true. In the two years since she'd been diagnosed with cancer, rarely did Naomi hear her complain. Except sometimes in the night, when the drugs did not quite reach the pain. Or if she'd been having a bad dream. Never, when she was awake though. Although she knew by the little frown on her forehead that the pain was bad, and would give her the pills, sometimes a little before she was supposed to take them. Naomi was grateful to have the responsibility taken over by the nurses.

Soon she was alone again. The only sound in the room was her mother's shallow, raspy breathing. Once, a gurney rattled by out in the corridor. Someone paged a Dr. Johnson, and then it fell silent.

"Naomi."

Naomi had closed her eyes without realizing it. "Mom, hi." So little to say to her now.

And yet so much— years of conversations they would not have.

"Is Edna here, dear? I thought I heard her voice."

"She was, Mom. She just left a while ago. She didn't want to wake you."

Her mother nodded. "I'm so blessed to have you," she said, her voice weak and thready. Her hand trembled as it reached for

Naomi's who covered it with her own. Beneath hers, her mother's hand felt fragile as a sparrow's wing. It was hard to talk past the thickness in her throat.

"I'm the one who's lucky, Mom."

Her mother spoke slowly, with difficulty, struggling for breath between the words. "Have you been happy, darling, being my daughter?" The effort of making a full sentence had exhausted her and she closed her eyes.

"Of course I have. You're the most wonderful mother any girl could have. You know that." Her voice broke and despite her best efforts, the tears seeped out, but her mother had looked away and didn't see them, for which Naomi was grateful.

When she turned to look back at Naomi, her faded eyes were full of confusion, as if she'd been about to say something and now could not remember what it was. A faraway look came into her eyes. Naomi searched her eyes, as blue as a summer's sky before she got sick, and wondered what she saw down that long corridor of the past. Maybe she sees Thomas. Maybe he's waiting to guide her into the next world, his hand reaching out to take hers.

She couldn't know of course if that's what happened when we leave this world, but the thought warmed her and gave her a measure of comfort. She envisioned Thomas' young, smiling face -- the face in the photo sitting on her night table, from where, according to her mother, she got her own looks. It was true she had her father's eyes, wide, bracken green. She also had that hint of a cleft in her chin. 'He was even more handsome in person', her mother had said.

She wished she could have met him, her hero father. His full name was Thomas James Waters and he went missing in action in the final days of the Vietnam War.

Although she missed having a father growing up, her mother had told her wonderful

stories about him, and she felt as if she knew him. Besides, she had his picture to talk to and his medals to remind her of his bravery.

Her mother had drifted off again, her breathing raspy, labored. The lights in the corridor dimmed, a cue that visiting hours were over, although if someone wanted to stay on, there would be no problem. Knowing time was short for most of the patients in here, the rules were relaxed. She heard the elevators going down, many visitors leaving, to return tomorrow. The quiet on the floor deepened to a hush.

As the clock ticked toward midnight, Naomi fell asleep in the chair as she sometimes did before removing herself to the cot. And she dreamed the old dream. It had been lying in wait for her:

She is running across a field, small sneakered feet flying, the long grasses brushing her legs. Above her, the flapping of giant wings is as loud as wind-whipped sheets on a clothesline, filling her heart with terror. But no matter how fast she runs, she cannot outrun the great shadow-wings that darken the grass before her, like a black cloud obscuring the sun.

She let out a small cry and it startled her awake. Sitting straight up in the chair, she could still hear the beating of wings echoing in the air around her, as if they had followed her here from some other dimension. What did it mean? Was the winged creature a symbol of death? Was it as simple as that? Yet she couldn't recall any past deaths associated with the dream she'd been having off and on since childhood.

She glanced at her watch; 12:05 a.m. She had been asleep only a few minutes. Her cry, if she'd indeed cried out in her sleep, hadn't sent anyone running into the room. So perhaps it was part of the dream.

Her mother's breaths were coming at longer intervals now, with long, frightening silences between. She drew her chair closer to the bed, the leg making a small scraping sound on the floor.

She found herself trying to breathe for her mother. Pushing the breath from her lungs, breathing it in, exhaling. *Breathe, Mom.* At the same time, she prayed for it to be over.

At twenty past one, her prayer was answered Her mother simply stopped breathing. The quiet of the room had not been quiet at all. Now it was.

Naomi sensed the instant her soul abandoned the still, ravaged body on the bed. The shell that lay there was no longer her mother. But Naomi could feel her life-spirit lingering close by, close and warm, saying goodbye, then she was gone. She remained at her bedside for a good minute before she went to fetch the nurse.

She called Edna from the nurse's station. "She's gone." Those two words seemed to burst the dam within her and all the tears she'd been saving up these past months flooded over, and she was sobbing into the phone, unable to stop herself.

"Pull yourself together, Naomi," her aunt said. "It's for the best, you know that. It's not as if we weren't expecting it. You go on home now. I'll take care of things. I'll take the obituary into the paper in the morning."

Obituary. She mopped her eyes with a wad of tissue a nurse handed her, touching her shoulder gently before moving on down the corridor. Naomi blew her nose noisily. There were things she must attend to. "I'll do that, Aunt Ed..."

"No need. I already have it written up. You go home and get some sleep. We'll talk later." Naomi didn't have the heart or the strength to argue with her. Let her have her way, what did it matter? Even if she won her point, what would be gained? If Edna wanted to write the

obituary, let her. Regaining her composure as best she could, she made her second call, this one

to Frank Llewellyn, her mother's longtime friend and attorney.

Frank lived in a large Victorian house at the edge of town with his black Labrador Retriever, Sam. He'd never married and Naomi suspected it was because he'd always been in love with her mother. But though her mother valued Frank's friendship, had even come to rely on it, she had not loved him back in the same way.

She heard his heavy sigh over the line, but he registered no surprise at the news. He'd been waiting for her call, had been here earlier in the day. His voice cracked a little as he said, "If there's anything you need, Naomi..."

"I'm okay, thanks, Frank. I just wanted you to hear it from me, not read it in the paper. Aunt Edna has the obituary written up and plans to take it in in the morning."

"Thanks, honey. I appreciate the call. I know how tough this is for you." "I know you do, Frank. I feel like I'm six years old. I already miss her."

"Did she say anything before...?"

Does he want me to say she spoke his name? No, she wouldn't lie. "Nothing. Well, other than to ask me if I'd been happy being her daughter. Such a foolish question." Her eyes brimmed over again.

There was a long silence, then, "Sam wants out, Naomi. He's scratching at the door. We'll talk tomorrow." With that, the line went dead.

Naomi frowned at the phone and replaced the receiver.

Chapter Three

Naomi chose her mother's favorite indigo blue dress with the cream lace collar and cuffs to lay her out in. She'd worn it just that one time to the dinner given in her honor by the nurses' union. The pearl earrings Naomi had given her for her last birthday went perfectly. Everyone said she looked beautiful, just like she was asleep. And it was true: death had erased the pain lines from the cancer. She looked at peace.

The funeral parlor was filled with flowers from co-workers, friends and neighbors. At home, saran-wrapped food covered the counter-top and was crammed into every available space in the fridge.

Over the years, Lillian Waters had been a fearless advocate for better working conditions for nurses, friend and mentor to many. And the letters and cards at home from grateful patients gave testimony to the fine nurse she had been.

Naomi was reading the note on one of the cards tucked into a lovely basket of summer flowers positioned at the foot of the casket when a voice said softly at her shoulder, "She looks so lovely, doesn't she?"

Naomi could only nod her agreement. She felt drained and constantly on the verge of tears, and doing her best to keep it together. Mrs. Devers smiled sympathetically through the dotted veil of her little black hat. Connie Devers ran one of the last surviving corner stores in River's End, and was a fount of information on its inhabitants, both living and dead.

"You know, Naomi," the woman said, lowering her voice conspiratorially, "I didn't know you were adopted until I read it in this morning's paper."

Naomi looked at her, at a loss. "Adopted? I'm not adopted, Mrs. Devers." What was she talking about? "What paper?" she asked foolishly.

"The local paper, of course, dear. Your mother's obituary. Oh, dear." She thrust out a hand in a futile gesture of self-correction. Drew it back. "Oh, I'm so sorry. You didn't know, did you? You haven't seen it yet." She leaned closer to Naomi. "You know, dear, I didn't think you wrote that piece up when I read it. It seemed very odd to me that you would have put your own name last in the list of survivors, even if you were adopted..."

Mrs. Dever's mouth was still moving behind the dotted black veil but Naomi could no longer hear anything she was saying, as though all sound had been sucked from the room. And then she heard herself saying, "There's obviously some mistake, Mrs. Devers. They must have gotten it mixed up with someone else's obituary."

The woman blinked pitying eyes at her. "Yes, yes, dear. Of course. That would explain it. God knows, they make plenty of mistakes in that newspaper."

It was then that she caught Edna's eye across the room. Edna quickly turned her head away and began talking to a woman next to her.

* * *

Naomi let herself into the house, picked up the newspaper from the hall floor on her way out to the kitchen. She dropped the paper on the table, took two Tylenol for a throbbing headache and plugged in the water for tea. She had slipped away from the parlor shortly after talking to Mrs. Devers. The woman had obviously made a mistake, yet Naomi needed to reassure herself.

She sat down and opened the paper. The pages rattled as she turned them, seeming to echo in the empty house. Strange, she'd been living alone in this house for weeks now and this

was the first time it seemed empty, as if its owners had been away for a long time. As if even her own presence made little impact. She might have merely been the woman who had come to water the plants and feed the cat. Speaking of which, here she is now, silent as a little shadow. "Hey, girl. How you doin'?" She reached down and scratched her behind the ears. She was grateful for Molly, a sweet-natured grey and white ball of fluff who, one night in the dead of winter ten years ago now, had shown up on their doorstep, cold and hungry.

Molly wandered over to her empty dish and looked expectantly up at her. Naomi left the paper and went to the fridge. "Hungry, girl?"

Opening the door, she retrieved the can of Whiskas from behind a saran-wrapped plate of brownies. The cat wove her silky soft self around Naomi's ankles, purring like an old washing machine as her mistress dished out her food.

The water bubbled in the kettle and she made a pot of tea. The Tylenol was kicking in, taking the edge off her headache. Leaving Molly contentedly eating her dinner, Naomi sat down again with her cup of tea and turned to the obituary page. At once saw the picture of her mother that Edna had taken into the paper. Taken months after she was diagnosed with cancer, she looked older than she was, drawn, the illness already taking its toll... It was not the photo Naomi would have chosen. There was nothing of her mother's achievements in the obituary, either. Only a brief paragraph stating that she'd been a nurse at River's End General Hospital for many years and that she died after a lengthy illness, survived by a younger sister, Edna (Harold), Bradley, two nephews, Brian and Theodore (Ted), niece Charlotte, and an adopted daughter, Naomi Lynne.

Adopted? She had to read the word a few times to be sure she'd read it correctly. Mrs. Devers was right. But it made no sense. She wasn't adopted. And why was there no mention of Naomi's father, Thomas Waters, Lillian's late husband, a war hero? Why was his name excluded? Confused and frightened in a way she didn't yet understand, she got up from the table.

Her hand was shaking so hard she had to punch in her aunt's number twice before she got it right. Why did she write it up this way? She thought of Edna watching her when Mrs. Devers was talking to her, and a cold, hard fear slid just beneath her rib cage.

Her aunt picked up on the first ring. She's been waiting for my call. Of course she would be. She must have left the parlor right after me.

"I just read Mom's obituary, Aunt Edna. I don't understand..."

"No, I don't suppose you do. I know this isn't easy for you, but it's time the truth be told, Naomi."

"Truth. What truth? What are you talking about, Aunt Edna? What's going on?" The headache was back full force.

"Lillian was remiss in letting you live a lie all these years. In living one herself, and making the rest of us go along. It wasn't fair to you, to any of us."

Her hand tightened on the receiver as she tried to ignore the chill around her heart, the lump of fear that worked its way up into her throat. "What do you mean, Aunt Edna? What are you talking about? What lie?"

After a hesitation, she said, "Ask Frank Llewellyn. He handled everything at the time. Lili always could wrap him around her little finger. I have nothing more to say on the matter, Naomi. I'm sorry if you're upset, but I know I'm doing the right thing and one day you'll thank me." With that, the phone clicked in Naomi's ear. She could only stare in disbelief at the dead receiver in her hand. She's making this up. She just wants to hurt me.

The latter was no doubt true. But as much as she wanted to believe she was lying about

the rest of it, needed to believe she was, she couldn't deny the ring of truth in Edna's words. Naomi was about to dial Frank's office when the doorbell rang. She opened the door to see her mother's old friend standing there, looking both miserable and furious, clutching the rolled up newspaper in his hand, and unwittingly confirming everything. Yet she could not take it in. It wasn't possible.

"I'm so, so, sorry, Naomi," Frank said. "I don't know why Edna did that. She's a spoiled, wretched woman and I'd like to kill her. It was a terrible way for you to find out."

Each word was a hammer striking her heart. It was true then.

She took in Frank's familiar features beneath the prematurely white hair. Frank, who had always reminded her a little of Dick Van Dyke, without the shtick. He was a smart man, a tough lawyer, but also a good man. An honest man. Or so she had always thought. But it was clear he'd been part of the conspiracy. *Lili always could wrap him around her little finger.*

"Come in, Frank. I've made tea. I hope you're hungry." In times of stress, people eat. She'd read that somewhere. Silently, she proceeded to set out small plates of sandwiches and cakes from the array of food neighbors had provided, glad to have something to do with her hands. Some distraction from the bomb that had just been dropped on her. As she poured the tea, steam rose invitingly from the cups. But sitting across from Frank, the cup of tea held in both her hands, its warmth could not penetrate the coldness that had gripped her since reading that obituary. No. Correction. Since Mrs. Devers approached her at the funeral parlor. It should have softened the blow. It didn't.

She set her cup of tea down on the table and folded her

hands under her chin. The round maple table at which she and Frank sat was still the same. Still solid under her elbows. The eyes of the owl clock ticked back and forth back and forth as they had for years. The wallpaper with its geometric pattern with randomly space tiny orange squares, hadn't changed. Yet everything was different now. The earth had shifted beneath her feet, and she was hanging on for dear life to keep from spinning off into space.

"So," she said, with just the slightest tremor in her voice. "Lillian Waters was not my real mother."

She saw him wince. "Don't say that, Naomi. Don't even think it." He leaned forward and looked deeply into her eyes to give his words added weight. "She loved you more than life itself. She may not have given birth to you, but no could have loved you more. Wanted you more." He tried to smile and fell short. "Even before she laid eyes on you."

In a kind of frantic move, he was opening his briefcase, producing what she recognized as her mother's Will. He slid it tentatively across to her, like a peace offering. "But for some generous bequests to Edna and her children, and a couple of charities, everything she had in the world she left to you, Naomi. Including this house, of course. I've made some decent investments for your mother over the years. You're far from wealthy, but we're still talking about a considerable amount of mon..."

"Surely you can't imagine I care about any of that, Frank. Tell me everything now. Please. Enough lies." Edna was right about that much at least.

Frank sighed, raked a hand though his hair and slid the Will back into the briefcase. He sipped his tea, then set the cup down on the saucer; it rattled lightly. He sighed. "It's an old story," he said finally. "A teenager gives birth to a child she can't take care of. Your mother was working on the maternity ward at the time. She wanted you. It's as simple as that, and as complicated. Nothing would do until you became hers. I made it happen. She took some time off and went When she returned, she told everyone she'd been secretly married to Thomas

Waters, and that he was killed in the war. No one questioned her. Lili was a pretty straight arrow. I suppose there were any one of a dozen ways the truth could have come out, but strangely it never did. Her only mistake was in confiding to Edna."

"I see." But she didn't. She didn't see at all. Such a bizarre story. "My-- my birth mother. Who was she?"

After a long pause during which he stared into his tea cup, he said, "I knew. She admitted herself into the hospital under a false name. And the day after you were born she slipped away in the middle of the night. Just disappeared into the streets, and no one ever heard from her again. End of story."

Naomi didn't think so. The story, as it stood, held a false note, seemed too pat.

"One good thing has come out of this," he said, trying for a cheerful note and not quite managing it.

"Oh? And what would that be, Frank?"

He pretended not to hear the sarcasm in the question as he

said, "You can cut all ties with Edna Bradley. And without any guilt whatever. I don't think anyone would blame you if you never spoke to the woman again. In fact, if she phones you, I'd advise you as both your friend and your lawyer, to hang up on her."

You're not my lawyer, she thought. You were Lillian's lawyer. And why don't you want me talking to Edna? "Edna was against the adoption, I take it."

"Sometimes I think she was against Lili, period. It was a kind of love/hate thing. She's always been jealous of her older sister while at the same time she looked up to her. It's complicated. Lili practically raised Edna after their mother died, you know. Edna was nine, Lili seventeen at the time."

"Yes, Mom…she told me."

"Lili spoiled her rotten, I'm afraid. I'm so sorry, Naomi." He shook his head in dismay, then glanced at his gold Bulova watch. "I have an appointment. Will you be okay?"

"Sure. I'm great." The bomb exploded, she felt as if she were standing in the middle of the debris, recognizing nothing. Most of all, herself. She nodded, then asked the question to which she already knew the answer. "Then my father. Thomas Waters. He's a lie, too. Waters wasn't really Mom's name. It's not my name."

This had to be a bad dream. Any minute now she would wake up and find out she'd had another of her dreams. A different one. Worse than any so far.

"No, it is. I legally had it changed to Waters; it's what she wanted." Frank's eyes had shifted from hers. She felt her heart breaking into pieces. She wanted to claw his unspoken answer from her brain. As Lillian Waters was not her birth mother, neither was Thomas her father. Her mind flailed about for an answer she could accept.

"But his picture, the medals...?"

Seeing the misery on Frank's face, she just shook her head, waved a hand at him to stop his talking. "Okay, don't stress yourself, Frank. I think I've got it. Mom invented an entire history for me and went to great lengths to make me believe it. Including the lie about meeting and falling in love with Thomas. Their marrying, his going off to war. Finding herself pregnant. All of it, a lie."

How often as a child she had gazed into the face of that young man in the photograph and imagined she saw traces of her own features there? Not in Lillian, who was fair and quite unlike her physically. But like Thomas with his dark hair and eyes, his crooked smile. The cleft in his chin. Her hero father who died in the war. The father she took into her heart and soul, wove into

the very fabric of her being. The whole thing was a charade. A joke. A horrible joke. How could she?

She interrupted Frank in the midst of another feeble apology. "Who was he? The man in the picture?"

"Lili picked him out of a photo gallery of boys missing in action back then." "But the medals?"

"They weren't that hard to come by," he murmured, his head down. He swirled the tea in his cup, looked as uncomfortable as she hoped he was.

She was relentless. "A second-hand shop? Or was it a garage sale? EBay wasn't around

then."

"I don't even remember," he said helplessly. "It was a long time ago. What does it matter? She made a poor judgment, Naomi. One of the few poor judgments of her life. But she did it for you. She wanted you to be proud of who you were."

"Proud?" Her laugh held a bitter, hollow sound. "My life is a lie, fashioned out of whole cloth, and you helped design the pattern. I don't even know who the hell I am, Frank."

"Hey, you're Naomi Lynn Waters," he said, laying a hand over hers and giving it a brief squeeze of encouragement. "The same terrific girl you always were, and don't you forget that. Honey, I can only imagine what a shock all this has been for you. You need time to digest it, live with it awhile. And please try to remember that your mother did what she thought was in your best interest. She did the best she knew how. Try to understand how it was for her."

"Why didn't she just tell me I was adopted? I would have accepted that, and been grateful she chose me." Why such an elaborate fabrication? And why did she still get the feeling Frank was holding something back? That this was only the tip of the iceberg. Who would have thought her mother was such an accomplished liar?

Chapter Four

Upstairs in her room, Naomi picked up the small framed picture of Thomas from her nightstand, trailed her fingertips over his face. Instead of losing one parent, she had lost two. She may have known him only from his picture, and her mother's stories of him, but he was her father, in every way that mattered. Growing up, she'd had many conversations with the young man in this photograph. Told him her problems, listened to his advice. Like talking to God, in a way. But now to find out he was a stranger to her, chosen at random to fit a scheme, seemed unthinkable. Impossible to grasp. She felt as if she'd been cast asea with no stars to guide her homeward. Even the medals she'd been so proud of were picked up at an estate sale. At least Frank had the good grace to look ashamed when he told her that.

She set the picture back down on the table and heaved a sigh. No wonder Mom told me you were an only child and that you'd been orphaned as a boy. She was making sure I wouldn't ever try to look up your family.

You know all my secrets. My teenage angst. My dreams.

Now she wondered who she'd been talking to throughout all those years. Did he have other family? Yes, of course he would have. But she was not among them. She was nothing to him. He'd merely been cast in the role of her father, without his permission.

Naomi lay awake for most of that night, staring at the ceiling, thinking, questioning, trying to come to terms with this new reality she'd been handed. A mirror to see herself in, as she really was. She'd been duped, made a fool of. Given a background that didn't belong to her. A family that was not hers.

At a sudden weight at the foot of the bed, she looked down to see Molly making her way up the blanket like a stalker. The cat licked her face, as if to say, I know who you are. A stray, like me.

"Love you too. We're each other's family, aren't we, Molly?" she said, and kissed the soft, furry face.

Chapter Five

Faint morning light was filtering through her lace curtains when Naomi slipped out of bed and padded across the hall to the bathroom. Passing the medicine cabinet mirror, she got a glimpse of herself, the hollowed, dark circles under her eyes. Ignoring them, she stripped off her pajamas and stepped into the tub. Turning the shower on full force, she stood beneath the needle hot spray and let the water beat down on her, turning her face up to it until the water ran cool and she thought she might be able to get through the funeral service with some semblance of composure, providing Edna steered clear of her. They should be comforting one another, and would be if they had a normal aunt and niece relationship, if they were a normal family, but they didn't and never would. And now she knew why. She supposed she should be grateful to Edna for laying the truth out there for her. But she wasn't. Not even a little bit. Which didn't mean she would have wanted to go on living a lie. It was the way she did it. Using the obituary to lash out at her. To let the world know that she was of no significance in this family. That she didn't belong.

The memorial was scheduled for ten o'clock. The service would be short, and that was something to be thankful for. Though her mother Lillian believed in God, she wasn't particularly religious and rarely went to church, so a religious ceremony didn't seem like something she would want, although she never said one way or the other.

Dressed in a navy suit over a plain white blouse, her hair brushed into a loose twist at the nape of her neck, she drove to the parlor.

Throughout the solemn proceedings, her emotions ran the gamut of confusion, anger and grief. The sadness at losing her mother undercut with the pain of betrayal.

The profusion of flowers in baskets and bouquets of every kind and size emitted a cloying sweetness. It was hard to breathe. A drone of soft murmurs, occasional sniffling issued from various corners of the room. She herself remained dry-eyed. Defensive.

Through a small clot of people, she got a glimpse of Charlotte standing at the casket, recognizable by her mane of kinky blond hair. She was dabbing at her eyes with a handkerchief, accepting condolences from a friend who had a comforting arm around her shoulders. I should go to her, she thought. But she couldn't make herself move from the spot where she stood, near a huge brass planter spilling over with large leafy greenery that looked artificial, not so different from the way she felt herself. She felt cut off. An outsider. Charlotte actually is more family to Mom than I am. She's Edna's daughter. She's blood.

But she managed to smile at those who offered their sympathy, who hugged her and said they were sorry for her loss. At one point, Charlotte came over and put an arm around her. "You okay, Naomi?" she asked, her voice filled with sympathy, and Naomi knew she was talking about more than the death of her aunt, which after the months of suffering was really a blessing. Naomi said she was fine and Charlotte nodded, patted her arm, and said she'd see her later.

Near the close of the service she spotted Edna, an expression of defiant self-righteousness on her face, heading in her direction. What more could she possibly have to say to me? Before panic could blossom fully, suddenly Frank was there whisking her away, for which she was thankful, despite not feeling too warmly toward him at the moment. Yet, looking at him, her heart softened. The man looked like he had aged ten years overnight. This was rough on him too, even if it was his own doing. At least in part.

"We need to talk again," he said quietly, his hand at her elbow. "Come on. I'll follow you home." He glanced at his watch. "The crowd isn't due at your place for another hour. We'll have some quiet time."

Crowd? And then she remembered that she'd invited people back to the house after the funeral, to partake of the food people brought to the house, to thank them for their kind condolences. But that was before she'd read the obituary. She was quite sure she couldn't possibly face more people today. Would Edna show up? Apparently she still had more she wanted to say to her. Uncle Harold? Even though she'd always been fond of him, she didn't want to see him, nor anyone else today. She didn't want to feel their pity. Poor little orphan girl. No, she didn't need that.

Despite mixed feelings where Frank was concerned, she was glad he was a take-over kind of person. She sensed his resolve, and tried not to think about what more he needed to tell her. Deep down, she knew it wouldn't be anything good.

She sensed whatever it was, Frank wanted to get it out in the open before Edna got to her. At least he'd be able to control how she heard it. But Naomi couldn't imagine what more there could be that would make her feel any worse than she already did. While another part of her braced itself for an aftershock.

This time around, they sat in the living room on the plush olive sofa with its curved legs, Frank with his forearms resting on his navy pin-striped clad thighs as he stared at the rug with its soft, faded shades of olive and rose, then up at the photo of her mother hanging above the fireplace, as if hoping she might offer him some advice on how to handle the situation. You should have thought of that sooner, she thought bitterly. Mom had to know the truth would come out eventually. She knew her sister better than anyone. Or maybe she really didn't. Didn't expect the viciousness Edna was capable of.

She let her own gaze drift to the photos on the mantle, mostly of herself taken at various stages of her life. At seven, standing with a baseball bat poised for a home run, the peak of her hat casting a shadow over her small face. Next to it, her high school grad picture. She'd worn a blue satin dress she'd ached to wear and her mother had gotten it for her, surprised her with it. She went with David Callaghan, a nice kid who had since become a lawyer and married one of their classmates. She had wished them well.

And there was one of her with her mother that Frank had taken the summer they went to Old Orchard Beach. She had just turned fourteen. They looked happy. So long ago.

Frank's own attention had shifted to the little wooden clown on the parallel bars, sitting on the coffee table, a birthday gift she'd given her mother years ago. Sighing again, he idly flicked the top of its red hat and as though on command, the clown went into his series of somersaults. "Naomi…"

"For God's sake, just say it, Frank, please. I think I'm pretty much past being shocked by anything."

He looked skeptically at her. "Don't be so quick to say that. But yes, I suppose there is no easy way. I wasn't entirely forthcoming when I told you your birth mother walked out of the hospital never to be seen again."

This wasn't exactly a revelation. She waited. He was obviously not looking forward to telling her whatever it was he was about to tell her, and she wasn't sure she wanted to know either, but she needed to hear, needed to know all of it.

"She died just five days after you were born. I knew if I told you that, well, you'd want to know more about her and that would lead to what I'm about to tell you."

"Then you know who she was. You know her name."

He nodded his head, barely perceptively, then he said, "Yes. Her name was Mary Rose

Francis. She was a native girl, Mi'kmaq. She lived on Big Salmon Reserve with her grandfather. The reserve is no longer there, of course. As you know, the land was confiscated by the government in the late eighties when they built the dam up there; the band dispersed to other parts of the country after that. Some migrated to the states. But that's where she lived."

Naomi said, "Then I'm part native Indian. She must have been ashamed of my origins, not to tell me."

"C'mon, honey. That's not fair and you know it. Nor true. You know your mother didn't have a racist bone in her body. No. That wasn't it."

Interesting he would talk about what was fair. "Then what?" He had steepled his fingers and appeared to study them. His deep sigh seemed to hold all the weight of the world. Then, in a monotone, as if he'd needed to remove himself emotionally from the story, he began to speak again.

"She'd been visiting at a friend's house after school. It was getting on to dark when she left to catch the bus home. A car drove up beside her, began to follow her. There were two men in the car."

He stopped and cleared his throat. Naomi sensed what was coming and didn't want to hear it. "Go on."

"One of them forced her into the car. They drove to the outskirts of town. No point in my trying to sanitize this, you can read the write-ups in the paper yourself. She was beaten, raped. When they finished with her, they tossed her out of the car, left her for dead. I'm sorry, Naomi. I'm so sorry to tell you this."

"I know. I know you are, Frank. Go on, please."

He sighed again. Stared down at his fingers in his lap, intertwined, now spread them helplessly. Resigned to his unpleasant task. "A man out walking his dog discovered her the next morning, lying unconscious by the side of the road. He called an ambulance, and she was rushed into the hospital where she remained in a coma for eight months. At the end of that eighth month, with the help of labor-inducing medications, she delivered a baby girl. Routine tests had already revealed the pregnancy. It was a rare case, but not unheard of. They'd considered a Caesarean section, of course, but it was decided that that would pose more hazards because of the risks of anesthesia and the potential difficulties of healing after the surgery. Not that it would have mattered. As I said, she died five days later, never regained consciousness. Almost as if she willed herself to stay alive long enough to give life to the precious child inside her. That child was you, Naomi."

I am a child of rape.

"Mary Rose's grandfather?" she said. My great-grandfather, she thought, and tried to take

it in.

"He died months before you were born. Of a broken heart, Lili said. He never knew about you. Matthew Francis was a fine man, Naomi, gentle, strong, kept his grief private. Anyway, there was no one left to take you in. You would have gone into an orphanage, and who knows where you would have ended up. The girl's parents were dead, which was why she'd been living with the grandfather. Your mother begged me to start adoption proceedings."

He seemed to be waiting for her to make some comment or ask another question. When she didn't, he looked down again at the fading rug under his black, shiny shoes. Strange, she'd never noticed before how faded the rug was, even a little threadbare here and there. The old Persian rug had been here as long as she could remember, centering the hardwood floor. It belongs here, she thought, as Frank began to speak again. As she listened to his words, Naomi

had this strange sensation of being in a far corner of the room watching the scene unfold, like a scene in a movie in which she'd been unwillingly cast.

"It wasn't as common then for single mothers to adopt children as it is today. Bring them up alone. I wanted your mother to marry me so we could raise you together, but she turned me down." He smiled sadly, self-deprecatingly. "She was a dear friend. But she didn't love me in the same way that I loved her."

Naomi touched his arm. Being mad at him seemed almost silly and certainly futile. He'd done what he did out of love for Mom. But it was a house of cards bound to fall. How could they not know that? Silence broken, the words hung in the air, set up a strange buzzing above her head. Then, even that stopped, bringing more silence. The silence after a bomb blast. Not so far off.

The one part of the story Naomi couldn't quite absorb was that her birth father, rather than being the war hero she had grown up adoring, was in fact a vicious rapist, and ultimately a murderer. That one was just a little too heavy to take in all at once. But yes, that might be something you'd want to hide from your child. Knowing that didn't make her feel any better.

"Thanks for telling me the truth, Frank. Even if it has been a while in coming."

"Don't thank me. I wouldn't have told you at all if not for Edna. I knew she'd tell you all of it, eventually. Maybe not today, next week, or even next month. But she would tell you. It was just too delicious a secret for someone like her to keep."

"You'd think Mom would have known that."

"Your mother loved Edna. She saw her through a big sister's eyes. Though she wasn't oblivious to Edna's faults, she would never have expected this kind of betrayal."

How she must hate me, Naomi thought, finally understanding Edna's hostility toward her. She's never considered me her niece, really, only a dark secret to be tolerated. The native child whose very existence, in her opinion, brought shame upon the family. And who, as she perceived it, replaced her in her sister's affections. Which was never true. Mom had always loved Edna. She was very protective of her.

Naomi envisioned another little girl, one not so lucky. She saw her in her mind's eye walking to the bus stop that night, so terrified, unable to escape her tormentors. No one to stop them. To save her.

"Did they ever find the two men who ...?"

"No. The caretaker of the cemetery said he heard her screams that night. He told the police he reached the top of the hill just in time to see a man forcing her into the back seat of a car and the car speed off. Unfortunately he wasn't able to give a description of either of them, or of the car, except to say that it was a navy or black in color. It was too dark out, his glimpse of them too brief. He only knew there were two of them. No. They never did catch those animals."

On the word animals, the doorbell rang, jolting Naomi's heart as she stared at the door, panic washing through her. She couldn't do this. Not now.

"Your first arrival," Frank said, getting to his feet with some difficulty. "I'll put the tea and coffee on. You might want to put out the food."

"Oh, no, please, Frank. You answer. Tell them I'm sorry. I can't..."

"Of course you can. You must. I happen to know you're made of sterner stuff than that." He placed a gentle hand on her shoulder. "It's your duty as Lillian Water's daughter. And you are her daughter," he added firmly. "Whatever you're feeling right now."

* * *

It wasn't as bad as she had imagined. A matter of pasting on a welcoming smile and going through the motions of being a gracious hostess. Easy for the most part, since those who came were themselves so kind and sensitive to her feelings, no one even mentioning the write-up in the paper. But everyone had read the obituary, and the fact of it was as large as the proverbial elephant in the kitchen, and curiosity and pity, even bewilderment, was behind every smile.

The only one of the Bradleys to show up was Charlotte,

Edna's daughter, who despite Naomi's protests, insisted on staying to help her clean up, then hugged her hard in the doorway. "I'll miss Aunt Lili," Charlotte said. "I loved her too, you know, Naomi. She was my aunt."

She nodded. "Did you know, Charlotte?" she asked softly. "Did everyone know but me?" To her credit, she didn't pretend not to know what Naomi was talking about. "No, Aunt Lili swore Mom to secrecy. And she did keep the promise until Aunt Lili was gone. You have to

give her that. She really does believe she did the right thing in telling you, you know. She thought you had a right to know. But I know how hard it must be. We all feel horrible for you, Naomi. It's why Ted didn't come. He couldn't face you after what Mom did. Dad feels the same way."

Naomi said she understood, was somewhat mollified that to know the entire family wasn't in agreement with Edna's tactics. But she knew 'having a right to know' had nothing to do with why Edna told her. Let Charlotte keep whatever illusions about her mother she had. None of this was her fault. It was good of her to come.

Alone now, the silence of the house crowding in on her, she wandered into the living room and sank down on the sofa, where just a short time ago, she and Frank had sat. Where he had told her the rest of it.

Looking up at her mother's portrait above the fireplace, a heaviness the size of a truck, settled in her heart. I didn't know you at all, she thought. She sat for a time. Then she wearily climbed the stairs to her room.

Standing before the vanity mirror, she gazed at her reflection in the glass. She examined the shape and color of her eyes, the fine arch of her brows, her near black hair, her cheekbones high in an oval-shaped face. A face she had convinced herself bore a likeness to her father's, who Mom told her, had Hawaiian ancestry in his background. 'A great-great-grandmother, if I remember correctly', she had said. Naomi smiled faintly now at the lie. You couldn't say she wasn't creative. She had chosen her surrogate father well.

Frank told her she was terrified someone from around here would make the connection between that tragic young woman and Naomi, so she couldn't take the chance of telling her she had native blood in her veins. 'She had to keep that from you, Naomi, and I know how much that bothered her. She didn't think she had a choice,' Frank had said.

She looked around at the room she had occupied for all of her life, the room that bore witness to girlhood secrets, hurts and triumphs, hopes and dreams. Her eye fell upon the books in the bookcase a biography of Emily Carr. Jane Eyre, her favorite book ever. She'd reread it not that long ago, and found new layers to be appreciated as an adult.

On the lower shelf, more treasured books from her childhood by authors Judy Blume, E.B. White, Lewis Carroll, Charles Dickens' Christmas Carol and others that had informed and entertained her, and helped to shape her view of the world, and of herself.

She'd updated the decor over the years from the little girl pink and white to the earth tones she'd come to prefer as she grew older. She painstakingly stripped and sanded each piece of the white-painted furniture in here -- bed, vanity, a vanity stool she'd found at a yard sale, and

the two night tables and stained them a rich warm oak, almost the exact shade of the floor. Forest green scatter mats lent color to the room. The dresser itself was a heavy old antique treasure, hand-crafted with decorative carving that she loved. She remembered what a hard time the moving men had getting it up the stairs.

Her room. All the things in it were hers. The pictures, the books, the teak monkey totem 'see no evil, hear no evil, speak no evil' that she kept on the dresser, another yard sale treasure. A small print of Edward Hopper's Nighthawks hung on the antique white wall. Yes, despite all this, she felt now as if she were occupying the room by default. She felt like a fraud.

* * *

Over the next few days, other than to drag herself to the bathroom and feed Molly, who had settled herself on the bed in mournful sympathy, Naomi did not leave the house. She ate little, ignored the doorbell and the persistently ringing phone downstairs. She was glad there was no phone in her bedroom. She tried to bully herself out of her self-pity party, but that wasn't working either. It just made her cry more. Then, one night the old childhood dream returned, this time more vivid than ever before, the voice insistent, commanding, refusing to be ignored.

The beating of wings came softly at first, from somewhere far off, gradually growing in volume, and the pounding of her heart thundered in chorus. She felt the familiar rise of panic and tried to wake, but the dream held her captive. A dream she'd had off and on since she was a little girl. One that both drew her in and at the same time, terrified her. In it, she was always trying to outrun the great beating wings, and each time, barely escaping to wakefulness before it could descend on her.

Whap…whap…whap came the creature in pursuit of her. Only this time a voice was urging Naomi not to run away. A gentle, yet commanding voice. Despite the fear, she obeyed, stopped running, slowly turned. Then, as the great shadow-winged creature settled on a nearby tree, the closing of its wings as soft and warm as a velvet shroud, she finally understood that the creature was an eagle, and that it meant her no harm.

"Find the evil ones," it told her.

Just a dream, she told herself the following morning. It means nothing. You're stressed out, not yourself, whoever the hell that is. You can't put too much stock in dreams. But the next night, the dream came again, and all her arguments fell away.

"Find the evil ones, 'Ntus," the eagle repeated.

Chapter Six

Early next morning, dressed in jeans and a grey baggy sweatshirt, Naomi came downstairs with a rather vague idea of learning more about what happened to her birth mother, and why her attackers were never found and punished. She was quiet inside, thoughtful, as she made herself a mug of coffee and took it with her into the studio, which was just off the living room. Once one room, it was now divided into two closet-sized spaces, a sound-proofed door between them, the first serving as her office, the second as a recording studio. It suited her purposes fine.

This was an old house with gingerbread trim, set above and well back from the road, with a gravel horseshoe driveway and a hilly lawn. There was a lovely spreading chestnut tree in one corner of the lot.

At the back of the house, what was once a grassy field had grown wild with brush, weeds and alders. Her mother had purchased the modest-sized Victorian 'fixer-upper' on 233 Elizabeth Avenue, years ago, apparently while awaiting Naomi's birth. Aunt Edna thought the house was too big for just the two of them, but it wasn't. It was exactly right. Naomi grew up in this house and had always loved it. And these two little rooms were her corner of the world. Her den. Den. Such an apt word. A place for an animal to hide away. For her, a place where she felt safe and content. Not so different. She liked the analogy. Here, she could tuck herself in, away from the world, yet connected to it in a way that suited her temperament.

This room was originally intended as a guestroom, but since they rarely had overnight guests, her mother suggested she take it as her own. When Naomi began to get work narrating audio books, Lillian had a man come and put up a soundproof wall, with a door erected between the computer workspace and the recording studio to isolate the hum of the computer and other noises the powerful mic managed to pick up. One wall in the recording studio had built-in floor to ceiling bookshelves, every space filled to bursting with books.

For the window facing the street, she'd bought wooden shutters and hung heavy drapes to further muffle any noise, although the sound of traffic could barely be heard this far back from the road. If she was recording, and a big, noisy truck did happen to rattle by, she would just wait until it passed before continuing, later editing out any offending noise.

Now, seated at the computer, its familiar hum welcoming her, she brought up the Google search engine, typed Mi'kmaq Dictionary into the box and clicked enter. She sipped her coffee and waited. Almost immediately, a couple of promising sites came up, the second one down owned by a professor of native languages at the local university. She clicked on it and scrolled down the alphabetical list of native words on the screen. The word 'Ntus jumped out at her. Beside it, was the English translation: 'My daughter'. Under the sleeves of her sweatshirt, goosebumps rose on her arms. 'Ntus.

Find the evil ones, 'Ntus.

Find the evil ones, my daughter.

She sat quietly for a time, letting the revelation take its full effect. Her birth mother had spoken to her in a dream. What other explanation could there be? How else would she have known the word 'Ntus? *I know no Mi'kmaq.*

The first stirrings of curiosity and of wonder rippled through her, mixed in with the myriad of emotions she was already dealing with.

She found herself distracted by the amount of information on the net about the Mi'kmaq (often spelled MicMac) or First Nations people as they had come to be known. One site linked to

the next. And the next. She learned about sculptors like Randy Simon of Big Cove, painters like Leonard Paul, and writers, including the late poet laureate Rita Joe of Nova Scotia. Naomi had read some of her haunting yet joyful poetry. Words that told of her life, her response to that life. A spiritual, yet down-to-earth woman.

It was the spiritual aspect of the Mi'kmaq culture that most captured her interest, however. For example, the Mi'kmaq did not make a distinction, as the white man did, between what was natural and what was supernatural. They believed, at least those who still held to the old ways did, that not only people, but animals, the sun, river and even rocks could have a spirit. The Mi'kmaq believe that all of the universe is filled with a spirit called mntu or Manitou, with the sun holding special significance. They hold great respect for animals, and all nature. The eagle in particular is highly revered, believed to be a sacred messenger sent from the Spirit Creator, Gisoolg. When she finished reading many stories and poems about eagles, any lingering doubt that Mary Rose had visited her last night, as she had on other nights, left her.

She thought of herself growing inside of the young girl's womb for those eight months that she lay in a coma, hooked up to tubes and machines to keep them both alive. *She didn't hate me for being there. On the contrary. She wanted me to live. To avenge her.*

I never heard her voice. Only her heartbeat, the pumping of blood through her body. Sustaining me until I could survive in the world on my own. It gave Naomi a strange feeling imagining herself the daughter of this young woman, who, until only recently, was unknown to her. She had no doubt that at some deep level, Mary Rose, even as she lay in a deep sleep, was aware of the child growing inside her. Aware of me.

"She's been trying to communicate with me for a long time, Molly," she said to her friend who was curled up at her feet. "Ever since I was a little girl. I was afraid and closed myself to her spirit. She wants me to find her killers."

Molly raised her head and blinked green eyes at her as if in understanding. Naomi turned back to the computer. But her efforts to find some mention of Mary Rose's abduction went unrewarded. She found nothing on the case. Although she did find an alarming number of rapes and murders of other native women across the country in which their perpetrators had escaped justice. One case in particular, involved the brutal murder of Betty Osborne, a native of

Saskatchewan. The nineteen year old girl had been picked up in a car by four men, gang-raped, then stabbed to death with a screwdriver. 'Evil' was really the only word to describe such a heinous act.

The gentle command played in her mind. "Find the evil ones, 'Ntus." "I will," she whispered. "I will."

The fish-tank screen saver popped up and she realized she'd been sitting there for a full fifteen minutes without touching the keyboard. She shut off the machine and went out to the kitchen, her mind swimming with thoughts and half-formed thoughts, her resolve strong to find justice for Mary Rose. She could only imagine the terror and pain her birth-mother suffered at the hands of her killers. Why had nothing been done to find and punish those men? she thought in sudden fury.

You don't know that nothing was done. You don't know anything about it. Well, she would know. She'd make it her business to know.

She opened the fridge door and took out the last quart of milk on the shelf, eyed the expiry date and sniffed the contents. Grimacing at the rank sourness that rose up to her, Naomi poured the milk down the sink, turning on the cold water faucet to wash it and the smell away. Through the window over the sink, she could see big blue patches in the clouds. Should be a nice

day, she thought, as her eye wandered across the abandoned field to the backs of the houses on Keel Street. Some ambitious woman had hung out a line of snowy white sheets and pillow cases that blew gently in the breeze. It was rare to see clothes on a line nowadays, with most people preferring the convenience of dryers, herself included. But she remembered her mother would sometimes put out a line of wash on her day off from the hospital, when Naomi was at school. You could bury your face in them, they always smelled so nice.

For some reason, this thought brought a lump to her throat. She must be in bad shape to get emotional over laundry?

Naomi checked the cupboard and saw she was down to her last can of cat food. There was a pan of cakes no one had yet touched, that she'd put in the freezer.

"How do you feel about brownies, Molly?" she said aloud, even though the cat was nowhere to be seen. She'd do a little grocery shopping while she was out. She'd also pick up some cleaning supplies and scour this place. Her mother, Lillian, would be appalled at Naomi's slovenliness. Maybe I take after my father, she thought, and laughed aloud. A hollow, bitter sound in the empty house.

Chapter Seven

Less than an hour later, she was at the library. From the first time she had climbed these wide grey stone steps and entered through the heavy oak doors of River's End Public Library, it was a magical place for her a hushed, warm haven where, through the pages of a book she could travel to far off exotic lands. She could experience vicariously the characters' lives through the author's words. Naomi loved books, loved their smell, their feel, their secrets.

But now she paid little mind to the books on the shelves as she made her way to the row of wooden filing cabinets against the far wall, the same cabinets that had been here when she was still in school, each labeled *River's End Tribune*, with corresponding dates. The sun shining in the high window polished the dark wood, the knobs on the drawers. A grade school girl sat at a far table, reading, and the same sun turned her hair a lovely molten gold, like doll's hair.

Naomi quickly spotted the drawer she was looking for, 64C, and pulled it open. She scanned the row of films in their boxes, selected four of them. Closing the drawer, she headed for the only machine in the bank of five not in use.

Removing the first film from its box, she placed it on the spindle, slid the film under the roller and glass and threaded the film into the take-up reel. She adjusted the controls until the page came into sharp focus. As she began turning the knob, the pages whisked past her eyes in a blur and she slowed the speed, so that she could scan each headline before the next page came up.

As if lying in wait, long before she was ready for the emotional impact the words would have, the headline jumped out at her:

Unidentified Girl Found Unconscious on Black Pond Road.

The blood rushed warm to her cheeks, and her heart beat faster as she read the write-up beneath the headline.

RIVER'S END - An elderly man out walking his dog on Black Pond Road this morning discovered a young woman lying unconscious by the side of the road. But for her socks and one white sneaker, she was unclothed. What is assumed to be her clothing lay beside her, likely tossed there, police say, by her assailant(s). The items included a denim skirt, white shirt, underclothes, and a right sneaker matching the one she wore. The young woman had been badly beaten, apparently left for dead. She is approximately five foot four inches, 110 pounds, and is believed to be aboriginal.

Police are asking for the public's help in identifying the victim.

Reading that, thinking about how she looked when the man discovered her lying there, sent the strangest sensation through her. Something like shock, as if the attack just happened and she had just now heard about it. A sadness welled up in Naomi.

Mary Rose was a petite girl, while Naomi herself was five eight and ten pounds heavier. Marking the article for copying later, she scrolled to a second write-up, published three days later.

Victim of Brutal Attack Identified by Grandfather, the headline read. This write-up had merited a brief additional paragraph, along with a school photo of Mary Rose. Looking at the girl in the photo, Naomi felt an instant connection.

She has an interesting face, almost pretty. Perhaps too serious for making friends easily. Protecting her tender heart with a necessary detachment from those who would hurt her. A survival technique, that couldn't, in the end, save her.

She looked out at Naomi with gentle dark eyes, intelligence shining through. Naomi

could see something of herself in the oval-shaped face. Not of Thomas now, she thought, but of this young woman in the photo.

Her blood flows in my veins.

So does his, came the grotesque thought. The monsters who ... No. Don't go there. Not yet. She pushed the thought away. Focused instead on the small crescent moon with the man-in-the-moon profile nestled in the vee of the white shirt Mary Rose was wearing in the photo.

Did she have on that same denim skirt the day this picture was taken she wondered. But you could only see the top part of the picture.

She sat back in the chair, let out a long shuddery sigh. This tragedy had actually happened. It seemed surreal. But this was how her own life had begun. She knew this intellectually, of course, but now she knew it emotionally. She read the second write-up:

The victim of a brutal beating and rape has been identified as Mary Rose Francis of Salmon Cove Reservation by her grandfather, Paul Francis, also of Salmon Cove. "When she did not return home from school on Thursday," an obviously distraught Mr. Francis said, "I called the police but no one called me back until yesterday."

Mary Rose Francis lies in a coma at River's End General Hospital. Though doctors say recovery is always a possibility, they are not holding out a lot of hope in this case. "She suffered massive head injuries," Doctor James Melick said. "It's a wait and see situation."

Students at River's End High School were shocked by the news of the attack on their schoolmate. The victim had been visiting at a friend's home earlier that evening.

"She was really nice," said a tearful Lisa Cameron. "I should have let her go home earlier when she wanted to. But we were having fun, listening to music and stuff, and we just lost track of time."

Naomi moved on to the next write-up, published two weeks later.

NO LEADS IN VIOLENT ASSAULT ON NATIVE GIRL - Police are frustrated in their efforts to solve the case of a brutal assault against a native girl, says lead detective, William Keys. "We'll be doing all we can to track down the perpetrators, but there's nothing new to report at this time. The investigation is ongoing."

That was about it, followed by a rehash of the few known facts in the case. Naomi could find nothing further after that. The case had apparently been dropped. She scrolled back to the second write-up in which Charles Seaton, the caretaker at the cemetery told police that he'd heard screams that night, and crested the hill just in time to see a young woman being forced into a car. 'It was enough to curl the hair on your head,' he told them. But he was too far away to help, he said, and could offer no further information, except to say that there'd been two men in the car when it sped away. Mr. Seaton said he would hear that poor girl's screams for the rest of his life.

Did you yell out? Naomi asked the man who wasn't there to answer for himself. Did you try to warn them off? Let them know they'd been seen? Did you do anything at all?

She was being unfair to Mr. Seaton. The abduction probably happened so fast it barely had time to register on him until it was over, and everything was quiet again. It must have seemed dreamlike in that moment. The story was pretty much as Frank had related it to her. Nevertheless, she jotted down the man's name. Couldn't hurt to talk to Mr. Seaton, providing he was still alive. How old would be now, if he was still around?

She wondered if the police had ever considered hypnotizing him? He might have

remembered more details, maybe even the car's license plate number. The subconscious mind can store information the conscious mind is not even aware of. At least, it works that way in the movies. The car itself would be long gone of course, to some scrap heap in the sky, but the license number could provide the name of whoever owned it at the time. Would there still be a record of that somewhere?

All her instincts told her that her next stop should be the

police department, where she could put these questions to whoever was in charge of cold cases, and demand the justice for Mary Rose she'd been denied all these years. But she knew that before she could hope to gain their attention, she'd have to make a few waves first. Just walking in there with some old write-ups wasn't going to do it. She needed a lot more.

Beneath Mr. Seaton's name, Naomi jotted down the name of Lisa Cameron, who was probably long married and going by a different name. But she shouldn't be too hard to track down; this was a small town. As an afterthought, she added the name of Dr. James Melick to the short list, followed by Detective William Keys, although they could both be dead by now.

Naomi had been in the library longer than she realized. Three of the stations had been vacated while she did her research. The girl was gone. Just one elderly woman left in the last one, perhaps researching her ancestry, which in a way was what she herself was doing. Although her ultimate purpose was different.

Armed with her notes, and copies of the news items that had run in the Tribune during the investigation, Naomi left the library and drove to the faded red brick building on Corona Street which housed the River's End Tribune.

Someone must know something, and there was only one way to find out.

Chapter Eight

"Good story," Editor-in-Chief Len Hayward said, leaning back in his chair far enough to make it squeak. Lacing his fingers behind his head, he studied Naomi over his bifocals. "You sure you want me to run it?" One scraggly salt and pepper eyebrow raised slightly.

"Of course I'm sure. It's why I'm here. I realize it happened a long time ago, but..." "Twenty-eight years ago."

"I know that. But cold cases have been solved before. Someone might know something. Maybe saw something and chose for one reason or another not to come forward at the time. From what I've read of the case, there sure wasn't a big push to solve it. It seems a native girl was not all that important a loss."

He nodded slowly, brought the chair forward with another hard squeak, picked up a pen and twirled it in his hand, his eyes never leaving her. "I knew your mom. Your adopted mother, Lillian Waters. Not well, mind you, but we were acquainted. You realize, of course, you'll quickly go from being the daughter of a respected nurse and labor leader to being a child born as the result of a vicious rape on a native girl."

Heat flooded Naomi's neck and face. His words brought a sting of shame at her very existence, something only her Aunt Edna had ever been able to make her feel. Was this how certain people made Mary Rose feel?

Her reaction wasn't lost on him. "Please, don't be upset, Miss Waters. I didn't say I felt that way. But bigotry still exists in this town, and anyone who thinks it doesn't, is dreaming." His voice had softened. "I assure you, I don't. We're all children of God, if he's up there at all, and I have my own issues with that. But you need to know what you're up against. Your mother guarded you against the circumstances of your birth for good reason."

With that, he got to his feet, a big man in dark rumpled pants, rolled-up shirt sleeves. He swept a hand over thinning hair.

"I'm happy to run your story, Ms. Waters. Why not? It's got all the elements that sell newspapers. Sex, violence, even a minor celebrity angle considering your mother was well-known in River's End, and you yourself are not an unknown quantity. In fact, you're my granddaughter's favorite books-on-tape narrator. She'd kill me if I didn't get an autograph." He pushed a sheet of paper across the desk at her. "Emily," he said, smiling. "She looked you up on the net so I recognized you from your picture."

She addressed it *To Emily*, wrote a brief note, signed her name and passed it back to him. He folded the paper and slid it into the pocket of his brown Columboesque trench coat

hanging on a rack by the door. "I just wonder if you're prepared for the fallout, that's all."

"To be honest, I didn't give the matter much thought beyond finding her killers," she said. Now that she did she knew just the briefest hesitation, and felt cowardly for it. "She deserves some justice," she said with a sudden welling of anger. "It's right that I should be the one to try to get that justice for her."

Len Hayward shrugged an okay, then gestured to someone walking by the glass cubicle

office.

The door opened and Naomi turned to see a bearded man in battered brown suede jacket in the doorway clutching a handful of papers, other hand on the doorknob. He gave Naomi a nod. "Yeah, Len."

The phone rang and Hayward picked up, cupped a hand over the receiver. "Eric here'll

take down your story, Ms. Waters. Get a couple of good head shots, Eric. Should be a piece of cake." With that, he dismissed them both, growled into the phone, "Hayward, yeah." Then he bellowed at his caller, "What do you mean, you can't track him down. I need that Wallace story on my desk yesterday. Where the hell...?"

The berating of some unfortunate continued as they left his office, cutting out as the door closed behind them. Naomi idly wondered who Wallace was. She hadn't been paying too much attention to the news lately.

"One of our town councilors is up for embezzlement," the reporter said, as if reading her thoughts. "A corrupt politician. Now there's something you don't hear about too often." He grinned to show he was joking as he ushered her past the row of desks to his own office at the back of the big room.

On the way there, they passed half a dozen people working

quietly at computers, a couple on the phone. No clacking typewriters here, or hard-nose reporters with rolled-up sleeves, filling the air with blue cigarette smoke, wearing rumpled soft hats with press card tucked into their bands. Nothing to suggest deadlines, or big 'scoops', like in those old black and white movies her mom had had a penchant for, (along with old radio shows) one of her favorite being the 1931 version of The Front Page starring Pat O'Brien. They had watched it shortly before she went into the hospital for the last time. She sighed without being aware of it, and Eric Grant glanced at her before opening the door to his office, which was considerably smaller than Mr. Hayward's, but neater.

"Please, have a seat." He set the sheaf of papers he'd been carrying on top of a grey metal filing cabinet in the corner, shrugged out of his jacket beneath which he wore a blue denim shirt. "Coffee?"

"No, thanks."

Closing the door, he went round behind his desk and drew the small tape recorder toward him and sat down. His finger hovered over the button. "I'm afraid my shorthand leaves a lot to be desired, mind."

"No. It's fine."

He pushed record. Recording was second nature to her, but this particular narration wasn't anything she was looking forward to. Only by mentally erecting a wall between the words and her emotions, was she able to get through her story a second time. In the same way Frank had managed to relate the story to her.

A half hour later, her story told, all that she knew of it

anyway, he clicked the recorder off and looked thoughtfully at her. "And you had no idea you were adopted before that?"

"None. Not until I read it in the obituary column. Although the woman at the funeral parlor I told you about prepared me to some degree, I suppose."

"Mrs. Devers."

"You have a good memory."

"I try. Comes in handy in my business. It's beyond tragic what happened to your birth mother. I don't remember reading about it. But then I would have been four at the time. I'd like to make copies of these articles if it's okay. Quicker than digging them out of the morgue...sorry."

"No need to be."

He slipped the thin sheaf of paper from the envelope, smiled at her. He had a nice smile. Taking in the scruffy gingery-blond beard, and hair long enough to curl at his denim shirt collar, she'd almost expected he'd have blackened pirates' teeth? Or maybe a stray tooth or two like that guy in Deliverance.

"I covered a couple of nurses' union meetings when they were voting to strike and had the pleasure of meeting your mom. It was a few years ago, I was a rookie cub reporter back then, but I remember her. You were a lucky little girl to be adopted by such a special lady."

"Yes, I know that," she said coolly, her defenses rising at the comment, which sounded to her like a veiled criticism. But then he didn't know what it was like to wake up one morning and realize your whole life is a lie. God, did everyone in town know her mother?

She was overreacting. It was an innocent enough comment, and it was also true. She had been lucky. She just didn't feel very lucky at the moment.

He flashed her another smile and stood up. "It'll just take me a couple of minutes to copy these. She noticed then that his eyes were almost the same shade of blue as his denim shirt. He was good-looking in a rough-hewn sort of way, though definitely not her type. He reminded her of one of those Vikings she'd read about in school. All he needed to complete the picture was a horned helmet and a sword.

Eric Grant returned shortly and handed her back her copies of the articles. He seemed quieter, thoughtful. If he had any further comments he was keeping them to himself. At least he wasn't a total dork. In his favor, he'd tried to talk her out of including her phone number and email in the write-up, but she held her ground. What was the point of doing this at all if people couldn't contact her?

"They can contact you through the paper," he told her. But she knew that by the time she got back to whoever had written they could have changed their mind about talking to her.

The interview over, Naomi thanked him and left his office. He offered to walk with her to her car, but she said no, that was fine. She'd taken up enough of his time.

With each step she took across the wood-grained laminated floor, she imagined eyes burning into the back of her neck like thin, hot lasers. As if receptionists, journalists, even customers standing at the counter already knew her secret, which of course was impossible. She was being paranoid. If she felt like this now, what was she going to do when the article came out in the paper? Crawl under the bed?

Stepping into the bright afternoon sunlight, the world tilted and her head spun. She had to grab onto the wrought-iron handrail to keep from tumbling down the stone steps. When the dizziness passed, dread grew inside her at what she had just done. The railing was slippery under the dampness of her hand as she made her way down the stairs.

Had she made a mistake coming here? Acted too impulsively, putting herself out there for public fodder? Maybe Mr. Hayward was right and she hadn't thought it through well enough. Well, too late now for regrets. It was done. The die was cast.

Whatever she had set in motion so be it.

Chapter Nine

Eric Grant had noticed her as she came through the door. Impossible not to. Even in casual pants and jacket, she was striking. Yet it was a quiet beauty she possessed. A certain exotic aura about her. Great cheekbones. She wore little makeup, (or was expert as making it look that way), and her thick sheen of dark hair was pushed back in a careless way that gave the impression her looks were not of major importance to her. But more, it was the purpose in her step that had captured his attention. The erect shoulders, the stride. This was a woman on a mission.

Now Eric watched from the office window as she emerged from the building. He tensed seeing her grab the railing, hesitate on the steps. But then she seemed okay. As okay as she could be considering what she had to be going through. An attractive, self-contained woman who in that moment looked like a lost child separated from all that was familiar to her. As he watched her descend the steps, he could feel her uncertainty, her confusion. He wanted to rush out there and tell her to forget the story, he'd toss the tape in the trash, but somehow he knew she would resent it, that any such grandstanding on his part would only stiffen her resolve to have the story published.

He wondered if she was already having second thoughts about going public and half-expected he'd get a call asking him to pull the story, which he would do in a heartbeat, no matter what the boss said. But she didn't call. It couldn't have been easy coming forward like that. She didn't strike him as someone who sought the limelight.

"She's a grown gal," Len said, when Eric shared his concerns. "It's her choice. And who knows? She might get lucky and nail a killer. That's the reason she's doing this." He grinned at Len. "You got a thing for the lady? Not that I blame you."

Eric just gave him a look and left the office, quietly closing the door behind him.

Chapter Ten

On Monday morning, Eric Grant set the story on his boss's desk. While Hayward read the article slated for the front page of the local section of the paper, Eric placed both palms on his desk, drawing Hayward's gaze away from the paper. He leveled his gaze at him.

"What?"

"I'm still not feeling good about this, Len."

Len Hayward frowned. "Why not? It's a damn good write-up. Great shot," he added, checking out the photo attached to the story. "It's not like we're paparazzi. She came to us. She asked us to write the story."

"I'm not sure she's in any condition to make that decision. A month from now maybe. But aside from the fact that she's got to be traumatized, just losing her mom from cancer, learning what she did about her beginnings. I also think running this story could put her in physical danger. Her birth-mother's attackers could be still out there."

"Did you share those concerns with her?"

"More or less. She's taken a bit of a defensive posture." He didn't mention that he'd already managed to tick her off with his dumb comment about how lucky she was that Lillian Waters had adopted her. Like she wouldn't know that, and what in hell did it have to do with the price of tea in China?

"We're not therapists here, Eric, me lad," Len said. "We're reporters. We're running a newspaper." He waved the story at him. "And this is news. Local news, but news. And human interest. AP will probably pick it up. People love human interest."

Chapter Eleven

Naomi waited on pins and needles for the story to come out in the paper, her heart in her mouth, torn between wanting it published and terrified it would be.

Which, on Tuesday it was. She heard the small thump as the paper came through the letter slot and hit the floor.

Seeing her own face looking up at her from the hall floor made her feel ill. She picked up the paper, feeling naked and threatened, as if she'd been tied to a tree and smeared with honey. It didn't help that she'd done it to herself.

She was a private person, and here she was laying herself out there for all of River's End to feast upon. At the same time, she wanted people to know her story. There had to be someone still around who would remember what happened to a native girl all those years ago.

And one of two of those people just might remember details long buried. She was counting on it. And at the same time, praying this wasn't all for nothing.

She sat down on the living room sofa with the paper, acutely aware of her mother's eyes gazing down at her from the photo above the fireplace. She had an eerie feeling that if she looked up she would see disappointment on her mother's face. Maybe even accusation. I'm the one who should be angry, she thought. And I am. I'm damned angry. But she didn't look up at the photo, or into her mother's eyes.

Instead, she read the article:

WOMAN LEARNS SHE IS A CHILD OF RAPE

Oh, God. Knowing everyone in town who subscribed to the Tribune was reading this too, didn't feel good. But what had she expected? Get over it, she told herself, and continued to read:

28-year-old Naomi Waters was born and raised in River's End.

She is a talented voice actor and adopted daughter of the late Lillian Waters, nurse and labor leader, who died recently after a brave and lengthy battle with cancer. Shortly after Ms. Waters passed on, Naomi learned she was adopted and that her birth-mother, Mary Rose Francis, was in fact, aboriginal, of Mi'kmaq descent.

Twenty-eight year ago, on a warm June night, Mary Rose was abducted by two men in a car, brutally assaulted and left for dead on Black Pond Road, an isolated area approximately ten miles east of River's End. The victim was sixteen years old at the time.

Says Waters, "The two men have never been identified. My birth-mother spent eight months in hospital in a coma, and died just five days after giving me life. I've read all the write-ups that appeared in this paper at the time, and it seems to me not much effort was made to find her killers."

Naomi Waters vows to correct that injustice. She is determined to find her mother's killers and bring them to justice.

She is asking for the public's help. If anyone has any information..."

There was more in the sidebar, the location of the abduction, other quotes from people, more sparse details lifted from the articles she'd taken in to him. He'd also gotten a quote from a Sergeant Graham Nelson. "It was a difficult case at the time," he said. "The victim was chosen randomly and those are the hardest cases to solve. There were simply no clues to follow."

They didn't look hard enough, Naomi thought. More quotes from her and those who were interviewed back then. Naomi closed her eyes for moment. Were her killers reading this story, too? she wondered. Are they looking at my picture? I must come as a big surprise to them. God, she hoped so. She hoped they were shaking in their evil skins right now. And she was suddenly very glad the paper had carried the story. She was feeling better about things.

It was well-written. No errors or omissions, no twisting of words for dramatic purpose. Not that it needed it. Understated, letting the facts speak for themselves. At her insistence, he'd added both her phone number and email at the end. She thought about his warnings. "You never know what kind of sickos are out there.

That was kind of the point, wasn't it? Ferreting the two scumbags out from under their

rocks.

She set the paper aside. "Well, Molly, what's your guess? Think we'll rattle some cages?" she asked, mixing her metaphors. Molly blinked up at her from her patch of sunlight on the floor by the window. "You know everything, don't you?" Naomi chuckled. "You are so smart." Molly gave her face a quick wash and went back to sleep.

The phone rang and her heart jumped, the smile vanishing from her face as she sprinted to answer it. "Hello."

"How dare you?" came the familiar voice, her aunt's venom oozing through the phone line, tying Naomi's stomach in knots. Old head tapes played on cue and she mentally braced herself for the onslaught. You are not a child, she reminded herself, even though her aunt could still take her back there with a look or a word. At Frank's prodding, she'd almost managed to put the woman out of her mind. Putting her out of her life was another matter entirely. But she should have expected this reaction from Edna. She didn't think I'd have the guts to go to the paper. And maybe I just don't give a damn anymore what she thinks. It hadn't been her intention to embarrass anyone, but if that was part of the cost, well...tough...

She could hang up, but best to let her rant. Get it all out.

"How dare you drag our family through your own muck...?" Edna was saying over Naomi's thoughts, sounding like she was breathing fire and burning up with her own fuel. "Who the hell do you think you..."

"I'm sorry if this is uncomfortable for you, Aunt Edna. Isn't this what you wanted? For the truth to be told?" This she said calmly with a perverse satisfaction, surprising herself. "As I recall, you were quite adamant about that."

"You ungrateful little...My sister took you in and gave you a home. Damn little half-breed. You are nothing, a spawn of Satan. You..."

Unable to listen to more, Naomi hung up. Not banging the receiver down, she hurt too much for that, but placing it gently in its cradle. To hell with you, Aunt Edna. But her hands were shaking and she had to fight back the tears. Her mother wasn't here as a buffer anymore and Edna was giving full rein to the rage she'd always harbored where Naomi was concerned, a satisfaction denied her while her sister was alive. Still, Naomi was stunned at the depths of her hatred. Devil's spawn. She'd been speaking of Naomi's biological father, of course. The rapist. The monster.

She was devastated by her aunt's cruel words, and missing her mother more even than she realized. Why was she so surprised? She angrily mopped at the tears with a tissue from her slacks' pocket. She had seen her aunt look at her with that same hatred and disdain from the time Naomi barely came up to her waist.

The crying had given her a headache and she took two Tylenol and went upstairs to lie

down.

That's the last time I will shed tears because of Edna Bradley, she promised herself fervently as she climbed the stairs. The last damn time.

On silent paws, Molly padded up the carpeted stairs behind her.

* * *

"Don't you think you were a little rough on the kid, Edna?"

She'd just hung up the phone and now she whirled around to face her husband. "She's not a kid, Sam. Did you read this?" she asked, snatching the paper off the table, folded to Naomi's story, shook it at him, practically shoving it in his face.

He snapped it from her and tossed it back on the table. "I read it. She's got a right to try to find out who abducted her mother that night, raped her and beat her into a coma, if she wants to. I think it took courage to go public with this. Anyway, it wouldn't have happened if you hadn't told her she was adopted. But you couldn't wait for Lili to take her last breath, could you? So you could tell her. Damned if I know why. I don't suppose you want to enlighten me?"

Rage bubbled up like bile in Edna as she faced the tall, gentle man who was looking at her with such bewilderment and dislike. As though he had seen deeply into her soul for the first time, and was more saddened than angry at what he saw, serving only to infuriate her more. How dare he judge her?

"That's not true. I loved my sister. Naomi always was your favorite, wasn't she? More important even than your own daughter. Makes me wonder why, Harold?" she sneered, leaving no doubt as to what she meant.

"You've got a dirty mind, Edna. I didn't favor her over Charlotte at all. I just never understood your hatred of the girl, that's all. I felt sorry for her."

Chapter Twelve

It was late in the afternoon when Naomi came downstairs to find the machine's red light blinking. She had four messages. She hit the play button and heard Frank Llewellyn's familiar voice.

"Hi, Naomi, Frank here. As you can imagine, I was surprised to say the least when I opened my morning paper. I wish you'd spoken to me first about this before you went ahead. I'm worried about you, honey. I'm not sure this was a wise move on your part, although I can understand why you did it. Edna will have a conniption." She heard a soft satisfied chuckle, before he said, "Still, you're very vulnerable in that house all by yourself. Call me, okay? If you're determined to pursue this, maybe I can be of some help."

Thanks, Frank, she thought. I might just take you up on that. She wasn't sure just how at the moment. But Frank was smart and he had connections. He could probably get the case file for her if it was still in existence. She felt a stirring of hope.

The next call was from her cousin. "Hey, Naomi, I just wanted you to know that I've been feeling really crappy about your finding out like you did…about everything. I love my mother, but she can be such an ass sometimes. She does have a good side, you know. It's just that she keeps it hidden most of the time. Anyway," she went on, "I hope you nail the creeps. Let's hook up for lunch soon if you're not too ticked at the whole family, for which I wouldn't blame ya. But I hope not. See ya. Oh, great picture of you, by the way. You look like that actress, Jennifer Connelly. Well, take care, Jen..." She giggled and clicked off.

Yeah, right, Naomi thought, allowing herself a small smile. She had almost forgotten how irreverent Charlotte could be, and how much fun. Tall and athletic with kinky wild blond hair, she'd always been something of a tomboy, which had irked Edna no end. Charlotte was a fitness instructor at the Aerobics center. They might have been friends had Edna allowed it. She wanted to call her back, but it seemed to her getting between Edna and her daughter could only invite more trouble, which she definitely didn't need and neither did Charlotte.

Uncle Harold, with his quiet, peace-loving ways couldn't have been much help to Charlotte growing up. He sure was no match for Edna. Naomi liked him though, and as a child, sensed he liked her too, though he was careful not to let it show when Aunt Edna was around.

The third message was from her publisher. Angela Haines spoke in her clipped, New York accent, friendly but no-nonsense. She had a new assignment for her.

Being in New York City, it was unlikely the editor would have any knowledge of happenings here in Naomi's neck of the woods, which was just as well. The River's End Tribune wasn't exactly well-known in the Big Apple. Naomi called her back and accepted the new assignment. She couldn't afford to be without a job. And her work was important to her.

The last message was a hang-up. She replayed it twice. In the background, she could hear country music. Only a fragment, three or four seconds at most, and then the click. Cranks, she thought, but she didn't dismiss the call altogether. She replayed the message half a dozen times, listening for some clue as to who her caller might be, but the connection was too brief. Someone trying to get up the nerve to talk to her? A neighbor who perhaps lived on the street at the time and saw something out her window?

Another possibility was that there was another woman out there who had suffered at the hands of these monsters, but survived the attack, and now decided to come forward. Then chickened out at the last minute.

Whoever you are, please call back. But she tried not to let her hopes get too high. It was

well she didn't. For the next day she received no calls at all, or in the days following. When a week passed and still there was nothing, her disappointment came close to despair. Had it all been for nothing? She stared at the mute phone. Please, please, call back, she pleaded silently with her mysterious caller.

Not that she received no other responses to the write-up. She did, as well as numerous emails, mostly from other adoptees eager to share their own stories. A few from anonymous sources, but nothing relevant to Mary Rose's case.

And then, out of the blue, while Naomi was washing the kitchen floor, Lisa Boyce called. "I used to be Lisa Cameron," she said. Even before she related that information, Naomi knew instinctively who it was. Perhaps it was the warmth, the kindness that came through the line that made her so sure. A voice belonging to a woman who, as a girl, would be the one to reach out to another child, one who stood outside the hallowed circle and needed a friend.

Naomi went to bed that night eagerly looking forward to meeting Mary Rose's old school pal at her home the next day. There were so many questions she wanted to ask her about the girl who gave birth to her.

Chapter Thirteen

Lisa Boyce was a pretty woman with warm coffee-colored eyes and streaked blond hair. The few extra pounds she complained about, as far as Naomi was concerned, just added to her appeal. Her husband died three years ago of a sudden heart attack, she told Naomi, and she lived alone. Their four grown children were scattered around the country, with children of their own, she said.

It wasn't hard to see Lisa through Mary Rose's eyes. To see her as a trusted friend, someone to talk to, to share secrets with. She exuded warmth and compassion, along with a sense of fun. At the moment she was explaining that she was computer illiterate, saying it would have been easier if she could have emailed, then Naomi could have had a choice of whether to answer or not. "I suppose it's always harder for people to say no on the phone."

"Naomi laughed, "It's not like you're a telemarketer, Lisa. Of course I would have answered your email. With pleasure. I can't imagine anyone saying no to you."

"Oh, I'm sure there are any number. Anyway, the kids are always at me to learn how to use the computer so we can all stay in touch easier, and so they can email me pictures of the kids. I've finally decided to give it a try. The local library is running a course for beginners. I'm scared to death," she laughed. "I'm about as low tech as you can get. I can't even program my DVD player." She gave a soft self-deprecating chuckle and sipped her tea.

They were sitting at a round maple table centered with a cut-glass bowl of flawless red shiny apples, in Lisa's bright kitchen, enjoying tea and home-made cheese biscuits that were high and light as clouds.

The apples in the bowl looked waxen they were so perfect in shape and color, but their sweet apple smell told her they were real. As real as Lisa Boyce herself.

"You'll do great, Lisa. You'll surprise yourself at how quickly you'll learn with a bit of hands-on help. Just takes practice. Six months from now, I guarantee, you'll wonder how you ever got along without your computer. You'll love it, I promise."

"That's what everyone keeps telling me. Well, we'll soon see. But enough about me. You know, when I saw your story in the paper, Naomi, I could hardly believe it. I didn't know if I should call or not. I really have nothing helpful to tell you. I wish I did. And I didn't want to bother you for nothing..."

"Hardly for nothing, Lisa," Naomi reassured her quickly. "I'm really glad you called. Actually, I was planning to call you. You're the only person I know who can tell me anything about my birth-mother."

"I-- I suppose that's true. I hadn't thought of it that way. I only wish I could help you find out who did such a terrible thing to Mary Rose. But I'm so excited you're here, Naomi. That you exist. It's like a miracle." An embarrassed laugh held tears. "I'm so happy to meet you, you have no idea. You have her smile."

"Do you think so? Thank you for that, Lisa." Her words had sent a pleasant warmth through Naomi. Strange how easily the conversation flowed between them, as if they had known one another all their lives.

"I'm surprised some lucky guy hasn't grabbed you up by now," Lisa said, getting up to refill their cups from the Pyrex teapot on the stove.

"There've been a couple of close calls," Naomi said easily. "Things just didn't work out. I'm probably too independent." *I'm more like mom -- my adopted mom-- than I realized.* "I like my freedom."

"Ah, a cat who walks alone," Lisa teased, returning to her chair. "Then more seriously, she added, "You just haven't met the right one is all. But you're young yet."

"I'm not really looking. And speaking of cats, I have one who's wonderful company. Molly. The love of my life. And I keep busy." Even as she spoke the words, an image of Eric Grant's blue eyes smiling at her out of that bushy face leapt unbidden into her mind's eye, surprising her. Strange. Had revealing her story to him created some childish bond in her mind? Like someone who develops an attraction for her shrink? What did they call it -- transference? Whatever, it would pass. She was just another story to him.

"You must miss your husband terribly," she said, turning the conversation away from herself to Lisa."

She nodded slowly. "We were supposed to grow old together. The year before his heart attack we bought a yard swing and joked about spending our golden years sitting in it, talking and looking at the stars. For a long time I didn't think I could go on. But you do. Somehow you do. You don't have much choice."

Naomi sat quietly. She could see a part of the swing through the kitchen window. Wooden, old-fashioned, the kind that invited you to sit a spell and contemplate the stars.

"Sometimes I sit out there alone and imagine him beside me. I even talk to him. Do you think I'm crazy?"

"No, of course not. I'm sure he hears every word."

"Your mother's secret must have weighed heavily on her all those years. She clearly loved you very much, to want to protect you."

"Maybe she was protecting herself."

"Oh, I don't think so, honey. She would have been considered some kind of hero if folks around here knew she took in that poor girl's baby to raise as her own."

Naomi let the words sink in. They made sense. Made her feel a little better, too. "I can see why Mary Rose was drawn to you, Lisa. You're really something."

She just smiled a sad little smile that Naomi couldn't quite read. "It's nice of you to say

that."

"It's only the truth. Can you tell me about her, Lisa? I know it was a long time ago, but..." "Not so long that I don't remember like it was yesterday. I remember her very well. I can see her face so clearly in my mind. Hear her laugh. And that night still haunts me, and will for the rest of my life. I can still smell the nail polish we painted our nails with, hear the music on the record player. What haunts me most is that her killers are still out there, free for years now to come and go as they damn well please while Mary Rose lays in the ground... I'm sorry."

"Don't be. I feel the same way. What was she like?" Naomi prodded gently, wanting to know Mary Rose better, wanting to make a deeper connection through this woman who knew her. Who danced and laughed with her, when they were both girls.

Lisa looked thoughtfully at her, but Naomi sensed she was looking inward, at old memories. Eyes soft, a tender smile on her lips, she said, "She was quiet and kind of shy. She had a great laugh though. Infectious. Made you laugh too. Although admittedly there wasn't much for her to laugh about at school. Kids can be pretty mean. I don't think it's so bad now, the bigotry. Anyway, she handled it. She was very close to her grandfather, and I think that helped. He called her 'Little Bird'. Let me see. She liked to draw and write poetry. And she had a lovely singing voice, too, like an angel. Once, I tried to talk her into auditioning for the school variety show, but you'd have thought I suggested she jump from a plane minus a parachute." She laughed softly, remembering. "Imagine, here I am sitting across from her daughter who would

grow up to be an audio book narrator. How cool is that?"

"It is kind of, isn't it?" Naomi grinned, feeling a self-conscious pride in her achievements, modest as they were. "I'm very lucky to be doing work I love."

"Yes. You are. That's not to say you didn't work for it. But I think knowing how to be grateful is a gift too."

Her words caught Naomi off-guard. A kind of back-handed compliment that came off oddly as advice. Also made her think of Eric Grant; he wasn't all that off base in his comment about her being lucky. She'd just been particularly touchy in that moment that was all. "I'm really glad you called," she said again. "You're a special person, Lisa."

The sadness in the woman's eyes deepened. "Not so special. I went to visit her for awhile after ... but it was too hard seeing her like that. Unable to speak, even open her eyes. All those tubes snaking out of her ...machines beeping. After a beat, she said, "I never knew she was pregnant."

"Don't be so hard on yourself. You were just a kid."

"I know. But I still feel guilty. Oh, I have something for you. I'll just be a minute; it's in the bedroom."

Moments later, she returned with a folded sheet of paper in her hand and passed it to Naomi. "It's one of her poems. I kept it in an old chocolate box all these years. I want you to have it."

Naomi's immediate impulse was to snatch the paper from Lisa's hand and clutch it to her heart, but of course she didn't, just forced her hands to lie limply in her lap. "I couldn't. It belongs to you."

"No, not anymore. I guess I was keeping it for you anyway. I just didn't know it." Naomi took the paper. As she started to unfold it, Lisa put a hand on hers. "Don't read it now. Wait until you're alone."

"You don't know what this means to me."

"Oh, I think I do," Lisa smiled. The smile gave way to concern as she said, "You be careful, Naomi. Be very careful."

The warning sent an involuntary chill through Naomi. "I will. But I don't think there's too much to worry about. I haven't heard anything significant since the article came out in the paper."

"You will though. I have a very strong feeling about that. You will."

Chapter Fourteen

Naomi had barely gotten in the house and taken off her jacket when the phone rang, but by the time she snatched up the receiver and said hello, the caller had already hung up. She contemplated the silent phone for a few seconds, then replaced the receiver with a sigh of frustration. Was Lisa right? Could that have been the call that would change everything? Surely they would call back then, if that was the case. If it was part of the plan.

Lisa was sensitive, and open, and it was that that had given Naomi the courage to tell her about her dream of the eagle. She was the first and only person she'd ever told about the dream. Not surprising to Naomi, she didn't laugh or look skeptical as many would have, but was matter-of-fact in her assertion that Mary Rose had reached out to her from the spirit world. Her words affirmed Naomi's own belief that we exist on different planes, and that all things are possible. Spoken aloud, it might sound like so much fantasy and wishful thinking, but Naomi felt in her heart that there was more to a life than six feet of ground at the end. Otherwise, it was all some kind of cosmic joke, and that seemed far less likely. That made no sense at all.

It had been an afternoon of reveals. Lisa surprised her by telling her that Eric Grant wrote a book called "Freakhead". Lisa had noted his byline on her story, and said she was a fan. "It's a memoir.

About being raised in an orphanage, Greyland's Home for Boys, aptly named, I might add. The place had a less than great reputation and they finally tore it down. He got the title for his book from some kid who called him Freakhead all the time."

Not as bad as Devil's Spawn, she thought. Then felt ashamed of herself for even daring to compare her own childhood with someone who was raised in an orphanage. It explained totally his comment about her being lucky to be adopted. Which, of course, was true.

Lisa offered to lend her the book but for some reason she couldn't explain even to herself, Naomi declined, saying she had all she could do to keep up with the books her publisher sent. She didn't miss the oddly puzzled look Lisa gave her, and wondered at her own resistance to reading his memoir. "Why was he in Greyland's?" she asked. "Were his parents dead?"

"Divorced. Mother remarried, and the new husband didn't want to be saddled with a kid. She made a choice. Four year old Eric went to live with his father. A year later his father died of a heart attack, and Eric ended up in that hellhole. You oughta read the book."

* * *

Driving home, Naomi recalled reading that Eric Grant's articles on the middle-east had been short-listed for some prestigious award a couple of years back. She hadn't made the connection with his name at first. She should try to stay current. Pretty impressive for a kid raised in an orphanage. As she thought about Eric Grant, and what was perhaps her skewed first impression of him, she continued to listen for the phone, willing it to ring.

Being in Lisa's tidy house had given Naomi a shot of domesticity. She tidied the living room, fed Molly, pushed sheets into the washing machine, in the laundry room, which had once been a pantry. As she added detergent, she continued to listen for the ring of the phone. She'd just let the clothes soak awhile, she told herself, in case she didn't hear the ring over the sound of the motor. She didn't want to miss it again if it did ring.

They'll call back, she told herself again, casting a watchful eye on the phone. While the clothes soaked and the house stayed silent.

* * *

An hour later Norman Banks drained the beer in his glass, wiped the foam from his mouth with the back of his hand and once again left the barstool to make his way unsteadily to the phone out in the dingy, urine-smelling hallway of the bar where he'd been for the past few hours. It had been a very long time since Norman had hung out in bars, but reading that article had gotten to him, made him anxious and nervous, affected his sleep, and he'd needed to dull the edges.

Looking at the girl's photo, learning who she was, had brought back the memory of another girl all those years ago. Another lifetime. This girl's resemblance to her mother was slight, but it was there. He was just a kid himself when it happened, barely twenty, but he'd never forget the fear in her face, or her terrible cries for help that had often wakened him in the night. That he'd done nothing to stop the attack was something he could never forgive himself for. He didn't have the guts back then to help her. If he had it to do again, he'd take his chances and slam something across that bastard's head. But life didn't allow for do-overs.

In the next room, two old guys were playing billiards, balls clacking sharply over Willie Nelson's To All The Girls I Loved Before, giving him a headache. As Willie sang on, Norman rubbed sweaty hands down the sides of his olive green workpants, glanced over his shoulder a couple of times to be sure no one was spying on him. Satisfied he went unobserved, he managed to steady his shaking hand sufficiently to dig out the folded square of newspaper, now wrinkled and smudged, from being in his pants' pocket. Unfolding the paper, he held it up to the greasy light by the black wall-phone although he'd already memorized her number and tapped the number out, almost gingerly. But again, before anyone could answer, he hung up. Forget it, he told himself. Let it go. Let the past stay buried. If it was just him, he wouldn't hesitate. He might even go to the cops. But what about Deb and the kids? Thinking of how they would look at him; the shock, the disappointment and finally, disgust when they found out was too much to take. I can't, he thought. I can't do it. He went back to his barstool and ordered another beer.

His face in the mirror behind the bar was pale and haunted,

and accusing. You still ain't got no guts, Banks. You're just as much a coward as you ever were. He didn't like to think of the nickname Weasel some of the kids at school gave him, but now he thought it fit just fine.

Chapter Fifteen

Naomi lowered herself onto the kitchen chair, poem in hand. She felt a sense of wonder knowing she was about to get a deeper look into a young girl's heart, through her own words. Mary Rose Francis who had given her life.

The sheet of lined paper rattled as she opened it, and she realized her hands were trembling. The smell of years locked in darkness floated up from the paper. It was like opening a treasure chest, long buried in the earth. The writing was neat and cursive, in blue ink.

She let out a soft breath and began to read.

GRANDFATHER

Grandfather's mahogany face is like an old map very wrinkled tracing back through time and time to the teepee and circle fires and laughter,

and later the peace-pipes and white men that lied to his father and grandfather before him.

Crystal waters rush over pink and grey stones, sparkling like golden coins.

A speckled trout gives himself up for our supper. Grandfather's eyes remember other times

and he is sad. But the sadness does not stay.

When he sees me his eyes crinkle and he laughs.

Sitting on the stoop, carving the deer bone into treasures for the tourists.

I have the best one.

I wear the white moon around my neck and am never in darkness.

by Mary Rose Francis - Age 16.

The last line had brought tears to Naomi's eyes, because the white moon that she held dear had betrayed her in the end, proved impotent against the darker force of evil. Was merely a thing of decoration, lovely, but without powers.

Mary Rose wrote this poem on a day when the blood ran like sap through her young veins and the world held sweet promise, despite whatever challenges she faced on a daily basis. Naomi was no expert on poetry, but she thought this was a good poem, an honest one. Who knows what she might have accomplished in her lifetime.

Lisa said she had a nice singing voice. She might have written songs for others to sing even if she'd been too shy to perform them herself. And who's to say she wouldn't have gotten over her shyness, or just learned to rise above it in the way of many, if not most, performers.

But someone had ended those possibilities, silenced her song forever. Her tears were also for the man who inspired the poem Mary Rose's grandfather and Naomi's great-grandfather. She

felt as if she knew him a little now.

She would find a special frame for the poem. In the meantime, she slid the sheet of paper between the pages of a coffee table book to smooth out the fold marks. As she closed the book, she glared at the silent phone. Ring, she commanded it. When it obeyed, she literally jumped.

She snapped up the receiver, pressed it to her ear. Country music was playing in the background, nothing she could identify, but a familiar tune.

"Hello."

There was a long pause, in which she could hear only the music, coupled with his breathing over the line. Then, "Is this that girl whose picture was in the paper... Naomi...?" The caller's voice was whispery, frightened, as if he was worried about being overheard.

Her entire body hummed with anticipation, even while a cold dark wind swirled round her heart. This was it. "Yes, this is Naomi Waters."

* * *

Three beers after he made the call to the girl's daughter, whose name the paper said was Naomi Waters, Norman was heading home from the bar. Knowing he was well over the legal limit, he drove slowly, with caution. The last thing he needed was to get stopped by the cops. He wasn't supposed to be drinking at all what with the diabetes. Deb would be really mad at him for going against doctor's orders, but reading that story in the paper had really freaked him out. What if the cops could get a voice print, or trace the number? Had someone been watching him when he made the call?

He'd been careful to look around him, but you never knew.

His hands were sweaty on the wheel and his stomach was twisted like the pretzels he'd eaten; the beer he'd consumed burned like acid in his gut. He needed to talk to someone. Ordinarily, that someone would be Deb, but not this time.

There was only one person he could talk to about this. The one whose awful secret he'd kept all these years. The one he'd been with that night. The night they took a girl's life.

Spotting the McDonald's sign at the next corner, he slowed and pulled into the parking lot. Spotting an empty slot between a pickup and a green Volvo, he eased the car into it, turned off the ignition and sat for a few minutes. Then he got out of the car.

In the restaurant's alcove, he looked up the number in the battered phone book, was almost surprised to see it there. As if in reality, the man existed only in some nightmare place in his mind. On some terrifying alternate planet. But his existence was only too real. He was a part of Norman's past. A past he had tried to forget, but could not. The newspaper article had made it fresh again.

The phone rang and rang. Norman was about to hang up, like getting a happy reprieve, when he heard the pick-up, and his heart slipped down into his stomach as he heard the words, "Your nickel."

Same thing he always said when he answered the phone. Same thing he said more than two decades ago when Norman called him. The acid in his stomach was burning its way through the lining. He had a mother of all headaches pounding away in his skull. The smell of frying grease didn't help.

Ordinarily he would have been craving a cheeseburger, but now he wondered if he'd ever eat again. As it was he hadn't eaten anything but those pretzels all day. Not good for his health. Neither was this. He was swept back in time, to a cold, ugly place. It wasn't a good feeling.

Maybe this wasn't such a great idea after all. But it was too late now. He had no doubt his

old cohort would have caller ID. This is a public phone, for Christ's sakes. Maybe the number wouldn't come up. But he wasn't sure. Anyway, he'd already identified himself, already said hello.

* * *

The man who picked up the phone lived on River City's west side on the second floor apartment of a faded red-brick building, close to his work. He'd just stepped out of the shower and had a towel draped about his waist, a smaller towel in his hand. He admired his reflection in the long mirror in the hallway. He was a big man, trim and muscular at fifty-three, owing to many hours spent at the local gym, pumping iron. The hair-transplant he was leisurely drying with a second towel was a good one. Undetectable to the average eye. Should be; cost him enough.

As he clutched the phone, the blue and gold owl's eye tattooed on his left upper arm, winked at him in the mirror.

"Hey, Weaz, long time no see," he said in his good ole boy fashion. "What's up?" But he knew what was up. He'd read the paper.

He knew why the Weaz was calling.

"We gotta talk," his caller said quietly.

Same old Weaz. Scared of his shadow. "Yeah, figured you'd call. I have to admit, reading that story in the local rag hung me out there too. Who'd a thought the bitch would live long enough to have a kid. She sure as hell looked dead enough when we left her, eh, Weasel?"

When you left her, Norman thought, but didn't say. But that wasn't exactly true either. He was right. I left her too. "I wish you wouldn't call me that," he said. "No one does anymore." The beers he'd had all but worn off. Just the headache left. He felt cold, and sick in his gut, and it wasn't the beer that was making him feel that way.

"Yeah, sure, sorry. Take it easy, okay? You sound bad. Like you're coming apart at the seams."

"Maybe you shouldn't say things on the phone. Might be tapped."

He laughed that ugly laugh of his. Norman heard that laugh in his darkest dreams. How could he have taken up with him?

"Get a grip, man," he was saying now. "Why would the phone be tapped? It happened nearly thirty years ago. The cops don't know squat. You still living in the same place?"

The question caught Norman by surprise, followed by a jolt of panic. He sure as hell didn't want him knowing where he lived. Didn't want him anywhere near his family. "No, we bought a house out in ...the country. Look, I gotta go. I'll meet you somewhere.

Friday night, okay. The wife works until ten on Fridays."

"Sure, Weaz Norm. Whatever you say?"

Norman swallowed. Tentatively, he said, "She's your daughter, Mac." "Who? What are you talking about?"

"That girl. Naomi Waters. She's your child." He was hoping the reminder might trigger some normal human feeling in the bastard. Norman might not be any hero, but he had kids himself and he'd die for any one of them. But the icy vibes that came through the line froze any such hopes. He wasn't really surprised. He shouldn't have called, he thought again. Why was he meeting him anyway? What was the point? But he let himself be carried along.

Just like he did all those years ago. "Deb know you called me?"

Hearing his wife's name coming from this man's mouth to his ear made the hairs stand up on the back of Norman Banks' neck, terrified him. He'd met Deb only that one time, before they were married. How the hell could he remember her name? It didn't seem possible. Had he been keeping track of him all these years? Maybe he knew exactly where he lived.

"No." He could barely get the word past the boulder in his throat. "You never talked to her about that night?"

"You crazy? She's still with me, isn't she? Anyway, I didn't do nothin'. You know that." "Don't matter. They get me, they get you." Ice in his voice. It melted a little as he said,

"But it ain't gonna happen. So don't worry, Weaz...Norm. It'll be fine. We'll meet, like you said.

We'll talk, okay?"

Mac glared at his phone as if it were a black serpent with poisoned fangs, oblivious to the fact that he was dripping water onto the carpet that his eyes had narrowed to slivers of grey ice. He turned away, caught his reflection in the mirror and grinned. Like he always did, even when he didn't realize it, he admired himself in the glass for a couple of seconds, then headed for his bedroom to get dressed, and think more on his conversation with his old buddy. His dangerous old buddy.

He didn't miss the Weaz's surprise that he'd remember his wife's name after all these years. No reason he should have remembered. Nothin' memorable about her that he could recall. Pretty enough, but a mousy broad. But the Weaz was nuts about her, like she was something special. Even bought her a diamond ring. He didn't see much of him after that.

The Weaz was trouble. He'd cave. I'll die in a cage, and no way in hell that was going to happen.

Chapter Sixteen

On Friday night, while his wife worked the evening shift at Sears, Norman Banks waited in the designated meeting place down by the wharf for his old friend in deed. It was just 9:15 by his watch. They'd set a time for meeting at 9:30. He'd come early, wanting to get it over with. Part of him had considered going to the cops and confessing the whole damn thing, getting if off his chest, but then he got to thinking again about how Debbie and the kids would suffer if he did that. They deserved better than to have their lives turned upside down, be forced to feel the shame because they were a part of him. It wouldn't be so bad if he'd just been part of a bank robbery or something, but the rape and beating of a young woman who would eventually die of her injuries was something else again. That would be unforgivable. No, he'd have to carry the burden alone. He'd been a part of what happened whether he'd personally done anything to that girl or not, and having this awful thing on his conscience was his punishment. And would continue to be for as long as he lived. He was glad he'd at least got up the gumption to phone the girl, to warn her against Mac.

He just knew he'd needed to talk to someone about what had happened. He'd been frightened, desperate. But he was okay now. He didn't need this meeting. Dumb idea. He'd just hit a bad patch in the road, that was all. I'll just leave, say I waited and somehow missed him.

He was okay now. It was just seeing that girl's picture in the paper like that that got to him ...reading about her.

Norman shifted his feet in their heavy brown work boots, which he wore to operate the forklift at Mason's Woodworking. The crunch of gravel under his boots was amplified in the silence. It began to occur to him that it was creepy down here. The night sky was overcast, no stars showed through. Although dirty amber light glowed here and there among the wharves, it was dark where he stood. Between the long, low buildings, he could see the water gleaming black and oily, hear it lapping against the slick and creaking wood pilings.

Feeling a sudden chill, he zipped up his nylon jacket all the way, checked his watch again. Only two minutes had passed since he last checked it. To hell with this, he thought. I've changed my mind. A person's allowed to change...

Before he could complete the thought, a large powerful hand clamped over his mouth and nose and yanked his head back. For an instant, he tasted salty sweat and turpentine from the hand, and then he felt a mild sting across his throat, but when he tried to breathe there was a gurgling sound and he couldn't take in air. Panic rose up in him, eyes widening as his hand shot up to cover the grinning wound, but the blood flowed over and between his fingers and his knees went out from under him as he frantically tried to gasp in air through vital tubes, now severed and useless.

As he lay there on the ground, his body jerked convulsively

like a live fish tossed upon a bank, and then the darkness, darker than any night, rolled over him.

Norman did not feel himself being moved, nor hear the scrape of gravel beneath his body as it was dragged away.

* * *

Earlier that evening, Naomi went shopping for a frame for Mary Rose's poem and found exactly the right one, with a narrow light wood trim. Intent on her own purchase, she didn't notice the dark-haired sales-clerk a few aisles away in the children's department, smiling at an

elderly woman who was holding up a large, brown teddy bear for her approval. Neither the sales-clerk nor Naomi could know that they were fated to meet, or that Debbie Banks' life, like her own, would be changed forever because of what happened to a teenaged native girl all those years ago. Norman Banks' wife would later wonder why she didn't feel the exact moment when her husband's life had bled out of him, and his soul departed this earth. How could she not have sensed this?

At home, Naomi hung the framed poem in her room beside the vanity mirror and stood back to admire it. She had neatly cut out Mary Rose's photo from the newspaper and fitted it in the bottom, left hand corner of the frame. Perfect.

The room seemed more hers now.

Chapter Seventeen

"Take a seat right over there, Ma'am." The heavy-set policeman with his pewter-colored buzz cut said, gesturing to a row of forest green plastic molded chairs set against the wall. "I'll tell Sergeant Nelson you're here. He's with someone right now."

Naomi had been sitting in the hard-backed chair for about five minutes, by turns thumbing idly through an ancient copy of Reader's Digest she picked up off the low table in front of her, and observing the early morning traffic like the bleached-blond in a mustard-yellow leather micro-mini skirt presently being led by a plain clothes cop through to a room at the end of the hallway. Her wobbly spiked heels clicked out an uneven beat on the beige tile floor.

Off to Naomi's right, an old man was ranting to a female police officer about teenagers tormenting his dog. "I'da shot the buggers if that gun wasn't so damned old and rusted out."

But for the clientele and the uniforms, the reception area looked like any office waiting room. There the comparison ended. You couldn't disguise the faintly sour smell of human desperation and fear in the air. As she mulled over that thought, a bray of laughter issued from across the room, where a knot of policeman were in private conversation. The laughter had held a mocking undertone, and Naomi found herself instinctively looking around for the woman in the leather mustard skirt. Not seeing her, she went back to her magazine. She had just turned to the humor page, All in a

Day's Work, when a male voice spoke her name. "Miss Waters ... Naomi?"

She looked up, expecting to see a police officer standing there, but instead saw a vaguely familiar and very attractive civilian grinning down at her. He was tall, blond, wearing a dark blue suit and burgundy and cream-colored striped tie, and could have posed for an Armani ad.

"Yes?" Naomi said, trying to place him. His grin reflected amusement, a certain sheepishness. "You don't remember me."

"I'm sorry, I..." There was something familiar in the eyes, but no, she couldn't place him. "Reporter at large," he joked. "Eric Grant." He gave a small, mock bow, a twinkle in his

blue eyes.

At what must have been her look of surprise, he laughed and rubbed a self-conscious hand over his square, beardless jaw. "Can't say I blame you. My boss said I looked like a mangy buffalo when I walked through the door last week. Not particularly a good idea to shave when you're information-gathering in the Middle-East. At least I never found one. Any response to your story?"

Momentarily embarrassed, she quickly recovered her composure. "Yes, it's why I'm here. I received an anonymous call from a man who said he tried to stop the other one. And I did recognize you, Mr. Grant. Just not right away." The smile gave him away as did those eyes, even if not at a glance. She had only met him one time, after all. But she had to admit, he cleaned up spectacularly. "You're a war correspondent. Yes, I remembered your last book was up for an award. Are you home for good now?"

"For the time being anyway. I'm freelance now pretty much. I like being a free agent. Suits my temperament. Appreciate your mentioning the book. I'm trying my hand at fiction now. It's a hell of a lot harder. For me, anyway. Being freelance, gives me that time to follow a dream of writing a novel."

"Sounds like a great job."

"Pays the bills. Like I said, let's me work on my novel. I hope you're not pinning all your hopes on that phone call. It could be legit, but that kind of story also can bring a lot of weirdoes

out of the woodwork. They'll confess to just about anything to see themselves on TV, or read their names in the paper."

"Yes, you said," she replied stiffly, irritated at his assumption that she wouldn't know a crank call from a real lead.

Before he could annoy her further, the policeman called out from behind his desk, "Ms. Waters, Sergeant Nelson will see you now."

Naomi was glad for the interruption. Eric Grant must think she was very gullible and not too bright. "I'm sure, Mr. Grant. He was one of them. Excuse me. I have to go. Nice to see you again. Good luck with your novel."

"Thanks. Great to see you, too." He stepped aside to let her pass. "I really hope you're right about the call. Maybe we could have coffee after and talk about..."

* * *

But Naomi had already brushed by him and was now striding down the narrow corridor with its pale green walls to her meeting with Sergeant Nelson.

Conversation drifted from inside the second door on her left. The door had a brass plaque that bore the name Sergeant Graham Nelson. The door opened and an attractive black female officer stepped out. Her hair was cut close to her perfectly-shaped head, enhanced by gold-hoop earrings. She gave Naomi a nod and told her in a rich, contralto voice that she could go right on in.

"Naomi Waters," the big man said, rising from behind his desk and extending a hand to her. She shook it, conscious of the firm, practiced handshake. His muscular build was softening in middle-age, a paunch just starting to spill over his belt, but he was still a formidable man, an impression not lessened by the granny-type glasses.

He gestured to the leather chair in front of his desk and offered her coffee. "Thanks, coffee would be great."

The coffee-maker with all the fixings stood on a table off in a corner of the room. "Cream? Sugar?"

"Black's fine, thanks."

He returned with two steaming Styrofoam cups and handed her one, went back behind his desk. "Tastes bad but it's hot."

He grimaced over his own, but drank it anyway. She didn't think it was so bad. As he said, it was hot and she needed a jolt of caffeine. She was still feeling some residual anxiety she couldn't explain from her encounter with Eric Grant.

He pushed the glasses higher up on his large heavily veined nose, and gestured to the newspaper on his desk, folded with her story turned outward. "I read the article. Helluva story. Young fella from the paper was in asking for a quote. I wasn't much help, I'm afraid. I was in traffic back then. Though I recall the case."

He glanced down at the folded newspaper, gave her a half-smile that held sympathy. "Like they say, truth is stranger than fiction. I'm sorry for the loss of your mother, Miss Waters. I read she recently passed of cancer. "He was talking about Lillian, of course. "Yes. Thank you."

"Well, let's get to it, shall we? What can I do for you, Miss … okay if I call you Naomi?"

Of course. I think you probably already know why I'm here, Sergeant Nelson. I want you to reopen the case." She looked at him squarely across the desk as she said it, then took another sip of her coffee. She could tell by looking at his face that he was already thinking of a way to let

her down easy. He sighed and removed the glasses, slipped them into his shirt pocket. His eyes were hazel, intelligent, probing.

"You mentioned on the phone you received an anonymous phone call from a man you believe is one of the two men who abducted Mary Rose."

"That's right. I bought the tape with me."

"What makes you so sure it wasn't just some crackpot?" he said, smiling a smile that was both indulgent and sympathetic. "You must have expected when you made your phone number and email public, you'd get your share of those."

She retrieved the tape from her purse and slid it across the desk to him. "Please. Play it for yourself, Sergeant. Then tell me what you think."

At least he wasn't going to turn her away without a hearing. Not a stupid man, he knew she wouldn't be above going to the newspaper again if he blatantly refused to help her. He would listen. But she was hoping hearing the tape would garner a more genuine interest in her cause.

She appreciated his use of Mary Rose's full name, rather than dismissing her as merely 'the victim'. It gave her the dignity she deserved, rendered her as a human being worthy of respect and consideration. And justice, she hoped.

"Fair enough," he said, sliding the small black recorder on his desk toward him. He snapped in the tape and closed the lid. "Long time ago," he mumbled, and she heard the warning beneath the words. A cold, cold case. Don't expect too much. He pushed the button, turned up the volume.

At once, the whispered voice filled the room.

"Naomi Waters," came the near-whispered words, fearful...chilling even now, in this well-lit office with a policeman sitting across from her. "I'm sorry, girl...I tried to stop him. I just wanted to tell you that. I ... I couldn't do nothin'."

The country music played in the background. Something she'd heard many times she still couldn't put a name to. It didn't matter. Beneath the music, the tape recorder whirred on. The man spoke again. "You don't know him. You oughta leave it alone, honest to God. He's bad news. You wanna watch your back..."

The music went on for a couple more seconds before the message clicked off. "Well?" Naomi said. "You can hear the fear in his voice. He's terrified someone..."

"You asked me to tell you what I think," he cut in. She fell silent. Nodded. "Okay," she

said.

The sergeant replayed the tape, frowned as he listened, rubbed the bridge of his nose with thumb and forefinger.

"I know he's one of the two men," she insisted when it was over. "I know it. Maybe you could run the message on TV and radio. Someone might recognize his voice."

He gave a short humph to her suggestion, and she wasn't sure if it was in agreement or dismissal. He slid his glasses back on his face and leaned back in his chair.

"First, with all due respect, you don't know anything, Naomi. You think you know. Your caller sounds like he's 'been into his cups' as me grandma used to say. But let's not jump the gun, either way. I repeat, this could just be some nut case who read your story and decided to have a little fun," he said, pretty much echoing Eric Grant's assessment. "There's no end of whackos out there, and I'm in a position to know that. As to the men who actually grabbed Mary Rose, I wouldn't be surprised if they're long dead."

Well, that would wrap it all up nicely, wouldn't it? she

thought, anger building in her. She put a lid on it and spoke calmly.

"But you don't know that they are. No, I know I think they're alive, Sergeant Nelson. With everything in me, I feel it. I believe they were young men at the time. In their twenties, maybe. Predators, stalking the vulnerable." The lone travelers at the edge of the herd, she thought. "They'd be in their late forties now, maybe early fifties," she continued. "That's relatively young these days. Who knows what else they've done. They're animals. And I've already rattled one of their cages."

He sat forward, folded his hands together and like a kindly uncle said, "Supposing you're right. Unlikely, but supposing. I still can't reopen a case on maybes. We need some real evidence to do that. Okay, granted the caretaker of the cemetery said he saw two men, but he wasn't able to describe either of them, or the car, except to say that it was big and dark. And that old car has long since been turned into scrap metal. And Charles Seaton was the only witness to the crime."

She could feel the sergeant's impatience, feel him losing interest. But Mr. Seaton might remember something after all this time. At least the sergeant had read the article, no doubt the file too. Probably as soon as he was off the phone with Eric Grant. She needed that file.

"I plan to talk to Mr. Seaton," she told him. After a hesitation, she said, "Sometimes people remember things during hypnosis, don't they? Do you know if they hypnotized him back then? If they didn't, couldn't you have...?"

"No. No, I can't. I can't allot time and money on a case without more to go on. That's not going to happen. We don't even know if Seaton is alive. It's doubtful. He was well into his fifties at the time." He glanced at his watch. "I'm sorry, but I'll have to wrap this up. I've got an appointment with the mayor in ten minutes. Anyway, let me mull this over for a day or two, Nancy Drew. See what I can come up with. In the meantime, you be careful, you hear? Too late to tell you to leave it alone, I suppose. Not that you would." He removed the tape from the recorder. "But at least heed your caller's words. 'Watch your back'. Whoever this guy is," he said, tapping the tape with his forefinger. "It wasn't bad advice. You live with family?"

He was dropping the tape into an evidence bag he'd gotten from his desk drawer. Fine, she'd made a copy. She decided to ignore the 'Nancy Drew' comment. "No, not anymore."

"Your adopted mom. Right. Clumsy of me. I expect the house is pretty lonely with her gone. It's not good to live alone. Especially for a young woman like yourself. You might want to think about getting yourself a dog. A shepherd, maybe."

"I can take care of myself, thank you, Sergeant Nelson. All women aren't damsels in distress, you know." She spoke pleasantly but pointedly. Then decided to cut him some slack. "But you're right; I'm keeping my doors and windows locked."

Each time she heard her mother referred to as her 'adopted mom', it gave her a jolt. It hurt. It sounded so strange spoken aloud, as if the term 'adopted mom' couldn't possibly apply to her mom.

Clearly, she hadn't made the transition in her psyche yet. "Anyway," she said, "my cat Molly wouldn't take kindly to the idea of a dog, but I appreciate the concern." She thanked him for his time and told him she'd be back.

He walked her to the door. "You shouldn't be so defensive, you know, Miss Waters. No one is suggesting you're a damsel in distress or that you can't take care of yourself. But neither do you want to ignore the fact that you're a woman living alone and there are some very bad people out there. You don't want to be naïve and end up hurt. Or worse."

"I don't think I'm at all naïve," she said. "I came here asking for your help. I'm counting on it. I think your job is to catch those bad people, isn't it, unless I'm mistaken. I'll be in touch, Sergeant."

* * *

It was just past four when Naomi showed up at Frank Llewellyn's office. She took a chance he'd still be there and not too busy to see her. Not that he wouldn't have made himself available, but Frank was a busy man and she didn't feel good about barging in unexpectedly, although that's exactly what she was doing, taking advantage of the guilt she knew he felt about his part in the conspiracy. Not the most noble motivation. But he'd offered to help, and she needed the favor. She had promised to find the evidence Sergeant Nelson said he needed to reopen the case. So she needed to start with the case file.

Kay was at her desk typing at the computer, and didn't see Naomi right away. Kay Garrett had been Frank's right hand for years. A grandma now in her sixties, she was still a pretty woman, filled with energy and enthusiasm, makeup perfect, every platinum hair in place, smelling of gardenias. Or maybe it was a potpourri on the counter. Frank said he didn't dare suggest retirement to her, but he also admitted he'd be lost without Kay.

When she looked up and saw Naomi standing there, her face broke in a smile. "Naomi, how wonderful to see you. It's been a very long time. I was so sorry to hear about your mom, dear. And about all this other..."

"Thanks, Kay. And for the lovely card. How's that adorable granddaughter of yours? Kelsey...?"

"What a memory you have," she said, warming to a subject close to her heart, and no doubt one more comfortable than the matter of Naomi's background. She wondered if Frank had ever confided the secret to Kay, but then decided no, he wouldn't have. Kay knew only what she read in the paper, like the rest of River's End residents.

"Kelsey's four now, hardly a baby anymore," Kay was saying, reaching into her purse and producing an accordion of snapshots over which Naomi made all the appropriate comments. Not that it was hard to be complimentary. Kelsey was a pretty little girl with light brown curls, bright blue eyes and a mischievous smile. "She has your eyes," Naomi said. "Blue as robin's eggs."

Kay beamed. "That's what they tell me. She starts

kindergarten this fall. It has been a while, hasn't it?" she laughed, returning the photos to her purse. "Frank will be delighted you're here. I'll buzz him."

* * *

"I don't see a problem getting you the file," Frank said, a short time later as they sat across from one another at The Golden Dragon, the best Chinese restaurant in town.

"Thanks, Frank. I really appreciate it."

She hadn't meant to take up more than a few minutes of his time, but he'd insisted on taking her to dinner, saying, "If I remember correctly, Chinese is your favorite."

The instant they entered the restaurant and Naomi smelled the enticing aromas, she was suddenly famished, and realized she'd forgotten to eat today. She chose her favorite almond gai ding, eggroll and chicken fried rice. Looking around, she was overcome with a sense of déjà vu. She sipped her white wine which Frank had ordered, and remembered coming here years ago with Frank and her mother. She might have been nine. They'd ordered her a Shirley Temple and she'd felt like such a big girl. Almost grown up. Happier times.

The decor hadn't changed. Lots of red. Exquisite wall paintings depicted scenes of old China; men and women wearing shade hats tied under their chins, as they worked in rice paddies. Hanging silk and bamboo lanterns. A wave of loss swept over her, eclipsing the anger, which was already starting to wane.

"You're a good friend, Frank." "Then I'm forgiven?"

"I'm thinking on it." She grinned. A forkful of chicken chow mein mid-way to her mouth, she leveled her gaze at him. "I hope you won't tell me what an ungrateful person I am, that I should leave well enough alone. I've already heard that a few times and I don't think I can handle hearing it again. Not from you."

"That wasn't even close to what I was planning to say."

"Okay. I'm sorry. But to some people, it's as if my wanting to bring Mary Rose's killers to justice is some kind of slap at my mother. It's not. I loved my mother, and I know she loved me."

Frank's sigh of relief was audible. "You can't know how happy I am to hear you say that, Naomi."

"Oh, Frank, that will never change. I just wish she had trusted me with the truth." He took her hand. "It was a hard truth, Naomi."

"I know." Lisa had made her see things a little differently. "Anyway, this is something I have to do."

"I understand. I do. I admire you for it. And if Lili were here, so would she. She cared about justice and fairness. You know that. And if this is what you need to do to find some kind of closure-- that's an overused word and not the right one, but you know what I mean..."

She smiled thinly. "I think so."

"Like I said, getting the file shouldn't be too much of a problem. It's an old case. My biggest concern, and I have to say this even if you don't want to hear it, is that you're putting yourself in harm's way. Whoever is responsible for such a monstrous crime isn't going to want to see new attention being brought to it after all this time. Animals like that are capable of anything. Don't underestimate the capacity for evil in some people. I've been in this business long enough that nothing surprises me anymore. Remember, to these monsters, you're nothing but exhibit 'A' - like leaving your blood at the scene of the crime. You're evidence."

His words sent a prickling of foreboding through her. She hadn't thought of herself as exhibit A. But now that she did, clearly that's exactly what she was. The killer's DNA would match hers. The idea took a bit of getting used to. She considered telling Frank about the phone call, then thought better of it. He might change his mind about getting that file for her and she needed it. She wondered if Sergeant Nelson would tell him. She hoped not.

"I'll be fine," she said. "Frank, I really appreciate your help."

"You're welcome. Just answer me one thing, and please don't take it the wrong way." "Shoot."

"Well, you had the ground ripped out from under you pretty brutally, I know that. Are you sure you're not grasping at something to keep you grounded, I suppose, with all this dredging up of the past?"

"Please don't psychoanalyze me, Frank." There was no edge to her words; it was a fair question. "Anyway, even if that's true, it's only a small part of it. I think you were more right than you realize when you said it was like Mary Rose willed herself to live long enough to give birth to me. I believe that somewhere deep in her subconscious she made herself hang on until she somehow knew I could be delivered safely. She gave me life, Frank. I owe her to try to find out who took hers. It's like a covenant. In lawyer-speak, a contract."

"I know what a covenant is." He grinned and sipped his Chinese tea from the black

miniature cup embossed with a gold dragon. His shrewd lawyer's eyes studied her thoughtfully over its rim. She saw the sadness in their depths. He misses Mom too. They were dear friends long before I came on the scene. He's probably remembering them being in here together. She wished he could meet someone. Frank was too nice a man to be alone.

Setting her plate to one side on the crisp white tablecloth, Naomi picked up her fortune cookie and cracked it open, withdrew the strip of paper from within its shell.

"Good news, I hope," Frank said. "We could use a little." She read it aloud: "The way of the trouble-maker is thorny."

They both laughed, and she heard the trace of unease in the sound. Still, it had been a very long time since she'd heard her own laughter, and it was strange in her ears.

* * *

On the drive home, Naomi thought over her discussion with Frank. As she had wanted to tell Sergeant Nelson about her dream of the eagle, so she wished she could have shared it with Frank. The eagle was at the heart of her quest. But Frank was a lawyer, and like the sergeant, thought in terms of tangible evidence. Thank God for Lisa who hadn't needed anything, but had taken her dream to heart without hesitation or question. It was in her nature to believe that just because a thing cannot be proven doesn't mean it isn't real. Lisa had quoted Hamlet, smiling her warm, mysterious smile: 'There are more things in heaven and earth, Horatio, than are dreamt of in your philosophy." With a self-conscious laugh, she told Naomi she played a small part in the play in school, and remembered. Naomi thought Hamlet knew of what he spoke.

She wondered if the man would call again

Chapter Eighteen

"I need to report my husband missing."

The officer looked up from the John Grisham novel he'd been reading to see a thin woman with short, dark hair and anxious eyes looking down at him. He reached absently into the tray on the desk for a report form. "Yes, Ma'am. Name, please." Unaware, he ran a hand over his buzz-cut, which was still relatively new to him, and made him feel naked, at the mercy of a stray draft.

"Norman Banks. I'm his wife, Debbie Banks."

"When was the last time you saw your husband, Ms. Banks?" He picked up a fat, maroon ballpoint, poised it to write.

"Yesterday morning. Before he went to work. He hasn't been home since. No phone call. Nothing. I think something bad happened to him." Her voice broke. "I thought maybe an accident, but I've checked the hospitals...nothing. I called his work. He was there yesterday..."

The officer set the pen down, suppressed a grin. "Sorry, Ma'am. There's nothing I can do about a man who decides to stay out all night." He was thinking the guy was probably off on a toot somewhere, maybe shacked up with some little chippie, which was usually the case. He'd show up eventually, was his experience, probably with nothing worse than a bad hangover and an explanation that, however weird, his wife would buy because she wanted to. "You uh, maybe oughta be at home in case he phones. My guess is he'll likely be home by the time you..."

"No, you don't understand," she cut in, the intensity in her brown eyes willing him to listen. "It's not what you're thinking. Normie wouldn't do this. He's not that kind of man. We got three kids together. He's never stayed out before. Not once." Her eyes suddenly swam with tears. "But that's not the only reason. My husband's a diabetic and he needs his shots. He could go into a coma without them."

She had his attention now. Diabetes put a different spin on things. His brother's kid had diabetes and it was nothing to fool around with. He took down the missing man's description, and clipped the photo she'd brought with her to the form. "We'll call you as soon as we know anything, Ma'am. If he comes home in the meantime, please let us know."

"Please find my husband," she said.

As soon as she was gone, Officer Ramsay took the missing person's report into the sergeant. "Thought you'd probably get this one out to the public, Sarge," he said. "His wife says he's got diabetes and needs his shots. Might be lying in a ditch somewhere."

* * *

But it wasn't the police who found Norman Banks' body. Henry Wilkes found him. Henry was a homeless vet, who'd been down by the wharves stumbling about, nursing a bottle of wine in a brown paper bag, headed for his favorite out of the way shed where he intended to sleep. The stomach-wrenching smell hit him just seconds before he tripped over the body. A mouthful of the heavy sweet wine bubbled up from his gut, filling his mouth with the taste of vomit. He gagged and spat it off to one side on the ground as past horrors flooded Henry's mind, accompanied by the stench of fallen bodies halfway around the world in Vietnam. It took a few seconds to reorient his alcohol-fogged brain to the present. He flicked the head of a match with his thumbnail, and the flame caught the flatness in the dead man's eyes and the gaping slash across his throat.

He was out of breath and pretty much sober by the time he got to the phone booth near the main road and made the call.

He waited with the corpse till the cops showed up. 'Poor devil," he kept saying. "Poor son-of-a-bitch." His exact sentiments were noted in the report.

* * *

Poor devil indeed, Sergeant Nelson thought, glancing over the missing person's file that had just been brought to him, one he'd already read. Banks' wife's worries had been justified. Norman Banks didn't go into a diabetic coma, however, but he did come to a very bad end, with his throat slit from ear to ear.

There was no sign that he'd put up a fight or any resistance at all, and the consensus was that the killer came up behind him, surprised him. Why? And what the hell was he doing down there late at night, all by himself? He wasn't homeless like Wilkes. Not even a vet like Wilkes. He was, in fact, married with grown kids and operated a forklift for Harris Woodworking, a company run by a third generation of Harris'.

No smell of booze on him. Was he having some kind of secret rendezvous? A secret his wife wasn't in on. A lover? Drugs?

His wife didn't know yet that her husband was dead. She kept calling. He'd have to go out there and see her. Break the bad news. She probably already suspects, doesn't want to believe it. They'd need her to make a positive I.D. on the body.

"That's it, then," he said to officers Drew Mullin and Jerry Knowles. Jerry didn't have all his color back yet and his eyes looked glazed. He was a rookie and this was his first homicide. "You got nothing, no leads? Didn't come across the knife, by any remote chance?" A joke, of course.

"Nope," said Mullin, "just that article the vic had on him about that half-breed dame, all folded up in his pocket." Mullin was a big man, a Brian Dennehy lookalike, but without the actor's class or charm.

"Her name's Naomi Waters," Sergeant Nelson said coolly, not missing the look Jerry shot his senior partner's comment, though Mullin picked up on neither, "She's an audio book narrator."

Mullin looked blank on that one. "You think there might be a connection between her and the dead guy?" he asked.

Sergeant Nelson sighed. You can't bitch at a zebra 'cause you don't like stripes. "Maybe. Worth checking out." Was Norman Banks

Naomi Waters' mysterious caller?" Nelson wondered.

"You want me to go see the vic's wife?" Mullins asked. "Break the bad news?"

Hell, no. "No. I'll take this one myself. I'm going out that way anyway," he lied, pocketing the tape Naomi Waters had brought him. Telling someone their loved one was dead, worse, murdered, was not a job he looked forward to, but better him than Mullin. Drew meant well, but he was old school, with some of the same bigotries as the old guard. He'd be retiring next year, and in his opinion, not a minute too soon. Not that all the older cops shared those negatives; they didn't, as he himself didn't. At least not that he was aware of.

A half hour later he was headed out to the Banks' house in Rollingdam, feeling heavy with the task before him. But better she hear it from him than through the media. If Banks' name wasn't already out there, give it an hour and it would be. Even if she already knew in some deep part of herself that her husband was gone, it would still come as a shock. The last shred of hope

ripped away, she'd be left with a husband who presently lay on a slab in the morgue. Her life would be forever changed. That was the brutal reality.

Feeling the weight of the tape in his pocket, his thoughts turned to Naomi Waters. He envisioned her sitting across from him, all fired up about seeking justice for the woman she'd just found out gave birth to her.

Was it possible that the murdered man was one of the two who abducted Mary Rose Francis that night, all those years ago?

Would solving this cold case be that easy? Didn't seem likely. Banks probably had that article in his wallet for some other reason entirely.

Maybe he was just taken with the girl's story. Lots of people in town were. Although you don't usually cut a story out of the paper if it has no personal connection to you.

Well, he'd find out soon enough. Debbie Banks would certainly know her own husband's voice when she heard it. The tape in his pocket suddenly felt like a small, nasty animal.

Chapter Nineteen

Sergeant Nelson sat in Debbie Banks' neat, modestly furnished living room. The news he'd delivered minutes ago hung in the air like the silence following a terrible explosion. She sat across from him, folded in on herself, on the brown rust velvet-covered sofa reminiscent of one his mother owned in the eighties, but newer. Her eyes were swimming with tears and she was shaking, but trying to hold it together. She didn't scream or cry out when he told her, just whimpered and put a hand over her mouth, her eyes begging him to tell her it wasn't true. But she knew; he'd seen the fear in her eyes when she opened the door and saw him standing there. Then she'd wept softly. He hadn't shared with her the gruesome details of her husband's murder. She would learn them soon enough.

Now she was mopping at her tears again with an already sodden wad of tissues, getting shakily to her feet, asking him if he'd like tea. Being hospitable was apparently important to her, no matter the circumstances. A part of who she was. Strange how in times of great suffering, we adhere to our basic natures, reverting to old tribal practices that allow us to go through the motions of civility. Or maybe she just felt a need to do something with her hands.

"No thanks," he said quickly before she could disappear into the kitchen. She nodded and sank back down on the sofa.

"But I do need to ask you a few questions, Mrs. Banks," he

said. "I can come back later if you prefer, I know this is hard for you. But the more answers I have, the faster we'll find your husband's killer. And we will find him, I promise."

More promises he may not be able to keep. Story of his life. It was why Jeannie left and took the kids. They were grown now. She was married again, an insurance broker. A safe, predictable life. He couldn't fault her. And why was he wallowing in the past?

"I know this is difficult," he said. "I'll try not to take up too much of your time."

"No, it's okay. Take whatever time you need. Ask your questions. Please, Sergeant. I want his killer found and punished more than anyone." She sniffed into the tissue, then lowered the hand clutching the tissues in her lap and settled herself stoically, ready to do whatever she could to help solve her husband's murder and bring the man responsible to justice.

Everyone wants justice. It was his job to see that they got it. Unfortunately, his powers were sadly limited. But he would try his damndest.

Debbie Banks looked small and helpless sitting there on the sofa, eyes leaking tears, between questions, staring at her hands as if they might belong to someone else. Someone else whose husband had been murdered. She was trying so hard to stay strong. He fondled the tape in his pocket, eager for an answer, but if it was her husband's voice on the tape, she might come apart at hearing it, literally within minutes of finding out he was dead. It would be cruel to test her limits.

"I don't understand," she was saying. "Who would do this? We live a quiet life. Our kids are grown. Normie didn't have any enemies."

He had one, Graham thought. "That's what we aim to find out, Ma'am. It wasn't a mugging that much we know. He had money on him. Three twenties and a ten. A credit card. Did he seem different to you lately? Uptight? Nervous?"

Her thin shoulders shrugged and she shook her head. "I don't think so. But he was working a lot of overtime, so I didn't see much of him lately. I work evenings, Sears, the kid's department," she added vaguely. "I worked till ten Friday night."

"And you have no idea what he would be doing down by the wharves?"

She shook her head, still fighting tears. "No. None."

Sergeant Nelson could think of one reason for setting up a meeting down there at night: you didn't want to be seen together. He thought of the article in Banks' wallet."Mrs. Banks, do you know a woman named Lillian Waters?" It was always possible Naomi's adopted mother was the connection, and not the girl herself.

She shook her head. "Lillian Waters? No, I don't think so. Why?"

"Mrs. Waters was a retired nurse. She died recently. Cancer. She left a daughter behind. An adopted daughter, Naomi Waters."

A light of recollection came into her eyes. "Oh, that piece in the paper about that girl looking for her birth mother's attackers. I thought it was such a sad story when I read it." She wiped her nose into her tissue. "Why? What has she got to do with Normie?"

"Probably nothing. But that article was found folded up in your husband's wallet. I wondered if you might know why."

She gave him a puzzled look, then began sifting through a stack of newspapers in the magazine rack at the end of the sofa. She found the paper in question and opened it. The article was intact. She looked absently at the photo of Naomi Waters, then dropped the paper back onto the rack. It slid onto the floor. She didn't bother to retrieve it. "He didn't take it out of this paper," she said, bewildered. Questioning.

So her husband had cut the story out of another newspaper, which told Sergeant Nelson he didn't want his wife to know it had any meaning for him.

After a space of time in which Debbie Banks had drifted a million miles away, she said quietly: "Normie was sick a lot when he was a kid. He spent time in the hospital. Maybe she was one of his nurses. Was nice to him. Made him feel special." She blew her nose delicately into the tissues, then went on. "Some of those nurses can be bitches, you know, but there are some who are angels, too." She reached into her pocket and Nelson realized she was out of tissues. Seeing the box of Kleenex on the sideboard he rose and brought it to her, also picking up the newspaper off the floor and putting it back in the rack. She thanked him.

"The diabetes?" he asked, still standing.

"Yeah. Asthma, too, you name it. He grew out of most of it. But now he's -- he *was* okay as long as he got his shots." The tears spilled over again, giving way to gut-tearing sobs that made him want to get the hell out of there. He tentatively touched her shoulder, said he was sorry and quietly let himself out. He left his card by the phone. The tape still in his pocket.

He'd come back. A couple of days wasn't going to change anything. In the meantime, they'd interview neighbors, co-workers, see who might have held a grudge against him, if he'd been involved in activities his wife might not know about.

He sat in the cruiser a good five minutes, mulling over questions. For example, why would Norman Banks, at some point in their long marriage, not mention this nurse who had left such a lasting impression on him, if that was the case? Was she the sort of woman who didn't want to hear about other women in her husband's life, no matter their age or how innocent the association? He didn't think so. She didn't strike him as the type, and he liked to think he was a pretty good judge of character. Why then, didn't he cut the article out of his own paper? The answer didn't change: he didn't want her to know the story held that much interest for him. He was hiding it from her.

Why?

That's what he needed to find out.

Chapter Twenty

It was already dark outside her window when Naomi fixed herself a grilled cheese sandwich, poured a glass of milk and carried them into the living room. There was a small dining room adjoining the living room, but she rarely ate in there, preferring the kitchen, or here in front of the TV.

She watched some local news, heard about the stabbing of the man down by the wharves, but made no connection to herself, thought only of the poor man's family and the growing violence in the world. Later she watched an unfunny comedy that relied mainly on crude jokes for ratings. Or maybe it was just her. Not much was funny lately.

She needed new evidence if she had any hope of persuading Sergeant Nelson to reopen the case. She had hoped the tape would do that for her, but she'd obviously been wrong about that. Maybe it was best to leave it alone for a while and pray for the call that would shed new light on the case. After all, that man had phoned her out of the blue. Have a little faith, she told herself.

Around nine-thirty she switched off the TV and went into her studio, Molly padding behind her. The publisher had sent her a new teen mystery titled Secret at Fog Lake to narrate. She wasn't in the mood, but she'd read the book in bed last night and enjoyed it. It lent itself to a dramatic read. Just the sort of distraction she needed to get herself back on track. No more procrastination. She'd get to work.

What if the phone rang? She wouldn't hear it. She'd leave the inside door open. Edit out any noise later. If it didn't work, she'd just have to do it over. What the hell, she had nothing else to do. Not until she heard from Sergeant Nelson. Or her caller.

The story reminded her of those Nancy Drew books she'd read as a child, which also reminded her of the sergeant calling her by the heroine's name. She didn't think it was meant to be complimentary.

In this book, though, there were references to Hillary Duff, and the dialogue was sprinkled with computer jargon. And of course, the main character has a cell phone. Something Naomi didn't even have, probably should, but so far she'd resisted.

The protagonist, Lois, while trying to solve the murder of an old hermit, was also dealing with the divorce of her parents. It was a well-written story with believable characters, a creepy atmosphere, clever plot, and should do well for its author. She would do her best to do it justice and not let her own problems get in the way.

Like Mary Rose, the thought of performing in front of a live audience was far too daunting to Naomi. She much preferred imagining an audience of one little girl who sent her fan mail and called her the storybook lady. Aside from the pleasure of the work itself, and getting paid of course, there were other perks to her job. She loved getting fan mail from audio book lovers, but the biggest reward always was a happy author.

After booting up the computer, she brought up her audio editor, hit record and went into the studio. Tucking the errant strands of her hair behind her ears, she fitted on the padded headphones. After a sound check, she shut the door and settled down in front of her beloved ElectroVoice RE20 mic, and opened the book to the first chapter.

With the headphones snug against her ears, it was like being shut off from the outside world. Maybe a little like being inside a mother's womb, she mused, thinking of Mary Rose. Did she feel me inside her, growing, tiny hands closing into fists, feet kicking as her own body cradled and nourished me? Naomi believed she did. She believed they had connected in their

silent worlds. And she has never really left me. But my world was not really silent, was it? I would have heard her heartbeat, the blood coursing through her veins, and into mine.

Knock it off, she told herself, and removed the headphones. She wouldn't be able to hear the phone with them on. Quit naval gazing, literally, she told herself. Focus on the story. On Lois. Read!

And she began.

And was soon immersed in the tale, had slipped into Lois' skin and was sitting in the small rowboat, almost able to feel the chill of the air at her shoulders, hear the slap of water against the sides of the boat as the oars dipped and rose rhythmically, each stroke bringing her closer and closer to the shore of the fog-shrouded island.

* * *

The lone figure moved stealthily through the back field, coming off Keel where he'd parked the van. The night was moonless, dark, and smelled of rain. Perfect for his purpose. He drew nearer to the back door of 233 Elizabeth Avenue. Once there, he sat the gallon can of gasoline he carried in some nearby bushes; the liquid inside made a deceptively gentle sloshing sound.

"If they get the bastard," one of the guys at the gym said this morning, "he'll be easy to nail. His DNA will match hers." The conversation went on, but that was all he heard. The single statement made his bowels turn to ice that quickly melted.

Suddenly staring through imaginary bars, his hands had turned sweaty and he nearly dropped the barbell on his chest. Funny he hadn't thought about that. But it wasn't going to happen. He'd make damn sure of that.

Leaving the gas can in some bushes, he moved to the door and with a black-gloved hand picked the old lock easily. A skill he'd learned as a teenager and never lost. The door swung inward with a faint creak, and his stomach muscles tensed. He cocked his head, like a dog sensing danger. Then, hearing nothing, he let out his breath and stepped across the threshold. He stood silently in the dimly lit kitchen, listening, ready to bolt if she wasn't alone. But he didn't think that was case.

There'd been only one car parked in her front driveway when he drove past, a dark blue Cavalier, and he knew it was hers. He'd made it his business to know.

The kitchen smelled faintly of grilled cheese. He saw the frying pan upturned on the dish rack, and grinned to himself. He wondered what she would have eaten if she'd known it was her last meal. That she was his biological daughter meant nothing to him except that she could bring him trouble. That the Weaz had thought it would made him laugh. The Weaz was a sentimental fool. He'd taken care of that problem.

The fluorescent light above the kitchen window shone softly on the tiled floor beneath his

boots.

As he left the kitchen, and stepped onto the softness of the living room rug he became aware of someone talking in a far room, and froze where he stood. But there was no pause in the talking. No sign of alarm. Was she on the phone?

It took him a few seconds to identify what he was hearing; she was reading aloud. The paper said that's what she did for a living, make recordings of other people's books so you could listen to them on tape or CD. He wasn't much for books himself, preferred movies he could watch on his TV. Liked his action. All kinds.

He took another step, and another, testing each soundless footfall on the rug, until he was deep in the living room, just outside the door of the room from where her voice was coming.

The door was open a crack. The words were muffled, but slightly louder here. As he stood in the dim light from the lamp by the sofa, he glanced down at the clown on the coffee table, and barely aware of his action, compulsively flicked the yellow pom pom on its hat with a gloved finger, sending the clown into his predictable performance on its parallel bars.

Turning his back to its antics, he fixed his gaze on the door behind which the voice rose and fell. A voice that threatened to cause him problems. One he would silence forever.

She wouldn't be asking any more questions, nosing around, dredging up old bones. He stood very still. Very quiet. The sound of his breathing would have been hard to detect even by someone standing next to him. He was practiced at stealth, at being silent. As adept as he was in silencing others.

He continued to listen to the sound of her voice as she read, but had little capacity to appreciate its warm, melodious quality or gift of storytelling. Reaching into his back pocket and drew out the other black glove.

Calmly, taking his time, he worked his large hand into it. Then he flexed his fingers in the glove, smiling faintly. A smile that failed to reach his cold grey eyes. They should have aborted you. Well, better late than never.

His gloved hand gave the door a light push inward. In the same instant, the doorbell rang.

Chapter Twenty-One

At first, deep into the story, Naomi wasn't even sure it was the doorbell she'd heard, but then she saw Molly hissing at the door, hackles raised, ears flattened. Setting the book aside, the world of Lois and her adventures already fading from her mind, like rags of dissipating cloud, she stood up.

"What's the matter, Molly?" she asked quietly. The doorbell rang again, and this time there was no mistaking it.

Molly was scratching at the door, frantic to get out. It wasn't like her to get so wrought up over a ringing doorbell. As soon as she opened the door, Molly scampered out between her feet and leapt up on the back of the sofa, hackles still raised. Naomi had started for the front door when, out of the corner of her eye, she caught a movement and turned to see the little clown on the coffee table rocking to and fro, as he did when his flurry of somersaults had wound down. Strange. A draft from somewhere?

She peered through the peephole in the door before opening it, something she rarely had done before the article appeared in the paper. Frank. She unlocked and opened the door.

"I hope I'm not disturbing you, Naomi," he said apologetically. "I know it's late, but I wanted to get this to you before heading home. The file you wanted..."

"No, you're not disturbing me at all, Frank," she said, glad to see him, and especially pleased to see the file. "Thank you so much. Please come in." She took the manila envelope from his hand, noted with disappointment but not surprise, its thinness.

"I've been working too, but I was just about to quit so your timing's perfect. I'll put the coffee on. Did you have dinner? I can offer you a grilled cheese sandwich, which is what I had for my dinner, or scrambled eggs..."

"I've already eaten, but coffee would be great. I won't stay long," he said, following her out to the kitchen. "Sam's been out of sorts lately, so I want to get home. He's getting old. Hell, so I am. Anyway, I scanned the file and I wish I could say I uncovered something that would break the case open, but I can't. I don't think there's anything in it you don't already know."

She offered to take his coat, but he said he'd just leave it on, reiterating that he couldn't stay long. Naomi didn't press him. She was disappointed he'd found nothing significant in the file, but not surprised. Still, there could be something in there that would be helpful, something Frank or the cops, had missed. She was anxious to do her own read-through, but was careful not to seem to be rushing him. Frank had shown her nothing but kindness from the time she was a little girl; he was the uncle she never had. He was a good guy. Her mother probably should have married him.

"I made copies of the case photos. They won't be easy to look at," he warned. "I know. I'll handle it. Thanks for including them, for trusting me."

He nodded, then looked away from her, an eyebrow shooting

up "Why is your back door open?"

Naomi turned to see it slightly ajar and alarm shot through her like a sudden infusion of cold water into her veins. "I don't know. I hardly ever use this door. It's always locked." She closed and locked it now.

"You've had a lot on your mind. Maybe you..."

"Yeah, maybe." But she was sure the door had been locked, and even if she was wrong about that, she definitely wouldn't have left it open.

She put the coffee on, seeing in her mind's eye the little clown rocking back and forth on

his bars, Molly hissing at the studio door.

Someone unlocked that door from the outside, she thought, setting the cream and sugar on the table. Someone who meant her harm. Her shock at seeing that door open, left her with a cold weight of fear in the pit of her stomach. What she wouldn't have given for that German shepherd the sergeant suggested. One that adored Molly, of course.

Frank was looking worriedly at her; she must look shaken, which reflected the truth of it. "I'm sure you're right, Frank. I guess I just forgot to lock it."

He frowned at her, his expression telling her he was unsatisfied at her answer, and questioning his own initial assessment of her stability. "I'm not so sure. Don't take unnecessary chances, honey. You be careful. Always make sure your windows and doors are locked," he added unnecessarily, going to the kitchen window and peering out into the darkness, hands spread before him on the sill. He turned away after a moment and sat down at the kitchen table. "I think we're in for more rain," he said. "The sky looked pretty angry on the drive here."

Naomi nodded, poured them each a steaming mug of coffee, pushed the pitcher of cream across to Frank and sat down across from him. "And I don't want you driving home in a downpour. Please don't worry about me, Frank. I'll be careful. I promise." She made herself smile.

Questions went round in her mind as she looked at the manila envelope on the table. Did Frank interrupt an intruder? Was that why Molly freaked out? Was there a connection between what was in that envelope and her door being open? Or did she, Naomi, admittedly more than a little scattered of late, leave the door unlocked, not quite closed, and it drifted open on its own? Or was her first instinct right and someone else unlocked it? Questions coming full circle, then starting round again.

Had the clown really been rocking on his bars, or was her mind playing tricks on her? She didn't voice her questions to Frank though. It would serve no purpose but to worry him further, and delay the moment when she could be alone with the case file. Besides, she didn't want to keep him from Sam. You could tell he was really worried about his old friend. He'd got Sam as a puppy and was devoted to him. He was his family, like Molly was hers. That was the sad thing about pets, they left you before you were ready to let them go, not that you ever were. I can't imagine this house without

Molly in it.

* * *

After Frank left, Naomi returned to the kitchen, opened the manila envelope and slid out the file folder. Before opening it, she wedged a chair under the door knob. It didn't take long to read through the file. Frank was right, there was nothing here she didn't already know, or hadn't read about in the Tribune accounts. No clues, no crumbs she could follow that would lead her to a killer. If she didn't hear from Sergeant Graham Nelson very soon, she would start making some calls on her own. He could call her Nancy Drew if he liked, but if Sergeant Nelson wasn't taking her seriously, then it was up to her to find the evidence that would change that.

She might even take her copy of the tape to a few bars in town and see if anyone recognized the voice. In her business as a voiceover, making the copy had been second nature to her. She always backed up everything. A couple of near-disasters had taught her that lesson well.

Still averting her eyes from the photos in the file, not yet ready emotionally to look at them, she went back over the notes in case she missed something. At a sudden loud crack of thunder, her heart banged against her ribcage and she looked up from the faded yellow page.

At once, a flash of blue-white light filled the kitchen and lit up the back field like a surreal stage setting, complete with brush and scraggly trees. Almost simultaneously, the skies opened and the rain fell in torrents, battering the windows, sounding vaguely like applause in some great celestial amphitheater.

There'll be no one walking around out there tonight, she thought with some relief. She was safe for the time being. No guarantee, of course. It depended on how driven he was. How impatient. He would know she was alone. Stop it! she told herself. You can't even be sure you didn't leave the door open yourself. But she was sure. Deep down, she was sure. She had to find out who he was before it was too late.

A second read-through of the notes left her no better informed than when she began. Bracing herself, she let out a long, slow breath, then spread out the pictures on the table.

Chapter Twenty-Two

It rained for two days and then the sun came out. Despite a couple of sleepless nights, there were no further disturbing occurrences. On a more pleasant note, Lisa Boyce called, asking her if she was okay. They had a good talk, like old friends. She told her about her fruitless visit to the police station. Other than that, all was quiet. By Sunday Naomi still had not heard from Sergeant Nelson and figured he had probably dismissed her from his mind the minute she closed the door behind her. Tomorrow she'd call him.

That afternoon she drove out to Fernhill Cemetery. Winding her way up through the narrow path to the gravesite, she parked the car and got out. She retrieved the two bunches of forget-me-nots from the back seat, that she'd bought at the city market yesterday and proceeded up the narrow path toward the gravesite.

The air smelled clean after the rain, mingled with the faint scent of damp, upturned earth, the ground spongy beneath her feet. The sun shone weakly through a milky sky. But it was peaceful here, the silence interrupted only by an occasional birdcall, or a car passing by outside the cemetery gates.

She'd chosen for her mother's grave a pink marble headstone, with a dove engraved at the top, bearing an olive branch. As yet, only her name and the dates of her living and dying were carved on it.

Despite Edna's penchant for wanting to run things, the

obituary had really been all she was interested in. The responsibility of the funeral and the headstone had fallen to Naomi. Which was more than fine with her. She hadn't quite known what to have carved on it though and the man said there would be no problem coming back to the gravesite and etching into the stone whatever she decided. Beloved Wife of Thomas didn't work anymore. 'Beloved Mother of Naomi'?

Yes, that seemed exactly right. Frank was right; in every way that mattered, she was my mother. And to hell with Edna.

Unmindful of the wet grass, Naomi knelt on the ground and set one of the bunches of the tiny blue flowers, her mother's favorites, on her grave. Then she laid her palm flat against the gravestone. At once, a warmth seemed to emanate from deep within the marble, washing through her like a wave of love, bringing tears to her eyes. Her throat thick with emotion, she said softly, "I miss you, Mom. I admit I was really angry at first that you lied to me, especially about…Thomas. But I understand now."

Crazily, she still felt Thomas was her father. She had not come close to severing the ties. "You did what you thought was right. But now that I do know, please understand that I have to find Mary Rose's killers."

She thought of the horrible pictures she'd made herself look at, every detail burned into her brain. No way would those men get away with what they did to her.

"You were all about fairness, Mom. You were," she whispered. Then she touched her fingertips to her lips and transferred the kiss to her mother's gravestone. Sighing, she rose to her feet. The knees of her jeans were damp from the wet, bits of dirt and grass clinging to them. She brushed them off and looked around, scanning the rows of tombstones of varying sizes, and religious statues stretching before her toward the hill and beyond. Frank had said Mary Rose was buried not far from here and gave her directions. "Lili took care of it," he said.

The grave was only a few yards away, the gravestone facing the road, marked with a small ivy-etched white stone bearing only her name, Mary Rose Francis, and the dates of her

living and dying. As she set the second bouquet of forget-me-nots on the grave, propping it against the stone, she wondered what her favorite flowers had been. She would never know.

At a prickling at the back of her neck, Naomi stood up and looked off to her right, half expecting to see someone standing there, another mourner perhaps, come to visit a loved one's grave. But there was no one there. A fleeting shadow, come and gone in an instant. Someone crouched behind a gravestone? Kids playing? She stared at the spot for several seconds before she gave a mental shrug and looked away.

Maybe a bird or a small animal. But the sensation of someone watching her remained. She turned full circle, slowly, was about to look away from where she'd seen or imagined

the shadow when she caught a flicker of movement up on the hill, by the looming marble statue of Jesus on the cross. She stared at the place where she had caught the movement, but again, saw no one. The flicker of motion had come and gone in an instant. But the feeling that she was being watched stayed with her, clung to her skin like cobwebs in a dank cellar, and she knew it had nothing to do with simply being in a cemetery. She had no aversion to cemeteries. On the contrary, Naomi had always found walking through a cemetery a quiet, serene experience. Reading the names and dates on old grave markers, imagining the lives of the people buried there, wondering about their dreams and sadnesses, their triumphs, brought her a sense of peace and continuity to her own life.

Gazing toward the hill, she remembered that this was the same graveyard where Charles Seaton had once worked as a caretaker. It would have been right about there, near the statue of Jesus when he heard her screams, saw the men force her into the car. He would have been walking along the path, unprepared by what he saw, the full reality of what was happening not registering until it was too late. Maybe if the man had yelled out...if... She stopped herself. You can't change the past with what ifs.

But knowing the past, you can carve out a future. She had come into this life for a reason, to make sure the crime didn't go unpunished. She didn't necessarily think that was her only purpose for being on the earth, but it was an important one. She believed that. She also believed someone wanted to make sure she failed at her mission.

Naomi made her way down the slight slope of wet, slippery grass toward her car, and was glad to see a maroon Buick pull in behind hers, and an elderly man and woman get out. The man had his arm draped around the woman's shoulders. The woman smiled at Naomi as she passed. "Lovely day after all the rain," she said, and there was a small sadness in her voice. The man merely nodded, his attention on the woman.

Naomi could see the bus stop from here, glassed-in now. There was no one waiting on this warm, peaceful day. A light breeze came up and stirred her hair. Within its soft sigh, she imagined she heard the cries of a young girl. Cries that once rose from this very place, and now echoed across the vast plains of time to me, her child.

I hear you.

Chapter Twenty-Three

In the hallway, Naomi's took off her wet sneakers and socks and left them on the mat. She then went on into the kitchen and plugged the kettle in, some part of her already sensing something wrong in the house. Nothing she could identify. There were the usual sounds, the hum of the refrigerator, the tick of the clock, normally familiar, welcoming sounds.

But as she stood there idly watching the steam escape the kettle's spout, something darker began to eclipse the welcoming of home. The knowledge of what it was came suddenly, like a blow to the midsection. During the time she was at the cemetery, someone was here, in her house. The temperature in the room seemed to drop, and the clammy hand of fear crept up between her shoulder blades as she realized something else; Molly hadn't come padding out to greet her as she always did. Molly! Where was Molly? A cold dread tightened around her heart.

I've drawn a terrible darkness into my life, she thought.

Chapter Twenty-Four

"He was letting me know he can get to me any time he chooses," she told Sergeant Nelson the following morning. Even in broad daylight... he's telling me to back off."

After listening to what she had to say, Sergeant Nelson sat thoughtfully twirling a pen in his hand. He hadn't seemed altogether pleased to have her show up unannounced, but was pleasant enough to her, even sympathetic, she thought.

"He could have killed her," she said adamantly.

"You don't know that it was..." He drew a scrap of paper to him, and began jotting down notes with the pen in his hand. Or he might have been just doodling for all she knew, waiting for her to give it up and go home?

"Yes, I do know. She was upset. I think she's okay now." Molly mewed loudly from her travel carrier at Naomi's feet, as if to disagree with her diagnosis of her emotional state.

Naomi had been beside herself when she couldn't find her. Then she heard her cries. Upstairs in her room, the dresser drawer open a couple of inches, and she had been afraid to look, to cross the room, afraid of what she would see. Molly's glowing green eyes had peered up at her from her dark interior of the drawer and Naomi's relief that she was okay was overwhelming.

"No way I was going to leave her alone again."

"Apparently," he said, frowning down at Molly. "Well, you wanted evidence. I think he also came into my house the other night. A friend

rang the front doorbell and scared him off."

"Did you actually see him running away?" he said with maddening calm.

"No. But the back door was unlocked, open. I always lock it." She wasn't positive, but after what happened with Molly, she'd bet on it.

He put the pen down, looked at her with something between pity and annoyance. She thought he looked flushed, despite his calm demeanor.

"This is mere speculation on your part. I can't launch a manhunt, Miss Waters, based on this kind of non-evidence. As to this latest incident, if there was one, no one was killed or even hurt. Not even the cat," he added, with a wry grin down at Molly. At the look that must have been on Naomi's face, the grin vanished.

"Not this time," she said, not missing that he had gone from calling her Naomi to addressing her as Miss Waters.

"I think you're overreacting. Topsy probably jumped into..."
"Molly," she corrected.

"Molly probably jumped into the drawer on her own. Crawled up the back of the dresser and into the drawer. I've had cats; they do that. Or maybe you've got a mouse you don't know about, and she was chasing it. Look, I'm not surprised you're feeling a little jumpy. Who knows what kind of lowlife that story in the paper might have scared up. But I doubt they've been in your house while you weren't home and put the cat in a dresser drawer. What would be the point of that?"

"A warning. What else? And if she got into that drawer on her own, why didn't she come out on her own?"

"Why should she? She heard you calling to her. She was waiting for you come and get

her."

He had an answer for everything. But she had to admit that what he said made sense.

Regardless, she had no intention of leaving her alone in the house again.

Through the large window behind Sergeant Nelson, Naomi could see a man standing on a ladder working on a sign over the door of Aiken's Print Shop, across the street. Above him, the sky was enamel blue, marred only by a few fluffy clouds. A beautiful day. She barely noticed the weather these days.

The sergeant sighed. "Look, I know you're upset and Kitty is probably sensing that. The thing is, you opened this can of worms yourself. You mentioned someone coming into your house the other night. Did they break the lock?"

"No. The door was ajar when I went out to the kitchen."

"You've been a little distracted. You probably forgot to lock it."

"There's not a doubt in my mind that it was him. He's running scared; worried I might find out who he is and send him to prison where he belongs. Where he would have been a long time ago if the police had done their job."

He started to argue but she cut him off. "You have the tape I gave you. Couldn't you check out some of the local bars and listen for a similar voice?" She heard the plea in her voice. "I could go with you. I..."

"And which bar did you have in mind? We've got half a dozen in River's End. You could hang around for a month and get nothing. Your caller might have been home with the radio playing. Or sitting in his car. Look, if you get any more calls, note the date and time. Record them. We'll go from there. In the meantime, be careful. Maybe there's someone who could stay with you until..."

She stood up, her sigh of 'What's the use?' audible even to her.

She picked up the carrier by the handle. It seemed heavier somehow. "Thanks for your time, Sergeant Nelson."

"If you want my advice," he said to her back, "you'd put all this nasty business in the past where it belongs and move on with your life."

"I can't do that," she told him, without looking back. Suddenly more tired than she could ever remember being, hot tears pressing against her lids, she opened the door. She had her hand on the knob when he called her back. He had come out from behind the desk. "Please, Naomi. Hold on a second."

She could see him weighing his words carefully. Finally, he said, "Do you know a Norman Banks by any chance."

The name rang a bell, but no face came to mind. "No. Why?" Where was this going? she wondered. Norman Banks. She had had the feeling the entire time she was here that he was mulling over some something in his mind. Not quite listening to what she was saying.

"Well, it probably means nothing. You want to put Fluffy down. I've something to show

you."

She set the carrier on the floor. "Molly." "Yeah, I know."

Naomi studied the man in the photo the sergeant showed her. He was tall and thin with fair hair and he was smiling at the person taking the picture. His wife? She'd noticed a breeze had caught a lick of light hair in front and blew it off his forehead. Captured there for all eternity. He was gone now, murdered, the sergeant told her. "Look familiar?"

"Yes. This is the man who was found near Fisher Wharf, isn't it. This picture was in the paper. Why? What has he got to do with me?"

And then he told her the police had found a copy of the interview she did for the paper

folded up in the victim's pants' pocket. "It was wrinkled and dirty, he'd been carrying it around for awhile."

"Why would...?" She took a closer look at the photo, heard him in her mind speaking the words left on her machine. Sometimes when you hear someone's voice on a radio or phone and you imagine how they might look in person, what you imagined is so often way off from the reality. But not in this case

, she was certain. The voice and the picture matched. The voice on the tape and the picture she was presently holding, matched.

She looked squarely at the sergeant. "I'd bet money this is the man on the tape. The man who called me and said he was sorry about what happened to Mary Rose, and warned me about her killer. And now he's dead."

"He's dead, for sure. But we don't know that this is the man who called you. Now, don't go jumping to conclusions as you've got to admit you have a tendency to do. Though I agree it's possible."

"It's more than that. It's probable. Why didn't you tell me about this, Sergeant? Why did you let me go on? Never mind, it's easy enough to check out. Just have his wife listen to the tape. She'll certainly know if it's her husband's voice or not."

He told her he planned to do just that. "But she's in pretty rough shape right now. I'm going to give her a little time before I hit her with this."

"Why didn't you tell me?" she repeated, softly now, just wanting to understand.

"Norman Banks' murder is under investigation. I've already told you more than I should have. I don't want you interfering in this."

"Then you do believe me." But if he truly believed the implication of that call, wouldn't he have already played the tape for Mrs. Banks? Would he really wait a day or two until she recovered from the shock of her husband's murder to find out if it was the same man?

When did they give a damn about the victim's family? How much had they cared about my great-grandfather? About his pain? His loss?

"Look, I know that someone called you," he said. "But it's a big leap from that to Norman Banks being one of the two men who abducted Mary Rose."

She didn't see it as such a big leap. Maybe he even wanted to be found out. "A lot of years to carry such a burden, Sergeant. I think he read my story and became unglued, called the other one. That would have posed a threat to his killer. The alpha of the two."

The sergeant agreed her theory had some merit. He wouldn't go further than that, but she was encouraged. She felt a new excitement, new hope. They were going to solve this thing. She knew it. "I'm going to track down Mr. Seaton," she said. "Talk to him. Maybe he'll remember something more after all this time has passed."

"I thought we agreed you'd leave this to the police."

She ignored the comment. She'd agreed to nothing. "I take it you no longer think I should just put the whole thing behind me?"

"Would it matter if I did?"

"Not really. When are you going to let Mrs. Banks listen to the tape?" "A day or two."

"Will you call me right after she hears it?"

Instead of answering her question, he asked her if she knew a Frank Llewellyn. She heard the slightest trace of irritation in his tone and understood he wasn't exactly thrilled that she'd pulled strings to get the file. Tough. She also had a feeling he admired her tenacity.

He nodded. "I figured. Not much in it, is there?"

"No. I didn't really expect there to be. But naturally I hoped." At least he'd looked at the file, hadn't simply dismissed her as some kind of crackpot as she'd concluded.

Molly let out a yowl and in the same moment someone rapped at the door and the attractive black policewoman who could have been a high-fashion model, opened it a fraction, gave her a smile, said to the sergeant that the mayor wanted to talk to him.

The open door had let in the din of banter, laughter and ringing phones. Naomi picked up the carrier and left the police station, but not before getting his promise that he would call her as soon as he played the tape for Deborah Banks, whatever the outcome.

* * *

The mayor was gone, leaving him with the problem of citizens complaining about prostitution and drug dealings on Water Street, especially since they opened the strip club. So let the city close it down, he'd told her in the nicest way possible. In the meantime, they'd do their best to tone things down.

Now, setting the problem on the back burner, Sergeant Graham Nelson sat quietly at his desk going over his conversation with Naomi Waters.

Was she onto something solid here? Well, he'd know soon

enough. If she was, he had to consider the possibility that she was in very real danger. He had no illusions that the bastard who brutalized that girl all those years ago would have developed warm and fuzzy paternal feelings toward a biological daughter he had no idea of until he saw her picture in the paper, and read her story. In fact, if facts played any part here, it would be in his best interests to kill her and dispose of her body. But he also had to know that if she did go missing, he'd be hunted down like the cur he was. We couldn't be letting that happen to the woman and then to her daughter.

Let's hope he has a job to go to and didn't follow her here this morning. Better still, let's hope she's way off track on this whole thing and he didn't have to worry about finding her dead someplace.

He poured himself a cup of coffee from the dregs left in the pot.

He had to admit, she was damned convincing, not to mention pretty as a sunset, and kind of vulnerable in her determination, while fiercely focused on avenging Mary Rose Francis. She reminded him a little of his kid sister, Angie. He was proud of Angie, loved her to pieces, but once she got hold of something, she was like a dog with a bone. Try to take it from her and you might end up punching in your friends' phone numbers with a hook.

Speaking of phones. He picked up the receiver and called Deborah Banks, asked her if tomorrow afternoon was convenient for him to come see her. Sounding a million miles away, she said that was fine. He told her he had a few more questions, said nothing about the tape. He'd wait till he got there to spring that on her. By the time he hung up, the coffee in his gut had turned to oven cleaner, and he took the roll of Tums from his shirt pocket and popped a couple into his mouth and waited for the burning to go away.

Gotta lay off the coffee, he told himself.

Chapter Twenty-Five

More than a week passed and Naomi had no word from Sergeant Nelson. During that entire time she'd done little else but hang by the phone, and listen for strange noises in the night. She had also taken to keeping a knife under her pillow.

Disappointment tasted like ashes in her mouth. She had thought he finally believed her when she left his office. What happened since then? She answered her own question. The voice didn't belong to Norman Banks and therefore he saw no point in calling her. But he had promised he would, one way or the other.

The one phone call she did get was from Charlotte, and she let the machine take it. She felt mildly guilty about not returning the call, but the thought of evoking more of Edna's venom made her resistant. The last thing she wanted was to be drawn back into the woman's web. And she could be, through Charlotte. She knew intellectually she was too old to allow herself to be intimidated by Edna, but those old childhood tapes playing in her head didn't know that. No matter how old I get, I'm always that same little kid around her, eager to please, knowing I never will. I need to work on that. Aunt Edna is a racist; she can't help herself. Odd, though, considering Mom was the epitome of tolerance and compassion. Why would her sister be so different? Or maybe Frank was right and she just resents me for usurping her position with Mom. Naomi could even understand that, but it didn't make her feel any better. In the end, it was probably a combination of things. The truth was, she'd never know exactly what made Edna tick. And right now, she told herself, picking up the telephone receiver, Edna was the least of her problems.

"River's End Police Department, Detective Henderson," the pleasant-voiced woman said. Naomi introduced herself and asked to speak with Sergeant Nelson. After a slight pause, the woman told her that Sergeant Nelson had suffered a mild heart attack, and was in the hospital. Stunned, Naomi listened as the woman reiterated that it was a mild one, and that he was being released today, and would be taking early retirement. "Is there anyone else who could help you?"

She was remembering how flushed he had looked to her that day. Answering the question, she said, "No. No, thanks. Although...I may be calling you back."

The news had shaken her, but he must be okay if they were releasing him. A wake-up call. If he heeded the warning and changed his lifestyle, he could live a long and healthy life.

Since the case had never been reopened, it wouldn't be passed on to anyone else. So she was back to square one. Well, not quite square one. She still had the tape.

Naomi slid the phone book out from under the phone and looked up Norman Banks' number, dialed it.

Chapter Twenty-Six

"No," the woman answered in a frail, sad voice, no one had asked to her listen to any tape. "Last week the policeman I forget his name nice man, said he was coming out to talk to me, but he never showed." She'd agreed to see Naomi if she came along now.

"I have an appointment with my doctor later this afternoon," she said.

Naomi promised not to take up much of her time, said she'd explain about the tape when she got there. Now, fifteen minutes later, she was on the road, excited, hopeful. And at the same time, she didn't feel good knowing she was going to draw fresh blood from an open wound, but she didn't see that she had any choice. She would have preferred Sergeant Nelson did the deed, but through no fault of his own, that hadn't been possible. If he'd given the case to anyone else, she would have heard about it. No, she was quite sure she was the last thing on his mind.

As sorry as she was to hear about his heart attack, she was also relieved to know he hadn't simply written her off as an irrational, overly emotional female. She'd underestimated him. She knew she could have given the information to Detective Henderson on the phone, but then that would have meant more waiting. If they bothered to follow it up at all. No. She needed to know now, one way or the other if the voice on the phone belonged to the murdered man, Norman Banks.

Molly howled at her from the backseat, not at all happy with being back in the carrier, on her way to who knew where. "Sorry, girl," she said over her shoulder. "I know you hate this as much as I do."

Molly fell silent and Naomi's thoughts turned to Charlotte. It wasn't right to just ignore her like she'd been doing. Cowardly, to say the least. Maybe she'd drop in at the gym tomorrow and have a chat with her. Wouldn't hurt me to sign up for a Yoga class. No better stress reliever she could think of. And she could use the exercise. Then again, there were probably rules about bringing your cat to class. Still, nothing stopping her from dropping in for a couple of minutes and being up front with Charlotte. She owed her that much.

Molly complained and Naomi spoke to her in soothing sounds until she quieted again. Minutes later, she turned left onto Barnesville Road, where Debbie Banks lived. Most recently, by herself.

A hundred yards along, the car left the pavement and she was now driving over a rough, potholed dirt road, forcing her to ease off on the gas. All signs of the city were behind her now. She passed a couple of old barns, sway-back farmhouses that hadn't yet met the bulldozer. A silo. Saw an old rusting tractor sitting in the middle of a field. Here and there, more modern bungalows had gone up.

She passed a small grocery store with a Pepsi sign out front. The house was three miles past the store, Mrs. Banks had told her, small and beige with brown trim. Blue Toyota in the yard.

Focusing her attention on finding the house, Naomi didn't notice the light-colored van following her, keeping a fair distance behind her car. Once she looked in the rearview mirror, but saw only Molly standing on all fours in her carrier, paws against the door, eyes wide and unhappy. Feeling helpless, Naomi apologized again. Poor Molly, she hated the car. She's pure housecat. It wasn't fair that she couldn't be home where she was content. At the same time, she couldn't take chances with her life. She'd never forgive herself if anything happened to Molly. I've turned us into the hunted. Even the haunted.

There was the house, just as Debbie Banks had described it. She pulled into the drive

behind the Toyota.

Behind the house, a wedge of silvery grey-colored lake reflected the gathering clouds in the low-hanging sky. The damp air crawled inside her jacket. There was a saying in River's End: 'If you didn't like the weather, just wait an hour and it'll change'. She cracked the window open a little more and got out of the car, locked the doors.

"I'll just be a few minutes," she promised Molly through the window, who looked at her as if she were Judas in the flesh.

She had to skirt around a couple of mud puddles to get to the door. As she pressed the bell, a neighbor's dog began barking, sensing an intruder in its territory. Amidst the barking, the door opened and a woman with pink-rimmed eyes said hello. Her dark hair made her paleness all the more noticeable even beneath the makeup.

A powder blue coat was draped over her arm. A not so subtle hint, Naomi thought.

"You're Naomi Waters. Please, come in."

Naomi offered her condolences and her effort felt wanting. "I'm so sorry to bother you at this time, Mrs. Banks. I can't even imagine what you must be going through. I do know what an intrusion this is and I wouldn't be here if it wasn't important."

She nodded. "It's okay. You said something about a tape. Please, sit down." She gestured to the sofa, laid her coat over the back of it, and sat down. "I have a few minutes. I mentioned to you on the phone that I have a doctor's appointment. I haven't been sleeping too well. You've probably gone through a few sleepless nights yourself, having just lost your mother. Well, both your mothers, really."

She read the story, knows who I am. "It's not true what they say, that time heals all wounds," Naomi offered. "But it does get easier. If that's any consolation."

"Not much." She gave some semblance of a smile. "It'll help a little when I'm able to put my husband to rest. The police are still holding his body in the morgue. Please. This...tape."

She took the recorder from her purse, and slipped the tape in the slot. "I'll sit here by the window if that's okay," Naomi said. "I left my cat in the car." Without any change of expression, the woman told her to sit wherever she was comfortable. Without further preamble, Naomi hit play.

Deborah Banks didn't break apart at the sound of the voice

as Naomi had feared she might, but the paleness of her skin seemed to grow even paler. Her willingness to listen to the tape was costing her. It was obvious to Naomi that the voice on the tape was that of her husband. She was not surprised. But gratified to know she'd been right.

When the tape clicked off, Deborah Banks searched Naomi's face, bewilderment coming into her own sorrowful eyes. "I don't understand. Why would he be calling you? Who is this man he's talking about?"

"I hoped you might know. I'm sorry," she said gently. "I know this is hard for you. But I believe your husband was with the man who abducted Mary Rose Francis, my birth mother, on that June night twenty-eight years ago. You read about that in the paper?"

"Yes. It was horrible what happened to her, but you're wrong about..."

"Please, hear me out. I don't know what their association was, but you heard him say yourself that he tried to stop the other man."

She couldn't help wondering how hard Norman Banks had tried, or even if he'd been part of the attack on Mary Rose. If not, then what? Did he freeze in the face of such evil? Was he afraid to intercede? Perhaps not been all he might have been on a different day? She would never know for sure.

As Deborah Banks sat listening, Naomi saw fear creep into her eyes, mingling with her puzzlement and her grief. "You were his wife; you knew him," Naomi said. "You loved him. So I don't need to tell you he was basically a decent man." Whether this was true or not, she didn't know. Would never know. But she felt a need to say it.

"That's why he called to warn me. And I believe that's why he was murdered."

The last thing Naomi wanted was for Deborah Banks to be on the defensive with her. She would close herself off, along with any information she might provide to help her find the killer.

"So long ago," she said.

Naomi's saying that she believed her husband had been a good man seemed to have its intended effect, which in turn made Naomi feel less guilty about intruding on her grief. If Sergeant Nelson was on the case, he wouldn't have been too pleased at her intrusion, but he wasn't and someone had to ask the questions.

"I met Normie around that time," she said. "We didn't get married until a couple of years

later."

"Do you remember who his friends were back then?"

"I don't think he had any...well, no one special anyway. Normie's always been something of a loner. He learned to be on his own as a kid, being sick and all, like I told the policeman, Sergeant Nelson. Yes, that was his name. I remember now. As a child, Normie was small for his age, a little different. No, I don't recall anyone in particular. So long ago."

The outcast she was describing might be vulnerable to someone with a stronger personality, Naomi thought. Someone who befriended him, made him feel like he belonged.

She had to ask it. Be double-sure. "Then you're absolutely

sure the voice on this tape belongs to your husband. You could swear to it in a courtroom if you had to."

She looked surprised at the question. "Courtroom? Yes, And of course, I'm sure. Just a minute. She left the room and came back minutes later with miniature a tape exactly like the one in the recorder. She played it.

"Hi, you've reached the Banks' residence. We're not available to come to the phone right now. Leave a message at the beep and we'll get back to you."

A generic message, but definitely the same voice. A relaxed, easy voice, not afraid or secretive.

"Can I take the tape with me?" Naomi asked. "I know it's important to you and as soon as I make a copy, I'll bring it back"

"Okay. I took it out of the machine because hearing their dad's voice upset the kids when they called. I didn't mind for myself personally. I like hearing his voice. I imagine he's still here, that none of this...happened."

Naomi nodded. She had another thought. "Do you remember where he was working when you met him?" He'd crossed paths with this guy somewhere during his lifetime. They didn't just meet on the night they took Mary Rose.

Thin brows furrowed, trying to recall, Mrs. Banks finally told her he had worked in an auto body shop. "In River's End, on Pine Street. He quit not long after we got engaged and went to work for Harris Woodworking. That body shop was torn down years ago. I think there's a Wendy's there now."

She had to start somewhere. "That place where he worked. Do you remember the name?" The frown deepened and she shook her head. 'The Shop' was all I ever heard it called."

She glanced at her watch. Naomi stood up at once.

"I'm sorry. I'm holding you up. You've been a great help, Mrs. Banks. She scribbled her

number on a scrap of paper and handed it to her. "If you think of anything else..."

"Call me Debbie, please. I'll call you, of course, if I think of anything that might be helpful. I want Normie's killer found as much as you do. More, I expect."

Naomi didn't argue the point.

The woman put on her coat and picked her purse up from the sideboard, and the two women left the house together. Debbie Banks was locking her door when the neighbor's dog began barking again.

* * *

As Naomi drove back to town, Sergeant Graham Nelson was still in his striped pajamas and robe, sitting in the La-Z-Boy, half-watching CNN on TV, and mulling over the Mary Rose Francis case. And he was thinking of Naomi, which would have surprised her. Thinking how abandoned she must have felt when he didn't call her back. She probably knew by now what had happened; she would have called the police station. She wasn't the type to go away without answers. If she tried to engage anyone else's help at the station, he hadn't heard about it. He'd called a couple of times to see if there were any breaks in the Norman Banks case, and was told there was nothing. He mentioned the tape Naomi had left and the possible connection with the Banks' murder, but it didn't garner much interest, and he got the distinct impression that he was being blown off, that his opinions were not welcome, and tolerated at best. Enjoy your retirement, old man was what he heard loud and clear, though not in so many words. What was actually said were things like, "Get well soon" and "take care of that ticker". Oh, yeah, and they envied him. He heard that a lot. Lucky him, done with all this crap that never ended. Rest, they said. Only thing you need to catch now is fish. Ha ha.

A call came over the police band amidst crackle and static and he leaned forward, eager to catch the details, engaged in his day once again, grabbing onto the link to his old life. A service station had been held up over on Elm, near the baseball field. The perps, who appeared to be a couple of kids the owner thought he recognized, took off running when he grabbed a baseball bat from behind the counter.

Out of habit, he jotted down their descriptions in his notebook as they were related, trying to ignore the fragility of his body since the heart attack, that he felt like a very old man, shaky and weak, like his guts had been hollowed out. They told him he had to give himself time to recuperate. He had to take it easy. Well, he wasn't stupid; he knew that. Didn't mean he had to like it.

He sipped his green tea brought to him by his health-conscious, younger sister, Angie, grimaced at the fruity taste, and longed for a strong coffee. He was bored out of his mind with all the resting. Too much resting could kill you.

And he hated fishing.

* * *

The auto body shop was a long-shot, Naomi thought, but worth a try. She'd drop in at the library on her way home and check out the city directories from that time. Shouldn't be too hard to find an auto body shop that had been operating on Pine Street in the mid to late eighties.

As if reading her mistress' mind, Molly protested loudly from the back seat, and Naomi decided she'd had her fill of travel for today. "Okay, Molly, take it easy. We're heading on

home." The library would have to wait until tomorrow. Maybe she'd even get lucky and find something useful online.

The visit to Deborah Banks hadn't gone as badly as she'd feared. In fact, she wished Sergeant Nelson was still on the job so she could call him and give him her news.

Where from here? she asked herself.

She could still take both tapes to the police station, maybe talk to that Detective Karen Henderson, let her listen to them. But what did they really prove? Only that one of the two men who grabbed Mary Rose that night called to warn Naomi that she was in physical danger. A man who turned out to be one Norman Banks and who himself had ended up dead.

Maybe that's enough, she thought. Enough to persuade them to open the case again. But she wasn't convinced. I need to find out who killed him. I need a name.

Chapter Twenty-Seven

Had she continued on to the library she would have missed Charlotte, but as it was she found her waiting for her on the front doorstep, looking tentative but heels dug in, as only Charlotte could.

"If Mohammed won't come to the mountain, then the mountain must come to Mohammed, right? Ya gotta admire my timing."

Charlotte's grin was a tad forced, but she had an air of determination that Naomi had witnessed a long time ago in little skirmishes with Aunt Edna. She'd been ringing the front doorbell when Naomi pulled up at the curb. Her blue and silver mountain bike was propped against the house.

"Good to see you, Cuz," Naomi said, and it was. She could use someone to talk to. "I actually was planning to drop in to see you at the gym tomorrow."

"Sure you were. Here, let me take Molly. You get the door. I need a coffee."

"Me too." She had to admit, Charlotte was a breath of fresh air in an otherwise heavy-air day. You couldn't be with Debbie Banks and not carry some of her pain away with you. It didn't help that she'd intruded on that pain. "How are you?

"I'm good mostly," Charlotte said, letting a grateful, but indignant Molly out of the cage. "Have Molly to the vet?"

"No. We just went for a little drive."

In the kitchen, Charlotte slipped out of her blue nylon jacket with the gym logo on the pocket, a tiny barbell, and draped it over the back of her chair. "You didn't call me back," she said matter-of-factly. Smiling, but still accusatory.

Naomi plugged in the kettle and got the Maxwell House instant out of the cupboard. "I know. I'm sorry. I owe you an explanation."

"Hey, I didn't just fall off a turnip truck. I know why. You want to avoid Mom, and you think having lunch with me is a lousy idea for that reason. I get it."

Naomi shrugged lightly, spooned the coffee into their cups. "Something like that." "Something?"

The water began to boil and Naomi poured it over the grounds, releasing the aroma of roasted coffee into the room. They made great instant these days. "Actually, exactly like that. Everything seems so complicated ever since Mom died. I guess I always knew your mom had no love for me, but I never realized how deep it went." *Sure you did, you always knew, you just didn't know why.*

"You wanna know the truth, I don't get it myself. I was shocked when I read Aunt Lili's obit, and I'm not the only one. Poor Dad, he felt horrible. We all did. Mom can be difficult, believe me, I know. But I've never known her to be so vindictive. Maybe she's in the change or something."

Naomi smiled indulgently as she set their coffees on the table and sat down across from her cousin.

"No, I don't think that's it, Charlotte. Never mind, I'm glad you're here. It's good to see you. How are things with you? What's happening in your life? You said you were good mostly? "

"Same ole, same ole. Well, a few changes. I have my own apartment now, so my mother doesn't have to know my comings and goings, or that I stopped by, or anything else I don't want her to know. So you don't have to worry. I just want you to know I'm really sorry about all this. I've been thinking about you a lot and wondering if maybe I can do something to help."

"I appreciate the offer. But I'm doing okay." "Your vibe belies your words, my dear."

My vibe. A new age terminology. But, in truth, she wasn't that far off. I am feeling stressed out right now. "Okay, granted, I've been better," she conceded. I guess I just miss Mom."

"That's a given. You guys were close. But it's more than that, isn't it? Even more than finding out you were adopted. You seem haunted." She glanced at the chair propped under the back door knob, and frowned, but made no comment.

Charlotte was more than a little perceptive. Wonder what she'd say if I told her I thought a killer was stalking me. Or that I'd heard a young girl's cries when I was at the cemetery. A girl who'd been dead for nearly three decades. But what would be the point of that? It wouldn't help anything, and it would freak her out. Or she'd think I was losing my grip. And maybe she'd be right. *No, that wasn't true. I'm fine. I'm perfectly okay. Or I will be when they put that monster away.*

Ever since she found Molly shut up in the bureau drawer,

she'd been a nervous wreck, jumping at every sound, looking over her shoulder and finding no one there. Last night she was sure she'd heard someone outside her kitchen window, but when she moved the curtain aside to look, there was only the darkness to greet her, and her own ghostly reflection in the glass. Even turning out the light had revealed nothing ominous, no one lurking outside her back window. Once, she thought she saw the doorknob turn, but she was no longer certain about that either.

Unable to sleep, she even found herself getting up in the middle of the night, padding about the house checking on doors and windows she'd already checked, to be sure they were locked, that the chair was wedged firmly under the back door knob. And there was also that knife under her pillow. Would she even have the guts to actually use it if it came down to that? Hardly surprising if she looked 'haunted'.

She needed to find out who he was, she told herself again. That single thought was becoming a mantra for her. Find him. Put him behind bars. Until that happened, nothing would change. The situation could only get worse, dire. She wasn't fool enough to think a killer couldn't find a way into this house if he really wanted to. He'd already proven that much. But he hadn't hurt her, had he? Not yet, she thought. Could be the right opportunity just hadn't presented itself.

"Naomi? Hey, where did you go?"

"What? Oh, sorry, Charlotte. What were you saying?" "I asked if you've gotten any leads on the bad guys."

"Oh, no. Nothing definite. You look good, Char. Love that sweater. Blue's your color. And you should always wear jewelry."

"Thanks. But you're changing the subject."

Naomi smiled. "Matching lipstick and fingernail polish, too," she teased, knowing Charlotte had never been one for any kind of adornment. Her disinterest in fashion drove Edna nuts. Times changed. Maybe there was lover in the picture. Lucky her. She'd always been pretty sure Charlotte was gay. And she understood her reluctance to come out of the closet considering Edna was on the other side of the closet door. "You're in fantastic shape. I was thinking I should start back at the gym."

"If you need it, it doesn't show. But I'd love having you in my aerobics class." "Sounds like fun. But I'm more a yoga kind of girl," she grinned.

"We have a yoga class."

"One of these days I'll surprise you and show up. But I do want us to have lunch

sometime soon. And that's a promise. Just as soon as…"

"Forget lunch. We'll go someplace nice for dinner. My treat. Maybe Top of the Town. They've got a great blues singer this month, from Montreal. Really, she's terrific. Joanne LaRoche. You'll love her."

"Sounds good," Naomi said, meaning it in that moment. "But it'll be my treat."

Does that sound like I'm rubbing it in because Mom left me the bulk of her estate? Frank said Edna had already started legal proceedings to fight the will in court.

Against Frank's advice, Naomi was seriously considering offering an even split. But now she wondered if even that would satisfy Edna?

Chapter Twenty-Eight

Naomi was just getting out of the shower when the phone rang downstairs. With yet another promise to get herself a cell phone one of these days, she raced downstairs, tying her robe about her as she went, and grabbed the receiver with a damp hand as Debbie Banks was beginning to leave a message.

She hadn't found anything about the auto body shop online so she was headed for the Library, having made arrangements to drop Molly off at a pet daycare for a couple of hours. Better than leaving her in the car.

"Mrs. Banks -- Debbie, sorry. I was in the shower? Did you think of something?"

"Uh, maybe, I don't know. When I was at the doctor's yesterday, someone broke into the house. I called the police."

"What?" A cold sensation passed through her. Had her visit put Debbie Banks in danger? "Yes, they broke a back window and crawled inside. Nothing was taken but my photo albums were all out of place, and drawers had been gone through, some left open. Like whoever it was, was looking for something in particular. I have no idea what. The neighbor's dog set to

barking like crazy, but my neighbor, Mrs. Cross, said she didn't see anyone." He must have followed me yesterday.

"Maybe he didn't know what he was looking for either,

Debbie," Naomi said. "If he was who we're both thinking of, I think he was just blindly looking for anything that might connect him to your husband. Sounds like he's getting a little paranoid. Your photo albums, huh? Are there any pictures of your husband with male friends that you can recall?"

"None I've ever seen. Like I said, Norman wasn't one for going out with the boys. He's was a family man. But I did wonder if looking at his high school yearbook would be of any help. It's around here someplace. If I come across it, I'll take a quick look through but I doubt I'll find anything of significance. No reason I would. I didn't know Normie then. I'm on my way into town and if I find it, I'll drop it off."

Naomi thanked her, and told her to come ahead. She was suddenly afraid for the woman. Would he pay her another visit? Wondering if, in a weak moment, Norman Banks had confided his sin to his wife. With a sense of time running out, her eye drifted to the little clown on the coffee table and she saw it again rocking to and fro on its parallel bars, imagined the hand that had set it in motion. Hands capable of beating a woman to death. She suddenly knew he would not have left fingerprints on the clown, or the doorknob or Debbie Banks' photo albums or anything else he had touched. He would have worn gloves. He was no novice at not getting caught.

She might have passed him on the street over the years. Seen him in a grocery store lineup, or at the post office. What kind of work did he do in his regular life? Who sees him, talks to him every day, and has no idea of the monster behind the mask?

Who are you?

* * *

After Debbie Banks had come and gone, leaving her with the yearbook, Naomi drove to the library, returning home a short time later with Molly in the carrier, and a scanned page from a 1979 city directory in her purse, along with a borrowed copy of Eric Grant's book, "Freakhead". She was curious. He'd sent her a note of apology and asked her to lunch. He included his email and phone number, which she didn't respond to, but neither did she throw the note away. She

was hardly ready for a new relationship right now, and even if she was, she definitely didn't think becoming involved with Eric Grant was a good idea. But she couldn't deny the warm flush that came to her cheeks when she read his note.

The Body Shop, which turned out to be the actual name of the company, was listed in the directories from 1962 to 1984, always on Pine Street. It was possible Norman Banks and his pal had worked together at this place. She'd been excited to see the proprietor's name, Craig Kelly, included in the listing. Would he remember who worked for him back then? He might, especially if they were long term employees.

Thumbing through the phone book, something kept niggling at the back of her mind. Some important detail she had overlooked or forgotten, something in her subconscious trying to surface like a fish in murky water. But before it could, a woman answered the telephone. Naomi asked to speak to Craig Kelly.

"Mr. Kelly hasn't lived here in ten years," the woman said stiffly. "We're divorced. Who's calling please?"

Naomi introduced herself, told her she was trying to reach one of his old employees. A personal matter.

"Last I heard, Craig's in Mexico. I heard he's into stealing cars. Well, he probably doesn't steal them himself, he's too old for that. But he does the body work. I can't swear to that, 'course, just what I heard. Sorry I can't be of more help."

"You wouldn't happen to know who might have an address?" Naomi prodded, almost wincing as she did.

"Like I said, I haven't seen him in ten years. Who you looking for?"

"I uh, don't know his name. But he worked for your husband in the mid to late eighties, I believe?"

"Are you serious? You want me to remember who worked for my ex nearly thirty years ago. And you don't know his name?" She gave a laugh that sounded like a bark.

Naomi thanked her and hung up. That worked out well, she thought. Everyone had their story. To quote Tolstoy, "Happy families are all alike; every unhappy family is unhappy in its own way." A bitter woman with an axe to grind? she wondered. Or was her ex actually mixed up in some car ring in Mexico. Either way, it had nothing to do with her. Another dead-end. Lives change in nearly three decades. People moved away, got divorced, died. She had to change tracks; this one was going nowhere. She was beginning to feel like that guy who flung himself on his horse and rode off in all directions.

Does he feel me gaining on him? She hoped so. She hoped he was having a problem sleeping these days. She knew he'd be making new plans, since his first one had been foiled. She tried not to envision a scenario wherein he would kill her and dump her body somewhere so remote it would never be found. That way, her DNA could never be matched with his, which would let him run free for all time, hurting others as he chose. Not the preferred ending, from Naomi's point of view.

And she was having a lot less confidence in that knife under her pillow. False sense of security there. He'd probably use it on her. She'd have to think more on this. Think smarter. She needed a plan.

Definitely needed a plan.

In the meantime, there were still a couple of things she could follow up on. But first, she'd eat something. Not that she was all that hungry, but it was important to stay healthy. With

Molly contentedly eating her dinner, she opened up a can of tomato soup for herself. At the whine of the electric can-opener Molly looked up from her dish.

"Don't worry," she grinned, "I'm not having anything more exciting than your tuna. But you can lick the bowl." Molly loved anything tomato.

Even as she poured the tomato soup into a small pot, added a little milk and set the pot on the stove, her mind kept trying to grasp that forgotten detail, that nugget of information, but it stayed just out of her reach, like a word on the tip of your tongue. Whatever it was continued to nag her even as she set out her bowl and a few crackers on a plate, poured herself a glass of milk. It'll come, she thought. Don't try to force it.

She decided to make some notes to herself, retrieved a writing tablet and pen from the kitchen drawer and sat down at the table. In one column, she wrote: What I know for sure. (Or at least believe.) It was a short list, ending with the break-in of Debbie Banks' house on the same day she'd been to see her. She'd been hugely relieved when Debbie told her she was taking a little time to visit with her daughter out in British Columbia. The police had the number and would call when her husband's body was signed for release, so she could give Norman a proper burial. At least she'd be safe for the time being, Naomi thought, grateful not to have to worry about him showing up again and hurting her, or worse.

Sighing, she set the pen down and read over what she'd written. Norman Banks was murdered because he'd become a threat. Proof: none. But Mr. Banks did have her story on his person when they found him. And that was Norman Banks' voice on the tape. If not proof, then a hell of a coincidence. And she didn't believe in coincidences. She munched on a cracker, sipped her milk.

One thing was a definite. She knew a lot more now than she did when she read her mother's obituary in the paper, dear Aunt Edna's work. At thoughts of her aunt, the niggling piece of missing information began niggling again. Harder this time. Biting, clawing. Wanting out. I know something else. Why can't I remember?

It was when she absent-mindedly reached up to take the tiny gold earrings out of her ears, that she did. And it was like the breath was knocked out of her.

In the same instant she caught a whiff of something burning and jumped up from the chair. The soup. The pop...pop...pop sounds sent her flying to the stove as the scorched acrid stench filled the kitchen. Grabbing a potholder from the drawer, she lifted the furiously boiling red liquid off the burner.

* * *

Debbie Banks didn't miss the relief in Naomi Water's voice when she told her she was going out west to visit her daughter, and knew she'd been scared for her. She appreciated the concern. Although she, herself, had been surprised and alarmed that someone broke into her home, gone through her things, she wasn't really afraid. Mad? Hell, yes. But she didn't care enough to be afraid. Life without Normie seemed like a long grey corridor of loneliness, she thought, as she packed slacks, blouses and underclothes into the small blue suitcase lying open on the bed.

Naomi Waters seemed like such a nice young woman, determined to find her mother's killer, who she believes also murdered Norman. She'd hoped she might find some clue in the yearbook. She wouldn't have thought of it if someone hadn't broken in and gone through her photo albums. She went through them herself in case she'd forgotten some picture taken of him

with a friend, but there was nothing. And then she thought of the yearbook. It had taken her a while to find it.

Balancing precariously on the next to the top rung of the ladder, feeling a weakness in her limbs, she riffled through the mess on the shelf in their bedroom, sure that was where she'd seen it at one time. Norman had been something of a packrat and she had to move aside old bottles he'd saved, a pair of ancient binoculars, decks of cards no one used, flashlights minus batteries, a broken watch, old hats from work bearing the Harris Woodworking logo, before she found it. She'd pretty much left this shelf to him, ignoring the chaos, his minor fault.

Maybe that wasn't his worse fault; she immediately banished the traitorous thought. Normie wouldn't hurt a fly. It was in part his gentleness that drew her to him. Her own father had been a violent man, an abuser, and she wanted a different sort of man for herself, and her kids. She often heard that women are drawn to what they know; it hadn't worked that way for her.

She had found the book under a pile of old car magazines, pulled it out and blew off the dust. Sitting down on the bed with the book in her lap, slowly she began turning the glossy pages, some colored, many black and white. Photos of softball teams, cheerleaders, school musicals, prizes for leaders in academics, of the prom held in the school gymnasium, festive with gold and red ribbons, balloons. A band was playing on the stage, and the grads were frozen in various poses of dancing and laughing. They all looked so young and beautiful, the world their oyster.

Normie wasn't a part of the celebration. He never went to his prom, said he was too shy to ask anyone. His shyness. Another of the things she'd loved about him. She had thought she might come across a picture and it would be the other man and she would somehow know. She found nothing of course. How could she?

I want you, you son-of-a-bitch. I want you to pay for what you did to Normie. To all of us. She idly picked up his pillow and pressed it to her face and breathed in the faint scent of her husband, mingled with the hint of Old Spice he preferred to the more trendy brands. It faded a little more every day. Soon it would fade altogether. Too overcome with grief to sustain the anger, she could only weep and rock, and bury her face deeper into the pillow.

Chapter Twenty-Nine

Leaving Norman Banks' high school yearbook sitting on the coffee table beside the little clown, Naomi left the house, Molly in tow. Not exactly changing tracks, just boarding farther back on the track. She'd get to the book later.

The fitness center was a cacophony of noise, from the thumping music to the pounding of feet at various speeds on treadmills, bikes and other machines, a constant rumble of motors. The smell of sweat, dirty socks and perfume tinged the high energy air. The air-conditioning was on full blast. Underneath it all, there was talking and laughing. Socializing was a big part of hitting the gym for many of its patrons.

Some of the laughter was coming from the far corner of the room where Charlotte was working with one of the members, an overweight, sweet-faced woman in blue sweats who apparently found a lot to laugh at, mainly herself. The woman let out an exaggerated groan and flopped full out on the mat. Charlotte laughed too. She was helping her with her sit-ups, showing her a couple of variations that would be easier for her, but still effective. Naomi stood a short distance away so as not to interfere with their session.

"Lizbeth, use those stomach muscles when you curl up," Charlotte said. "Even if you just raise up off the mat a couple of inches, that will strengthen your abs and lessen the strain on your back."

Lizbeth followed her instructions without complaint. "Good, good, but don't forget to breathe."

The woman made a self-deprecating joke Naomi didn't hear, that earned another laugh from Charlotte. Seconds later the woman gave another exhausted grunt and flopped back again. Charlotte grinned, shook her head and tossed her a small towel to wipe her sweaty forehead.

None of the women were paying any attention to the middle-aged man who was sitting on a bench a few feet away from them, performing bicep curls with heavy free weights and watching Charlotte in the wall mirror. Charlotte in her black tights and white sweatshirt, lean, taut body. His eye swept over the long legs in their black leotard, a reflex more than anything else. He had other things on his mind. He was losing his cool, not like him, had to get it together. No one knew anything. The Weaz was dead. He'd searched his house and hadn't found anything that would tie them together, although he could have missed it. A photo, a note. Had he ever written the Weaz a note? He couldn't remember, but he didn't think so. He wasn't one for writing notes. Even if there was something, what did that prove? Without her, in the flesh, it was all circumstantial. He should have gone back that night and taken care of the problem.

His left arm was mid-curl when he saw her and his heart leapt as if he had seen a ghost. A slight turn of his head in the mirror and there she was. The vision of her standing there sucked the strength out of him and sent his rhythm off. The sweat turned cold on his flesh but he did not turn his face from the mirror. At first he'd thought he must be hallucinating. Because he'd been thinking about her, she had appeared, like some kind of phantom. But she was real enough. Wearing dark slacks and a suede jacket, long dark hair loose about her shoulders.

It's like that bitch waited all these years to crawl up out of the grave to get him. To get him through her kid. Well, it wasn't gonna happen. Rage born of fear made him unconsciously speed up his routine up, down, up, down ...arm muscles bulging, relaxing, bulging, the blue and gold tattooed owl's eye on his right upper arm opening, narrowing, like a thing alive, ready to swoop from its flesh canvas, bringing hot blood to his face and drawing soft animal grunts from his core. When she didn't look in his direction he began to breathe again.

She and the fitness instructor were hugging now, talking. It was not the first time he'd seen her in person, or heard her voice. A voice he would already have silenced had he not been interrupted that night. Later, he'd thought the doorbell ringing might have been a good thing. Safer for him if he could scare her into backing off. Everyone in River's End had read that article in the local rag. The Weaz's death would be looked at closer, maybe connections made.

So what? Let 'em prove it, he thought now, emboldened in his fury. Just because she didn't look at you doesn't mean she doesn't know who you are. Doesn't see you here. Fear washed through him like an icy bath. How dare she taunt him, thinking she's so damn clever, visiting his dreams, playing head games with him. Well, he'd show her who the master of games was; she'd be sorry she ever messed with him. He'd make the little bitch disappear forever.

"She's your daughter," he could almost hear the Weaz say. The thought generated the same surge of anger he'd felt the first time he'd heard him say it. To Mac, she was nothing but a crime scene with his prints all over it.

Keeping his head down, he feigned adjusting his weightlifting gloves as he continued to watch her in the mirror. She was a looker, you had to say that for her. He saw something of his mother in her; she didn't really look like his mother; his mother had been a blond, and not tall, but something. Maybe in the walk, the curve of her brow.

His mother died of a drug overdose when he was thirteen, and years before that his old man took off with some bimbo. He barely remembered him. His unmarried paternal aunt took him in, a good enough old broad, Gladys, and an easy touch. He pretty much came and went as he pleased growing up. She died a couple of years ago, left him a few dollars, along with the house, which was falling down and not worth a hell of a lot. He had it up for sale. He used to visit now and then to stay on her good side, but the chatter grated on his nerves, and he hated the dark furniture, the heavy drapes and the smell of camphor and dead roses that seemed embedded in the walls. He never thought of her as a mother, just an old lady who gave him a place to stay and something to eat.

"Takin' a break, Mac," one of the male trainers grinned down at him, startling him out of his unpleasant reverie. The guy was heading for the showers toting an armload of towels. "You're lookin' a little flushed, dude."

"Yeah," he replied, forcing a chuckle. "Must be old age." But his heart was thumping in a way that had nothing to do with the workout. Why was she here? What the hell was going on?

The two women left a few minutes later, heads together, talking. Charlotte, as he'd heard the instructor called, glanced in his direction as she passed him, smiled briefly, then looked away. Were they talking about him? Mocking him?

He did another set of bicep reps, the owl eye winking and opening with each curl, uncurl. He'd got the tattoo when he was sixteen. Just walking down the street one night when he saw a gallery of tattoos in a dirty storefront window and the one of the owl's eye spoke to him. One woman he'd dated a few times said she didn't like the tattoo, always felt like the eye was watching her. It made him laugh.

Made him feel good.

Chapter Thirty

They ordered coffee and muffins at a Tim Horton's drive-thru and Naomi drove the two miles out to Little River beach because she wanted some privacy when she talked to Charlotte. A few weeks from now this place would be packed, but now there were only a few cars in the parking area.

A lone young man in a blue jacket and dark pants was walking along the far end of the beach taking photographs, hair blowing in the warm ocean breeze.

She parked the car near a grassy knoll away from the actual parking area. They peeled the lids off their coffees, sipped and watched the big waves rolling in, crashing over rocks and sand, bleached driftwood, the beach a sweeping blue flared skirt with a long stretch of foamy hem.

Naomi was acutely aware of Charlotte waiting for her to say something, tell her why she was here. She cracked the car windows open and let in the smell of salty sea air, the raucous cries and mewling of the gulls.

It was a perfect day, blue skies, fluffy white clouds. The kind of day that inspired pleasant thoughts that relaxed you. But not today, not for her. The woman at the Pet Care center was surprised to see Naomi back with Molly so soon, but there'd been no problem leaving her, even if Naomi did feel guilty walking away.

"Good idea, this," Charlotte said cheerfully beside her. "I was surprised when you showed up today, but really glad to see you. Timing was great too; I was due for a break. And if I'm a little later getting back, so be it. I'm working through till ten tonight. I love these blueberry muffins. They're still warm. Great idea this, Naomi. The ocean is so beautiful. It would never occur to me to drive out here on my own."

Charlotte knew they weren't here just to look at the ocean. Naomi heard it in her voice. A mild curiosity, a certain wariness.

"Charlotte, I need to ask you something."

"Oh? So it's not my radiant personality that brought you to the center today." "That's part of it," Naomi smiled and touched Charlotte's arm affectionately. "But..." "If it's the Will, I think we've pretty much convinced Mom to give up on..."

"No, no, that's not it. I-- I need to ask you about that crescent moon you were wearing when you were at the house."

"Crescent moon? Oh, the pendant, you mean." She reached down inside her sweatshirt and drew it out. "What about it?" Charlotte asked.

Just then, another car drove up beside them and a young woman and two little boys got out. The boys raced for the beach, armed with plastic pails and shovels. The woman, wearing blue capris and a tee-shirt, followed behind, a jacket slung over her arm and clutching a paperback.

Naomi turned back to Charlotte, trying to conceal the horror and confusion that swept through her as she looked at the pendant.

She'd only had a sense of it before, but now she knew it was the same one, or one very similar to the pendant Mary Rose was wearing in the school photo. "Could you take it off for a minute, please. I'd like to look at it."

Charlotte shrugged. "Sure." Looking puzzled, she undid the clasp on the slim, braided leather lace and placed the pendant in Naomi's hand. "You really do like it. Hey, I'd give it to you gladly but it's not mine."

"Oh?" While she considered this statement, she turned the little crescent moon over in her hand. On the back, the letters SISIP were etched into the hand-carved bone. She ran her thumb over the shape of the letters. Her heart was beating double time. Dear God. Was it possible?

As she pondered the significance of the letters, a fluttery movement caught her eye. She looked up to see a seagull perched on the hood of the car, looking nervously in at them out of one beady eye. She should have brought treats. Sorry, little gull. It hopped from foot to foot, fluttered its wings. Then flew away.

"You wanna tell me what's going on?" Charlotte prodded. "I'm getting the message that this isn't just some piece of jewelry you covet."

"Any idea what those letter on the back mean?" Naomi asked.

"No. I figured somebody called Sis or something. You want to enlighten me, kiddo. I'm really in the dark here."

By way of answer, Naomi reached across Charlotte and took the sheet of paper from the glove compartment. It was a copy of

Mary Rose's school picture. She handed it to Charlotte. "Does the pendant look familiar to you?"

Charlotte looked at the photo for moment, then handed it back to Naomi. "This is the girl who was abducted all those years ago…your mother."

"Yes, my birth mother. Mary Rose Francis. Lillian Waters was my mother." Charlotte nodded her understanding. She examined the necklace again, looked back at the photo. "It's similar, I guess. You can't tell too much from this black and white copy though. Why?"

"Just something I'm working on. If it turns into anything significant, I'll call you. You said this necklace isn't yours, Charlotte. Whose is it?"

"Mom's. It's been in her jewelry box for years. She never wore it. Not her style. But I've always liked it." She grinned sheepishly. "So I…secretly borrowed it when I was at the house a few weeks ago."

"Charlotte, do me a favor. Don't mention our conversation to your mother, okay? Or to anyone else. Okay?"

She gave a quick shrug of her shoulders. "Sure." "May I borrow this?"

She shrugged again. "I guess."

"Thanks. I'd really appreciate that. I'll get it back to you shortly." She slipped it into her

purse.

"You think it's hers, don't you? Your birth mother's. That's pretty obvious. But you're wrong about that, Naomi. You can get this kind of jewelry lots of places, at the mall, online. There are reproductions that..."

"Yes, I know that's possible."

"There's no ways it's hers. I get why this is important to you, Naomi, I do, but don't you think you might be getting a little...obsessed?"

She was tiptoeing, not wanting to overstep her boundaries, and Naomi knew it. She took no offense. She supposed it could seem like obsession to someone who's never been where I am. Not that Charlotte didn't have her own share of problems. Naomi, wouldn't have wanted Aunt Edna for a mother on a bet.

"You could be right. Probably are. I don't know, Char. Like I said, I'll call you if I learn anything more. That's a promise. Your coffee's getting cold."

Charlotte looked her straight in the eye. "Why would Mom have something that girl Mary Rose Francis owned?" There was a coolness in the question, a defensiveness. Naomi wasn't surprised.

"I don't know. Maybe she doesn't. Right now all I have are questions." She finished off her coffee and sat the empty cup in the cup holder, noted that more people had come to enjoy a day at the beach, though it was not yet summer.

The two little boys were running to the edge of the water and back, squealing and laughing. It would be numbingly cold yet. A group of girls were setting up a net for a game of beach volleyball. "Either way," Naomi said, "I'll call you."

Charlotte nodded, not looking at her, but out the passenger

window. "I have to get back to work."

Chapter Thirty-One

The schedule for fitness trainers was pinned on the cork board by the counter. He ran his eye down the list of names, stopped at Charlotte Bradley. The only Charlotte on the list.

She was working tonight. He'd talk to her, that was all. Find out her connection to Naomi Waters. Just mention it casually, nothing to make her suspicious. She'd just figure he was interested in her; women were like that. She was cute, not half bad, but the jock-type had never turned him on. How did they know each other? he wondered, unable to dismiss the anxiety building in him, like a dog sensing a coming storm. Even while a small voice was telling him it didn't matter. All he had to do was make Naomi Waters disappear forever and his troubles would be over. No one could pin anything on him, no matter what they thought they knew.

No one knows anything, Mac. You're turning into the freaking Weaz.

Chapter Thirty-Two

Naomi couldn't get home quick enough. Locking the front door behind her, she let Molly out of her carrier, then rushed into the studio and turned on the computer. She sat impatiently, waiting for the thing to go through its paces. She'd bookmarked the Mi'kmaq dictionary and brought it up now, typed in SISIP, the letters carved into the back of the crescent moon.

She clicked find. When the words *small bird* came up on the screen, she could hardly get her breath, only sit there in wonder, the blood draining from her face. She had been staring at the words for what must have been a full minute before she realized she was crying, silent tears sliding down her cheeks that she didn't bother to wipe away.

It's hers. Not that she was all that surprised, and yet at the same time it seemed impossible that the pendant she held in the palm of her hand had once belonged to a young girl whose grandfather called her Little Bird, and who had made it for her. The same young girl who had given her life.

A myriad of emotions swam through her, setting every nerve ending afire and sparking. This was a gift she'd been given. A small miracle. Had Mary Rose not confided to Lisa Boyce that her grandfather had called her Little Bird, I would never have known. She asked the question Charlotte had asked of her, but with a little different take. How did the pendant wind up in Edna Bradley's possession? She'd have to find out. But not yet. First, she'd do a little more digging on her own. She didn't want to betray Charlotte's confidence without a very good reason. Right now she needed to know if Mary Rose had been wearing this pendant on the night she was taken. If she was, then why wasn't it with the rest of her clothing, to be returned to her grandfather at some point?

Lisa would know. Yes, she would know.

She started to get up just as the phone rang. She picked up in the living room, thinking for the millionth time that she should get a cell phone, but it wasn't a serious thought and she knew she probably wouldn't. As her mother often said, she had a foot planted in two worlds. "You're something of a computer nerd," she used to tease her, "but you're still an old soul, Naomi."

It was Lisa on the phone. Naomi smiled to herself, surprised by nothing today, as Lisa said, "You've been on my mind, Naomi. I just wanted to make sure you were okay."

"I'm fine, Lisa. I was just going to call you. I need to ask you something." "Sure, dear. What is it?"

"In the school photo of Mary Rose, it shows her wearing a pendant. A little..." "Crescent moon," Lisa filled in. "She always wore it."

"Then she was wearing it that night." "Yes. Why? What...?"

"I think I'm holding that pendant in my hand right now, Lisa. I want you to see it and confirm that it's the same one, although I don't think there's much question..."

"Oh, my God. How could...?"

"I'll explain when I see you. Can I come over now? Are you busy?"

A half hour later, Naomi pulled into Lisa's drive to see Lisa standing in her doorway, smiling, looking happy to see her. She also looked anxious.

"I'm so glad you're here," she said. "Hi, Molly. I was worried. Come in, come in. I've got dinner nearly ready. I hope you like tuna casserole. I know Molly will," she laughed, and closed the door behind them. "I've got a litter box already for her, so not to worry. I had a bag of the stuff left over from winter that I used for the driveway. Here, give me your coat."

Naomi unlocked the carrier, and Molly wandered about the kitchen warily, but not unhappily, and Naomi suspected the smell of tuna made the strange surroundings easier to take. Or maybe she was just becoming a seasoned traveler, looking forward to that next experience. She thanked Lisa for letting her bring Molly, and Lisa chuckled, saying, "Oh, posh, I love animals. Had a cat until the poor little thing died, twenty years old he was. His name was Hobo. So, let's have a look, shall we?"

Naomi had put the pendant in a small black velvet bag she'd found in her bureau drawer, that had once held a pair of crystal earrings, one of which went missing ages ago. Now she sat down at the kitchen table, took the bag from her purse, upturned it into her hand.

Naomi had often read of someone's jaw dropping, but Lisa's

actually did. "Oh, I can't believe it. But you're right, it is hers. Where did you...?" As she ran a thumb over the bone, tracing the letter with the pad of her thumb, as Naomi had done, her eyes shone with tears.

"My cousin was wearing it. My cousin by marriage, not blood." It was the first time she'd ever made the distinction aloud. "She said it was her mother's. That would be my Aunt

Edna...through adoption. Gets complicated."

"How did she get it?"

"That's the question I intend to ask Edna. But I wanted to be absolutely sure this was Mary Rose's before I went any further with this."

"Well, be sure then. We were in the same class for an entire year, and she always wore this pendant, every day. And she was wearing it the last time I saw her. She even let me hold it once."

"It apparently wasn't with her when they found her," Naomi said. "There was no mention of it in the paper."

"I remember her grandfather -- your great-grandfather, came to our house one time; he wanted to know about the pendant. He looked so old and broken standing in our doorway. Yet there was a strength about him, a special dignity that came from somewhere deep inside him, beyond the grief. My mother offered him tea, but he wouldn't come in. When I told him I didn't know where it was, he left. That was the only time I ever saw him."

Naomi surmised he probably told the police she'd been wearing it that night and they brushed it off, didn't believe him, thought he was an old man with an unreliable mind. And an Indian to boot. You couldn't ignore that possibility. Otherwise, they would have followed up on the lead. Because it was a lead.

"Things are somehow coming together, aren't they?" Lisa said.

"I think so. Somewhat. I'm getting a lot of help. Certainly from you."

"Mainly from Mary Rose, I'll bet," she said softly, the faintest smile on her face.

It was good to be with someone who had known Mary Rose back then, who knew what happened to her, and had cared. And besides, she liked Lisa for herself. Naomi liked being with her. "Being with you is like coming in from the cold, Lisa," she said impulsively, "and warming my hands over a lovely fire."

"Oh, honey, you sure you're not Irish," she laughed, but Naomi heard the pleasure in her voice. "What a sweet thing to say." She left the table then, and still smiling, opened the oven door to let out a blast of heat and more of the aroma of tuna casserole and homemade biscuits. "I hope you're hungry."

"I am now."

Molly echoed her sentiments in cat language, and later thanked her benefactor by licking the saucer clean.

Molly knew a good thing when she smelled it. The casserole was amazingly tasty, tender in a creamy dill sauce. Not to mention the green salad with cherry tomatoes, real bacon bits and chives. "I didn't realize I was so famished," Naomi said, dabbing at her mouth with a linen napkin, having polished off a second helping of the casserole with only a slight embarrassment.

"You're using up a lot of fuel with all this detective work," Lisa smiled. "You need to replenish. Anything would have tasted good."

"Not so. You're an amazing cook and you know it." She couldn't remember the last time she'd actually cooked a meal for herself. "My turn next. I promise. I'm no Lisa Boyce, but I make a pretty mean lasagna."

"I'll hold you to it. I love Italian. My favorite."

"Then we'll do it." How good it would be to live like a normal human being again. To have people over for dinner. Good conversation, a little wine, a few laughs. Would she live so long? Did Eric Grant like lasagna? Now where did that come from? She hardly knew him.

Lisa smiled at her, almost as if she could read her thoughts. "Let's put the dishes in the dishwasher and take our coffees outside. We'll sit on the swing."

They sat and chatted till the sun went down. The wonderful meal, the gentle motion of the swing, even its soft rhythmic squeak, lulled her into a peaceful state as she listened to Lisa telling her about her husband and their wonderful years together. She talked about her kids. In turn, Naomi told her about her mother, Lili, and how close they'd been. She answered Lisa's questions about her job as an audio book narrator, which seemed to fascinate Lisa no end.

Naomi told her how much she loved narrating stories, becoming each of the characters in the book, like performing in a one-woman stage play, except she imagined an audience of one. One rapt little face caught up in the story, rather than a sea of faces.

"One little girl writes me fan letters and calls me the storybook lady," she said. "She sent me a picture of herself. A serious little girl with braids and braces. She reminded me of myself as a kid."

"Your mom must have been so proud of you, Naomi."

"She was. She was my biggest fan. She's really the reason I'm in this business." She told her about her mother's fondness for old radio stories like The Sealed Book, The Squeaking Door and Suspense Theatre. "She had a stack of those old shows on CDs she'd ordered online. They instilled in me a love for the medium, and starting me thinking narrating might be something I could do."

She'd been right; her dream evolved into a career that she loved. Audio books were a big part of the publishing industry. She was lucky to have found her niche there.

She asked Lisa how the computer lessons were going, how she met her husband, about her kids. One thread of conversation leading to another, weaving the narrative of Lisa's life.

Soon, a sprinkle of stars appeared in the dusky sky. A hint of the bay was in the air, mingled with the apple blossoms growing on the lone tree in the yard.

"I really have to go, Lisa," she said. "It's getting late."

Lisa pleaded with her not to go, insisting she stay the night. "You have nothing you need to go home to," she said. "Molly's here with you, and she's fine. And you need some rest. I didn't want to say anything earlier, but you don't look good, Naomi. You've lost more weight and you've got circles under your eyes. You need a good night's sleep, and there's an excellent Posturepedic mattress on the bed in the guestroom. I have a nice Victorian nightie you can wear. You can even take it home with you when you go, far too small for me. One of the kids gave it to me for Christmas and I've never worn it."

"Hard to resist," she laughed softly. "Really, I'd love to stay, Lisa, but I have so much to do. I have to make a plan. I have to..."

"You'll think better once you've had a good night's sleep. Personally, I think you should take what you have to the police and let them handle it. But I know you won't do that. And I understand. But why can't it wait a little. It's waited this long. In fact, you could stay here with me for a while a week, two...."

"That's very generous. And I would leave it to the police if I thought they'd listen to me? They won't, Lisa, anymore than they listened to my great-grandfather all those years ago. There was a policeman who had begun to believe me, but unfortunately he had a heart attack and is no longer on the force. Though I'm told he's recovering nicely. No, I need more evidence. I need to solve the damn case."

The phone in Lisa's sweater pocket burbled. After it burbled a second time, she answered, hanging up a few minutes later, still smiling.

"My son," she said, the one in Alberta." He was checking up on her wanting to know if she was all right and relating his own news which was limited since he was working long shifts for a construction company. "He's a great kid," Lisa told her. "He hates being away weeks at a time, but the money's great. He has a girlfriend, Janet, and they're saving for a down payment for a house before they get married."

"They sound like a great couple."

"Yeah, they are. So, are you going to be my housemate for awhile?" "I can't, Lisa, I..."

"For tonight at least, then. I have such a bad feeling about you going home tonight. I really do. I don't think I could stand it if anything happened to you, too. I'd never forgive myself. And Mary Rose would never forgive me."

It was that last argument that persuaded her. And Lisa's unearned guilt over Mary Rose. The truth was she didn't want to go home at all. She wasn't brave, she was terrified. Maybe it was a good idea to stay away from the house for tonight.

Her hesitation gave Lisa an opportunity to reiterate the reasons why Naomi should not go home, and she seized upon it, though there was no need. She had already made up her mind. As soon as she did, a blessed sense of relief washed over her. It would be so nice to have one night where she didn't jump at every sound.

"I'll stay," she said. "And thanks, Lisa."

Despite the night sounds outside the screened bedroom window, a light wind, and once the moan of a foghorn out on the bay, Naomi soon slept.

When she woke, the plan was in place.

Chapter Thirty-Three

The Puffin Club was a hot spot in River's End, attracting a wide clientele, though tonight they were mostly a younger crowd.

When Mac walked in the place was jumping. The air reeked of booze and sweat and sex. The slick, gyrating bodies of women in scant clothing moving to the pounding, thrusting music, nightmarish in the strobe lights, sent a surge of fury through him. Made him want to go on the prowl. The thing that set him off, though, was showing up at that bitch's house and finding the car gone and no one home. Not even the damn cat, which he would gladly have slaughtered on the spot, just to punish her. Where was she? He could feel the vein pulsing in his forehead as he scanned the room. Easy Mac, he told himself. Be cool, man.

And then he spotted two of the fitness instructors from the center, including the one called Charlotte, sitting at a corner table with two other girls. She might know where her friend was. In fact, he was almost certain she would know. They knew him from the center, so it would be natural he'd go over and say hi. Maybe he'd ask Charlotte if she'd like to dance. He sauntered over to the table. Women were always wanting someone to dance with them.

He would have followed them from the gym today but someone might have noticed him leaving, and besides, they would have been long gone by the time he changed his clothes and got to his van.

"Hey, girls," he said, grinning down at them. He was wearing jeans, and a black shirt that showed off his physique. He felt confident.

They'd been deep in conversation when he approached. The girl with short, dark hair Blanche, he remembered suddenly, smiled up at him. "Hi, Mac." It pleased him that she remembered his name.

Charlotte echoed, "Hi, Mac." Asked him what he was doing here.

"Same as you girls," he said off-handedly. "Winding down after a rough day in the mines. Anyone up for a dance. Charlotte?"

The blond at the table, wearing a pink sparkly top that showed off a generous cleavage, slid hard eyes over him.

"No, no thanks, Mac. I did two aerobic classes back to back. That's it for me. Just having a beer then heading on home. "Della, you like to dance." Charlotte picked up her glass of beer, exposing the wet ring on the table, and grinned at her friend before taking a swallow. He suddenly felt himself the butt of an unspoken joke.

The blond was giving Charlotte a look that said 'I'll get you later', then with a sigh he perceived rather than heard, she pushed back her chair, gave him a horsey grin. He hadn't expected teeth as showy as her cleavage. "Sure, Mac, I'll give you a whirl around the floor."

The other two girls laughed, and Mac felt the heat crawl up his neck and face. As he guided the blond to the middle of the floor, behind him, he heard the softly spoken words 'aging playboy'.

Charlotte's voice.

It was Charlotte he'd wanted to dance with, an excuse to ask her a few questions, nothing more. She shouldn't flatter herself. He supposed he had no choice but to dance with the blond. Leaving her standing in the middle of the floor would only draw attention to himself. He was still feeling the sting of humiliation at Charlotte's rejection. Their private joke that wasn't so private, followed by her spoken insult, shot his anger up a couple of notches.

Where was the other bitch? he wondered again. He'd go back to her house later tonight. Maybe she'd be there then. He'd end this.

The blond said something into his neck and for an instant he was surprised to find himself dancing with her. The music was so loud he couldn't make out her words, but not wanting to encourage further conversation, he managed some vague reply, a smile.

The dance ended none too soon, as far as Mac was concerned. He ordered a drink at the bar and finished it off almost before the blond found her chair again. He hadn't bothered to walk her back to the table. He left shortly after, giving them a wave as he passed by their table. Damned if he'd let them think their opinion mattered to him, one way or the other. They stopped talking just long enough to wave back, an apathetic gesture, but he knew he barely registered with them. He was just the middle-aged guy who came to the gym. And apparently, who Charlotte thought of as an aging playboy. Horse-face had been doing him a favor by dancing with him. Bitches! Who in hell do they think they are? Bitches and whores, all of them. They didn't know who they were dealing with.

He'd worked himself into a mad fury by the time he reached his van. He got in and drove slowly around the parking lot until he found a parking place at the far end where he could see who came and went, but wouldn't be spotted. He'd been prepared to wait for however long it took, but less than a half hour later, the girls came out, hugged, and went to their separate cars. He watched Charlotte Bradley get into a silver Toyota and he followed her, keeping a safe distance behind the car.

Mac had no real plan thought out, but was just following instincts, wanting to hurt someone. Hurt them bad. He sat across the street from Charlotte Bradley's apartment building for more than an hour nursing the rage that coursed through him. His eyes remained riveted on the windows in the building from the moment she disappeared inside, and saw the light go on in an apartment on the second floor, and knew it was hers.

Every few minutes her silhouette would appear behind the blind as she walked past the window, and he fantasized about her, about taking her and letting her know he was much more than an aging playboy. He was her worse nightmare. He was still there, sitting in the darkened car, when she turned off the light.

When more time passed, he figured she was probably asleep. He pictured her in the bed, perhaps naked, trusting that she was safe. She was an athlete, a fitness trainer after all. She could take care of herself.

Two aerobic classes back to back, she had told him, so she wouldn't have to dance with him. Brushed him off on the blond like he was a joke, a laugh. But he needed to find out where Naomi Waters was. That was the important thing. I could make her tell me. Then take her. See the fear on her face, her eyes widen. She'd fight him; she was the type, but he would enjoy that. It excited him more when they fought him, gave him a bigger rush to gain control over them. He'd gag her, tie her to the bed. He smiled, picturing her in his mind. It pleased him knowing he could get into her apartment if he wanted to. There was no place he couldn't get into if he chose. He had the touch. He could do whatever he wanted to do.

His breathing rapid, his fists clenched and fire in his loins, he already envisioned himself halfway across the street. Until the saner voice spoke to him: You can't go up there. You can't touch her. Not tonight anyway.

The cops would have him if he did that. She'd been with two of her friends from the club, and they'd seen him, talked to him. One of them had danced with him. They would tell the cops about that. Tell them he asked Charlotte to dance with him and she turned him down. They'd figure out that he did exactly what he did do; sat in the parking lot and waited for her to leave, then followed her home.

He sat for a few more minutes, then let out a long breath and turned the key in the ignition. The van purred to life. He'd keep Charlotte Bradley on hold for the time being. Her time would come and be all the sweeter for the wait. But he needed satisfaction tonight. For the moment, his urges were under his control. But he was ravenous, and his hunger needed feeding. His rage demanded release.

Mac went hunting.

And he knew exactly where he would find his quarry.

Chapter Thirty-Four

It was past midnight when he drove back to the house on Elizabeth Avenue, slowed the van, but it was still in darkness. Her car still gone. From there he took off for downtown, squealing the tires only a little.

The girl was standing alone on the corners of Station and Harcourt, smoking a cigarette. She was young, eighteen, an addict who prostituted herself to support her drug habit. She was a natural blond and still had a pretty face in spite of the hard life. The work was shriveling her soul, would have gotten to her face in a few more years. Or maybe she would have got herself together, cleaned up and living a happier life. Unlikely, but possible. All things were possible if you were still breathing.

Her name was Marie Davis. She came from a broken home, had lived with a cousin and her husband when she was thirteen. One night the husband raped her, and her cousin threw her out when she told her what happened, and kept the rapist. So much for family.

Marie wore the requisite micro-mini and too-high heels to show off long, shapely legs. Her face was heavily made up, even though, according to one or two of the nicer johns, she didn't need it. When she saw the van slowing down, she dropped the cigarette she'd been smoking, and crushed it out under her shoe on the pavement, wiped the boredom from her face, and smiled. Thought how good it would be to get off her feet. These heels were killing her. And she was cold. Unfortunately, sweaters and leggings didn't do much for trade.

The van had stopped, was idling at the curb. She sauntered over to it, hoped this one would at least not be a fat disgusting slob who smelled bad. She was pleasantly relieved to see a very nice looking man smiling back at her from the driver's seat. His square, white teeth gleamed in the light from the dash.

"I could use a little company," he said. "How about you, gorgeous?" "Sure. You uh, gotta pay."

"How much?"

She hesitated. Bit her pretty lower lip. "You're not a cop, are ya?"

He laughed. "Nah. I hate cops. I do body work. Like you." He grinned obscenely.

She got the joke but didn't smile. "Fifty." She said it timidly, almost a question, like she was trying it on for size, ready to lower her price if she needed to.

"I like a girl who knows her worth." He reached over and opened the passenger door. "Hop in."

She paused only briefly as visions of Ted Bundy passed through her mind. He'd been good-looking too. "You're not a serial killer or something are you?"

He threw back his head and laughed as if it was the funniest thing he had ever heard. She laughed too, realizing how silly she had sounded.

"How do I know you're not another Aileen Wuornos?" he said, after she got in.

Her blue eyes widened. "That woman that shot all those men that picked her up in their cars? Wow, she was somethin' else, eh?"

Though Marie sort of understood how you could hate men that much, she was careful not to say so. "They made a movie about her called Monster. I got the DVD. That actress, Charlize Theron, was really good."

She moved closer to him, relaxed now in the warmth of the van, not worried, even amused that he'd thought he might be in danger from her. She toed the stilettos off her aching feet.

He pulled away from the curb. "Yeah," he said. "She was. Very good." "You don't need to worry about me, Mister."

He smiled without looking at her. "I know."

She heard the locks on the doors click. And there was the briefest moment when Marie felt the icy chill of foreboding creep inside her skin. And then, it went away.

Chapter Thirty-Five

Lisa wouldn't let Naomi leave without having breakfast first. Scrambled eggs, toast and orange juice. "I could get used to this," Naomi grinned, a forkful of fluffy scrambled egg midway to her mouth, and Lisa smiled at her.

The sun was streaming in the window, warming her face, throwing a warm path across the floor. She could stay here forever being fed and fussed over, forget all the dark stuff.

"You need to stay healthy," Lisa said, as she poured their coffee into stone mugs. "But I must say, you're looking much better this morning. Bright eyed and bushy-tailed. "

"I slept great. Thanks, Lisa."

"You're more than welcome. So is Molly. She slept great too. Didn't you, Molly?" Molly was curled up on an oval of sun on the floor, and merely blinked in contentment. "You've got a plan to catch him, don't you?"

Naomi smiled mysteriously. "I've got a plan. And you're psychic." "You're not going to tell me, are you? Please be careful, honey." "I will. I don't know how I can thank you, Lisa."

"No need. I love having you here. Molly too. And besides, it makes me feel like I'm making up a little for ... my lack back then."

"You have nothing to make up for. I know that's what you're feeling, Lisa. But it's misplaced guilt."

* * *

After leaving Lisa's, Naomi went to Home Depot and bought the hardware she would need to put her plan into action, along with a set of chimes she planned to hang just inside the back door. Then she drove straight to Edna's.

There was maybe a second or two, standing on Edna's front step, where she had rarely set foot, even as a child, when Naomi almost lost her nerve. Her finger was poised over the buzzer, hesitant. Now, ignoring that timid child within her, she pressed it firmly.

She heard her aunt's footsteps coming down the hallway and took a shallow breath. The door opened and Edna's eyes widened with surprise. "You," was all she said. Then came the tightening of her mouth, the flaring of nostrils as though detecting an unpleasant smell in the air.

She was dressed in a pearl grey suit, smelling of her L'Eau d`Issey perfume. Diamond horseshoe earrings enhanced a new flip hairdo. I really wanted her to like me. I tried. But that's all beside the point now. She suddenly realized she didn't give a damn what this woman thought of her, and the realization was freeing.

"Yes, it's me, Edna. I won't keep you long. May I come in?"

"I was just on my way out."

"I can see that." She held her ground, refusing to cringe under her cold, unbending glare. "As I said, it won't take long."

With a put-upon sigh, Edna grudgingly opened the door wider. "You've got a lot of nerve coming here after what you did."

After what I did. The door closed behind Naomi and she was standing in Edna's narrow gold and purple carpeted hallway, with the huge fern by the French doors, leading into the living room, reminding her of a hotel lobby. She made no response to the statement, but took the pendant out of her jacket pocket and held it out to this woman whose approval had once meant so much to her. "Where did you get this?"

She saw the fleeting shock in her eyes as she stared at the pendant in Naomi's hand. Then she looked up at her, defiance back, if not quite convincing. "I don't know what you're talking about? I never saw..."

"Yes, you did. I know it's yours. At least you've taken possession of it. I want to know where you got it. It's a simple question."

How did she turn out so different from her sister? Naomi wondered for the hundredth time. How could two sisters be so different?

"Now that I've taken a better look, I do seem to remember it. I found it years ago. On...on the beach. I don't know why I kept it, I never really liked it. It's of no value. You may keep the thing."

"Oh, I'm definitely keeping it, all right, and I don't need your permission. This is rightfully mine. It belonged to my birth mother."

The color left her face so that the rosy blush on her cheeks turned to splotches. "Whatever. Now I really have to ask you to leave. Or I'll have to call the police and tell them you've pushed you way in here and refuse to go."

"Go ahead, Edna. Phone the police. We'll wait for them together. Maybe they can get the truth from you."

"I've told you the truth. I found the damn thing on the beach. I forgot I even had it. There, that's it. So you can leave now." A flash of red scarlet fingernails as she ran a hand through her new hairdo. "Okay? Are you satisfied?"

She wasn't. Calmly, she said, "I don't believe you found this on any beach. Someone gave it to you, didn't they? Who was it, Edna? Who gave this to you?"

"I don't know what you're talking about."

But Edna's face said otherwise. Her entire body language said otherwise. "This pendant belonged to a girl who was raped and beaten and left on the side of the road to die. You know who she was. You read the article in the paper. You saw her school picture in which she was wearing this pendant

. She always wore it. She was wearing it the night she was abducted. It wasn't with her personal effects."

Edna's color had turned ashen. Only the blush splotches remaining. She was shaking visibly, but with anger now. "Yes, I read your damn story in the paper. We all did, everyone who lived in River's End has read it, and more. It's an embarrassment to leave my home these days. I'm sorry, but your early circumstances have nothing to do with me. I told Lili you'd bring trouble on this family, and I was right. I have told you I found that thing on the beach. How it got there, I have no idea. Now, please leave." She glanced at her watch. "I'm going to be late for my appointment. If you don't mind."

She did mind, but she knew she was not going to get any more out of her, not today, not voluntarily. Edna was lying, though. That much was clear. Surprisingly, she was not a very good liar. The panic in her eyes told on her. This pendant had meaning for her. Naomi didn't believe she wouldn't have kept it all those years if it held no significance.

The instant she got home, she phoned Charlotte at the gym and told her that her mother now knew the necklace wasn't in her jewelry box. "I didn't mention your name, but she probably figured it out that you took it. I thought you should know. I'm Sorry, Charlotte."

Charlotte muttered a mild curse over the disco music in the background. "I'll deal with it," she said, her voice edged with irritation and regret. "I've got to get back to work now, Naomi. Talk to you later."

But Naomi doubted that would happen. There would be no further courting from Charlotte's side. She didn't really blame her. Despite her problems with her mother, that was ultimately where Charlotte's loyalties would lie. Blood's thicker than water, she thought, and almost laughed at the bitter irony in the old adage. That's fine, I can live with that. But she had needed to confront Edna with the pendant, ask the question. And she had to look into her face when she did it.

She considered her options; she could take the pendant to the police. But running that scenario through her mind convinced her it would just be another dead end. They'd accept Edna's story that she found it on the beach and that would be that. Of course they would. They'd tell Naomi she was grasping at straws, to get on with her life. Yet, wouldn't it occur to them that that was awfully coincidental considering she was legally related to me? That the pendant had belonged to a victim in an abduction and had never been recovered. Would they follow it up? Take seriously the connection with Edna?

They might. But probably not. This was a cold case, hardly a priority for the police department. She could always call Sergeant Nelson and ask him to intercede, but she wasn't about to harass a man who'd just had a heart attack.

Two things Naomi knew for certain; Edna was keeping secrets, and Edna was afraid.

She suddenly thought of Frank. He knew Edna. Maybe he would have some ideas. She would ask him to go through that year book. He might have been acquainted with some of the people in Edna's life back then.

He was out when she called so she left a message with Kay. While she waited for him to call her back, she hung the chimes she'd bought above the back door. Eight feather-light butterflies in blues and yellows that would move at the slightest draft and warn her that someone had opened the back door. She was counting on it.

Having dubious mechanical skills, she spent the better part of an hour installing the bolt on her studio door, placing it well below the doorknob so that it wouldn't be immediately noticeable, and painted it toasted mahogany, the same color as the door.

She stood back and admired her work.

Chapter Thirty-Six

"You actually faced her down," Frank said, still appraising the pendant Naomi had handed him, turning it over and over gently in his fingers, obviously moved by its story. His glasses low on his nose, he looked like a professor of archeology, studying some recent find from a dig. He'd been stunned to learn all that Naomi had uncovered in her quest. That Sisip meant little bird, that Mary Rose's grandfather had made it for her. That she'd been wearing it the night of her abduction. He'd told her she missed her calling, that she should have been a detective. She didn't think so.

"You didn't know about the pendant, then, Frank?"

He looked up, hurt evident on his face. Incredulous that she would ask the question. Then something came into his eyes and the incredulity left. He conceded she had a right to suspect that more things could be hidden from her.

"No," he answered adamantly. "I swear I knew nothing about Edna having this pendant. Everything I know, you know," he said. "I've told you everything."

"Okay, Frank. I believe you."

"And you are absolutely sure this was Mary Rose's pendant?"

"Yes. Her name's on the back, like I said. The name her grandfather called her by. Sisip. Little Bird." She told him about Lisa Boyce, Cameron back then. "Lisa is positive she was wearing it that night. The pendant was supposed to protect her. I guess the evil was stronger."

He shook his head in wonder. "If you ever need a job as an investigator..."

"Thanks. I'll think I'll keep my present job."

He was back to examining the adornment that had been Mary Rose's talisman, running thumb and forefinger down the length of braided leather that held the crescent moon, and over the man-in-the-moon profile. "That couldn't have been easy, standing up to Edna," he said almost absently, merely glancing at Naomi. He held the crescent moon up to the lamplight so that the letters were more visible.

He was sitting in the armchair by the window, one leg crossed over the over, revealing a charcoal sock to match his pants. Due at a dinner for a colleague an hour from now, he'd donned a white shirt and blue tie beneath a navy blazer, and looked very dapper, much better than the last time she saw him, more relaxed and at peace with himself, apparently come to terms with his part in her mother's conspiracy, which more and more, she understood and forgave. As Eric Grant had said, she was lucky. God only knew what might have happened to her if Lillian Waters/Bradley had not adopted her. She could make a pretty good guess though. She wouldn't be here. They would have aborted her in utero. Eric was right. Two amazing women had fought to give her a life. She was indebted to them both.

"It wasn't easy, confronting her," she said. "Not at first, anyway. I'm sure someone gave her this pendant, Frank. She didn't find it on any beach." She picked up the yearbook from the coffee table. Here. This is Norman Banks' yearbook," she said. "Edna's picture's not in here, I already checked. I'm guessing she was probably a year or two behind Norman Banks in school, but I don't know that, of course."

What am I looking for?" He traded the pendant for the book, opened the front cover. "You knew Edna back then. She was living with Mom in the old house. You were there a

lot. Maybe you remember some of her friends."

"You're putting a lot of stock in my memory. That's quite a long shot."

"I don't know anyone sharper than you are. And I've been operating on long shots for a

while now."

He gave her a half-smile, nodded and turned the second page. Norman Banks' photo was near the front of the book, in keeping with the alphabetical order. A shy looking boy, he had a narrow, hopeful face, neatly combed hair, a boy who would sit on the sidelines until he met a woman who found much about him to love. But before that, he would meet someone who preyed on his vulnerabilities, and made him feel like he belonged. People reacted so differently to life's difficulties. She thought of Eric Grant who had been thrown to the wolves as a child, but he had stayed strong, believed in himself and accomplished his goals. She had a feeling he was going to write a fine novel.

Naomi sat in the chair opposite to Frank, leaving him to focus on the pages of students, while her thoughts lingered on the reporter. She imagined his smiling Viking face, with its wild beard, that she apparently managed to find attractive even if she didn't know it at the time. His clean-shaven face wasn't bad either, she thought, recalling their chance meeting at the police station during which he'd managed to really put her off. But he'd apologized for that, though he really had nothing to apologize for. She'd been overreacting, defensive.

With all she had on her mind, she hadn't had a chance to read his book yet. She would though. She was looking forward to it.

Frank was still turning pages. Despite the dinner he was due to attend, he was taking his time, giving attention to each face on the page. "No hand-written notes from school chums," he muttered. "Unusual." Then, "Was I ever this young?" He asked the question of the universe. "This filled with promise?"

"Sure. And you kept the promise. You're a very successful lawyer. And a good friend." He looked gratified at that, moved on to the next page. Scanned the rows of youthful

faces. Then another, and another. Soft whispers of turning pages in the otherwise quiet room. "And Charlotte was wearing the pendant," he said, again, more to himself than to her. But

she answered.

"Big as life, sitting in front of me at my kitchen table wearing it. She borrowed it from her mother's jewelry box, she said, where it's been for years. She said her mother never wore it. Didn't like it. Edna said as much to me."

"What the hell was Edna doing with it?" Frank said.

"'Ay, there's the rub. Like I said, I don't believe for one second that she found it on any

beach."

He turned the next page, not answering. Contemplating.

"She was frightened, Frank," Naomi continued. "I could see it on her face, hear it in her voice, though she was trying her best to hide it from me. Seeing that necklace in my hand really shook her. Do you have any idea why that would be?"

"Not a clue," he said.

Naomi realized something fundamental had changed in her; she'd always been the sort of person who took people at their word, things at face value. But she knew now things were not always as they seemed. Forgiving was one thing. Learning to trust again was another. But she would. She refused to live in the darkness.

About halfway through the yearbook, just as Naomi was beginning to think they were getting nowhere and was about to tell him to go on to his dinner, Frank turned a page, then flipped it back again, surprised recognition on his face.

"What?" Naomi said, leaning forward in the chair.

Frank tapped a tattoo on the photo and turned the book around so she could see it. She read aloud the name beneath the photo of the young man, "Marcus Leeland."

"Edna dated him at one time, years ago of course. Before you were born. He'd been out of school a couple of years then. Lili thought he was a jerk, but Edna was crazy about him. He had that kind of 'bad boy' aura some girls are drawn to. He had a reputation as a player."

"You're kidding. Edna?" But he wasn't kidding. Frank was dead serious. She examined the photo more closely. Good-looking blond boy, receding hairline even though he couldn't have been more than nineteen, macho type. Cocky grin. Marcus. Could it be? Edna dated him? Naomi had a hard time getting her mind around that, though her thoughts were travelling at super-speed, making connections that seemed impossible.

Aunt Edna? With her nose in air, always so critical, so proper. Dating someone so different from Uncle Harold. Edna had a side to her Naomi would not have suspected.

"God, Frank, are you sure this is him?"

"I wouldn't swear to it in a courtroom, but it sure as hell looks like him. The name's not quite right; I don't think Edna called him Marcus. Bud, Cal, something..." He stood up and re-buttoned his beautifully tailored jacket. "Gotta go. Don't go jumping to conclusions, okay? Even if it is the same guy, it proves only that Edna dated him at one time. Nothing else."

"Do you know anything else about him? Anything you remember?"

"Not off the top of my head. Uh, I seem to recall he was into restoring old cars. I've really gotta head out now, honey, but I'll think about it and get back to you."

"Do you happen to remember if he drove a dark car?"

"No. Sorry. I don't remember what kind of car I drove back then. Keep your doors locked, Naomi. Be careful. I don't like it that you're here alone. I'm worried about you."

"Don't be. I'm fine."

"Frank, did Mom know?" she asked, as he was starting down the front steps. He turned, frowned. "Know?"

"Did she suspect who Mary Rose's attacker was? Is that why she adopted me? Out of some misguided sense of guilt?"

"No, absolutely not. She would have turned him in if she had."

"I wonder. Edna wouldn't have been all that thrilled for people to know she'd been mad for a rapist. Ultimately a killer. And Mom really loved her little sister. And we both know Mom was good at keeping secrets. "

"C'mon, Naomi. Cut your mom some slack, okay?"

She conceded with a shrug but didn't give it voice. Edna had called her a spawn of the devil. But had Edna bedded that devil? "Are you sure that...?"

"Yes, I am sure. She didn't know. And she never saw that pendant. I swear it. Never." "If you say so."

"I do. I say so. I really do wish you'd let the police handle this, Naomi," echoing Lisa's sentiments on the subject.

"I don't have enough yet. Not to worry. It's okay. I uh, have a plan." "A plan. I don't suppose you want to enlighten me."

"I will. But not right now. Enjoy the dinner."

* * *

227

The thing that kept playing in Naomi's mind was Frank saying Marcus Leeland had an interest in old cars. In restoring them. Norman Banks once worked at a place called The Body

Shop. A place no longer in existence, but it was too big of a coincidence to think the two men didn't work there together, at least for a time. She had a name now. Marcus Leeland. But she still had no proof to take to the police.

Only a theory. Sergeant Nelson would have listened to her theory though, taken what she had into consideration. She wondered how he was doing. She would send a get well card, but had no address for him. She could always drop it in to the police station and ask them to forward it. Yes, she would do that.

That night she read in the paper about the murder of an eighteen year old prostitute named Marie Davis; it made the back page. Her battered body was found in a field in Lennix County, about twenty-five miles outside River's End. Though Mary Rose was an innocent schoolgirl, she couldn't help but make the connection. It happened on the same night she'd stayed over at Lisa's, though Naomi didn't think of that until later. She wondered how many people would have passed the item by, barely worth conversation at the breakfast table: *What the hell did those girls think would happen to them getting into cars with strangers, doing what they did?* But Naomi read the piece twice before she refolded the newspaper. A heaviness settled in her chest.

Only eighteen. She would have had family. A mother, father, people who loved her and would grieve for her. One could only hope this was so. 'There but for the grace of God', Naomi thought.

Later, she went back and read the write-up again. Wondering now if Marcus Leeland had killed her. Had he come here looking for me and frustrated, gone in search of other prey to vent his rage on? Easier prey? Was a young woman dead today because of her? Had the beast in Marcus Leeland unleashed its fury on someone else.

On the other hand, he wasn't the only predator around. Yet she couldn't shake the feeling that this was the work of none other than Edna's old boyfriend.

I want to see him, Naomi thought suddenly. I want to look at his face.

It was too late now, nearly eight o'clock, but in the morning, she'd call every body shop in town and ask to speak to a Marcus Leeland. Even if he wasn't pursuing the same line of work, someone might know him from the old days.

The sky outside her kitchen window was low and grey, threatening rain again, though the weatherman said sunny for most of tomorrow, a few cloudy patches.

Standing there, she imagined him walking across the back field, creeping up to her backdoor, and ripples of fear went through her.

She was about to leave the window when to her right a flash of red caught her eye. Wondering what it was, she unlocked the door and stepped outside, the little butterfly chimes tinkling madly behind her like excited little spirits.

It surprised her to see the gas can sitting near-hidden in some bushes a few feet from her back door. As the smell of the gas wafted up to her, the implication of its being here struck her full in the solar plexus, making her feel a cold that went straight to her marrow.

She hefted the can, heard the gentle sloshing of the potentially deadly liquid inside. Must be half full, she thought, feeling ill at the thought of what it could do. She cast a quick look around her, almost expecting someone to be standing there. But there was no one. He'd obviously intended to use this gas, which he left there in his hurry to get away when he heard the doorbell ring. That had to be it. Thank God for Frank's timing. She might not have been around right now but for that.

She considered what to do with the gasoline for a long minute. Then, hoping the gas had nothing else in it that would harm her car, but deciding to risk it, she walked around to the front

drive and poured the gas into her car's gas tank. Then she replaced the gasoline in the can with water, went around back again, and set it down where she had found it, in the bushes, by the door, but concealed a little better so that he would not think it had been discovered, and its contents tampered with.

He would come for her soon. There was no question of that. She had to be ready for him. One more thing to put in place, and it was done. But she was tired now. Mistakes get made when you're tired. She needed to rest for fifteen minutes or so. A power-nap, Mom used to call it.

She set down on the sofa and switched on the TV, keeping it low, a murmur in the background. A crime show, the plot of which eluded her. Molly jumped up on her lap, circled a few times before settling down. A comforting weight. Naomi patted her. "We're not going to be easy prey, are we, Molly? He's going to find himself in a fight, the bastard."

She didn't remember falling asleep. Only closing her eyes for a minute, having that power-nap and apparently went out like the proverbial light. Her dreams were more than vivid. Once, she thought she heard the crackle and popping of fire and smelled the acrid smoke filling the house, heard waves of heat stirring the little chimes by the door. Then stirring the hairs on her head. Sirens. Oh, God, the house was on fire. He'd done it. She woke in a panic, yet still hovering in that otherworldly zone between sleep and waking. Some other dimension that didn't want to give her up.

When she did sit up, she wasn't sure if she was still dreaming, or if her house was really on fire. But she saw no flames, and the smell of smoke was fading. And then she remembered she'd put water in the gas can. Even so, she found herself gasping for breath as her lungs tried to rid themselves of the choking dream-smoke.

Molly was no longer in her lap, and the room was dark, no light showing through the part in the living room curtains. The only light was from the TV. An old cop movie was playing. The sirens were far away now. How long had she been asleep?

Head aching, body stiff from the uncomfortable position on the couch, she made her way out to the kitchen, feeling like she'd been on a bender.

The owl clock on the wall told her it was twenty past three.

She put the coffee on and picked up the telephone book.

Chapter Thirty-Seven

Frank called around ten that morning to tell her he remembered Marcus Leeland had lived with a maiden aunt, but had no idea where she lived, or if she still lived. He expanded some on the relationship between Edna and Marcus Leeland.

"They fought a lot," he said. "Edna suspected him of cheating on her, and she was miserable, crying a lot. That was it. I know your mother was relieved when they stopped seeing each other."

"When did they, Frank? When did they stop seeing each other? Was it after Mary Rose was attacked?"

"I don't know, honey. So long ago. I'm surprised I remembered as much as I did."

She let it go, instead asked about the dinner, and he told her the chicken was rubbery, otherwise it was a good evening. Naomi heard a soft bark in the background.

"There's a pigeon on the window-sill," he said by way of explanation.

* * *

There were just five auto body shops listed in the phone book. She wrote the names down in her notebook. She'd changed her mind about phoning and decided she would visit each one and ask for him. Someone asking for him on the phone, then hanging up before he could answer might make him suspicious. Or he might answer himself, for that matter.

After writing down the addresses of the body shops, she looked up Marcus Leeland's name in the phone book. No Marcus but there was an M. Leeland listed. - 632 Watson Street. She glanced at her list of body shops and saw there was one maybe a block away: Mac's Auto Body Shop. Mac? Marcus?

Better than a good chance it was him. He owned the place. So he worked close to where he lived, down near the docks. If she remembered correctly, not that far from Fisher Wharf where Norman Banks' body was found. That he would arrange to meet his old pal so close to where he lived showed his boldness, his arrogance. His belief that he was smarter than everyone else. He'd been laughing at the police for years. And why not? He'd gotten away with murder. Three that she knew of, if indeed he did kill Marie Davis. How many more?

Marcus Leeland was a cold-blooded sociopath. Of course he'd be listed in the phone

book.

She opened the yearbook at the bookmarked page, and looked long and hard at Marcus Leeland's photo, memorized his features. There was not a doubt in her mind that this was the person who gave Mary Rose's pendant to Edna. Maybe he didn't even know it was hers, since he apparently slept with a number of women, but found it in his car sometime later and wanted to make up after some fight they'd had. It didn't really matter. Edna had to at least suspect her boyfriend's predatory nature. She would have seen the photo of Mary Rose in the paper and recognized the pendant. Maybe that's what finally woke her up and got her away from Leeland. Fear for herself. And to hell with anyone else.

So no one stopped him. I will, she thought. I will stop him.

Naomi had already found the crucial piece to her plan at the back of her closet shelf where'd she stowed it more than a year ago. Her mother had brought the gadget back from New York during some down time at a nurse's conference. Naomi had never found a use for it, until now. She read the instructions, ran a few test runs, and it worked great. A very special remote control that could allow her to operate her audio system from outside the studio. Everything was set.

First, I need to look in his face. Exorcise the bogeyman that had crept inside her psyche, and see him for the lowlife he is.

She dressed in jeans and a rust suede blazer, low heels, wore her hair loose. Free. It was important she appear undaunted, cool. Let him see she wasn't afraid of him. What if it's not him? a small voice asked. It's him, she answered.

Finding the pet center closed due to an outbreak of what was termed doggie-flu on the sign in the window, Lisa drove guiltily to Lisa's. Lisa was so sweet and obliging, taking Molly in as if she were a long lost friend, asking no questions as to why she was cat-sitting again. She didn't even question that Naomi had no time for even a cup of tea. I'm going to owe her a lot more than a dinner, she thought. "I'll tell you everything when I get back, Lisa," she said, and thanked her profusely before getting in her car and heading for the body shop on Watson.

The weather man had been right. It was a beautiful day. Blue skies, warm temperatures, a few scattered clouds, just the lightest of breezes. The perfect day to go looking for a killer. She had missed the entire spring in a way, instead travelling through the coldest and darkest of winters. At least that's how it felt.

With a little luck, it would be over soon.

Chapter Thirty-Eight

Eric Grant wasn't the one to do the write-up on the girl who was murdered, but when he read it he thought at once of Naomi Waters and what had happened to her birth mother. One woman dumped on the side of the road, the other in a field twenty-eight years separating the murders. Mary Rose Francis just took longer to die. River's End was hardly the murder capital of the world. It was a quiet town, mostly. Was it possible? Was this the same guy?

He knew, of course, that had he not met Naomi Waters and heard her story, he wouldn't have made any connection between the murders at all. Marie Davis would simply be an unfortunate victim of the high-risk life she lived. And maybe that's all it was.

He thought about calling Naomi, but was afraid she'd hang up on him. What a wimp he was. Yet, he had written, had apologized for acting like a jerk, for offending her, given her his email address and phone number, which she chose to ignore. It didn't take a rocket scientist to figure out she wasn't interested. Let it go, man.

But he couldn't get her out of his mind.

He wandered over to the office window, looked out on the front steps of the building, saw her as she'd been that day, as she was leaving the building. Standing out there on the steps in the bright sunlight that had turned her hair to black satin, looking frightened, confused as a lost child. He was sure he himself had worn the expression a time or two. And why wouldn't she be frightened? Her life, which was already ripped out from under her, had been about to be an open book for the residents of River's End to read at their leisure. And that included her mother's killer, who very possibly was still walking the streets of River's End. Maybe still preying on innocent women.

Naomi had guts. In the face of her fear, she was resolved to see this thing through to the end, no matter the consequences, and he admired that. In his own defense, he'd tried to talk her out of including her phone number and email address in the write-up. Yeah, you're all heart, Grant. Freakhead's a fitting name for you. Harold Barkley had good judgment. No, he didn't, he debated with himself. You're better than that. Just socially awkward.

Twice, he'd managed to upset her, make himself an irritation, and she cut him out like cutting out of a shirt a starchy label that rubbed your skin raw. She'd likely hang up the second she recognized his voice, and who could blame her. First he tells her how lucky she is to have Lillian Waters adopt her when it's clear she's going through a major crisis in her life. Hell, the woman had been lied to her entire life, understandable or not. And then I run into her, at the police station and instead of trying to redeem myself, I treat her like a child. Worse, a hysterical, gullible woman.

Hell, he'd hang up on himself.

And you can't blame it all on Harold Barkley. When he was a kid living at Greyland's Home for Boys, Barkley, two years his senior, never let up on him. The residue of all that, the names and taunts, the bullying, clung like vile-smelling fungi. Crazily enough, Harold later became one of his biggest fans, had stood in line at his first book signing, grinning from ear-to-ear proudly because he knew the author. He told everyone in line he inspired the title, "Freakhead", which he had. Nothing but pride. Life was nuts. Ya just never knew. To paraphrase Forrest Gump who said it far better than he ever could have, '...a box of chocolates'.

But Harold was the least of the hell of Greyland's Home for Boys, which they finally closed down two years ago, after his book came out. There were some things he would never put in a book. Anyway, who'd believe it.

Writing the book had helped a lot, diluted the power of the memories, though not entirely. Sometimes he regressed, and occasionally still had nightmares. Now that he was working on the novel, though, he found he was more at peace, doing what he was supposed to be doing with his life. What he'd always told himself he would do. Even on the darkest days, he'd held to his dream.

A new dream shimmered now, like a mirage, beckoning him. He picked up the phone to call her, then re-cradled the receiver like a teenager chickening out on asking a girl out on a date. But he refused to let her get away just because he was a scared chump. It wasn't in his DNA to do that. Besides, he was genuinely worried about her.

He knew he gave the appearance of being self-confident, but it was mostly sham. A cover. Oh, he knew he was a pretty decent writer; hadn't he won a couple of awards for his work? But sometimes that old insecurity he tried so hard to hide could come across as cockiness, betraying what was really in his heart. When you start out with sand under your feet for a foundation, things never really do feel solid under them, no matter how much time passes or how successful you get. And no one could tell him different.

He dialed her number. Got the machine, and left a message. He was still rambling when the machine cut him off. Shit!

He hung up, stared at the phone as if it had set out to conspire against him. He could send flowers, he thought, roses, but something told him his timing would be off by a mile. And also that roses weren't her favorite flower. Something smaller, more exquisite…a wildflower of some sort.

She needs help right now, not flowers. He remembered that she'd had an appointment with Sergeant Graham Nelson the day he ran into her at the police department. He could give Nelson a call, use his reporter status to fish out any fresh leads in the Mary Rose Francis' case. He didn't know him well, but they'd talked. He seemed like a decent enough guy, and had a reputation as a good cop. Grant dialed the police department. He'd check out this latest killing, too. See what information he could pick up. Maybe enough for a follow-up story. A Killer Among Us. Not that bad. If not original.

He identified himself to the officer who answered, but when he asked to speak with Sergeant Nelson he was told the Sergeant had suffered a mild heart attack and had taken an early retirement. Had he not been out of town, he would have known that.

No one else seemed to want to talk to him about any case, cold or otherwise, except to say that the investigation into the Marie

Davis case was ongoing. But he got a sense there wasn't a whole lot of activity being given to either case.

"You got a number where I can reach Sergeant Nelson?" he asked, without much hope of getting one. But surprisingly, the cop on the phone told him Nelson was recuperating at his sister's. "She's in the book," he said. "A.J. Nelson. And speaking of books, you wrote a damn good one, there, Mr. Grant. I got a cousin spent some time at Greyland's..."

Grant listened, was pleasant. But, anxious to talk to Sergeant Nelson, he cut the call short, agreeing cheerfully to drop by the station and autograph the guy's book. Good friends in the right places were necessary in his business. Besides, he appreciated his readers and couldn't afford to alienate one of them.

Chapter Thirty-Nine

Eric ascended the brick walk and rang the bell of the small, white house, with its profusion of greenery growing in white-painted window-boxes. The man who answered wore grey cords and a dark blue striped shirt, and looked like you'd expect a man to look whose body had turned on him. Physically fragile, a tad jowly with the loss of weight. But his steely-blue eyes were sharp and clear, and his color was good, and he seemed genuinely glad for the company.

The retired cop gave him an easy grin and opened the door wider. "I'm glad you called. C'mon in, Eric. My sister Angie is out doing a few errands. I practically had to arm-wrestle her to take her fingers off my pulse and get on with her life. Angie's a dietitian. What'll you have? Vegetable-ginger juice? Herbal tea...? Angie grows her own herbs and spices. You probably noticed some of them in the window boxes. Anytime you'd like a slip. I noticed a helicopter buzzing around over the house this morning, probably thinking she's growing weed." He grinned fondly.

Eric settled on instant coffee, decaffeinated.

They sat in the small, tidy living room in front of the TV, which his host had switched off, and they talked about the case. And their mutual concern for Naomi Waters. The sergeant said she was like a horse with blinders. "But I also think that girl has a good sense of direction," he added.

Eric was glad he'd phoned. The guy was going stir crazy and missed his work. He probably wouldn't have invited him to his house, and be talking so freely to him but for that.

Chapter Forty

Naomi drove slowly down Watson Street, checking the numbers on the houses. 632 was about halfway down, a few doors up from a dry cleaning shop. Most of the homes were wooden, not falling down exactly, but definitely on the way. The address was a two-story grey building with white trim, and relatively new siding. In better shape than some of its neighbors.

She parked a short distance past it, on the opposite side of the street. From here she could see the auto body shop up ahead, same side of the street. Big blue letters, spelling out Mac's Auto Body. He works close to where he lives, as she figured. He's probably there now. Her heart was pounding, and her hands on the wheel were damp. A heady brew of excitement and fear roiled inside her.

She sat in the car for several minutes trying to work up her nerve to face him. Up ahead, a half a dozen kids were playing dodge ball in the street, and she remembered that school would have let out for the summer.

Two young women, about her own age, passed her by going in the opposite direction, pushing baby carriages. They were laughing at some shared joke. Watching them walk away in her rearview mirror, she felt a pang of envy. They had family, were enjoying their lives, not chasing down killers. Worse, one who had sired them.

Never mind. All the pieces appeared to be falling into place, almost faster than she could process them. If she was wrong about this, she'd know soon enough, and no harm done. She'd just ask how much it would cost to dab up that scratch on her bumper. A legitimate reason for being there. Perfectly reasonable question.

She'd know by his face, just like she knew by Edna's face that she was lying about the pendant. Her breathing was shallow and she blew out a long shuddery breath. She wiped her hands on a tissue from her pocket. Would he smell her fear, like the animal he was? She took three more deep breaths, exhaled each slowly, then turned on the ignition. I'm fine.

She circled the block, came down Watson on the other side of the street and parked in front of the shop. She cracked open the window, could hear someone banging on metal, inside the garage. The office was adjoined. She got out of the car and went in.

An elderly man wearing a red plaid cap was sitting thumbing through a car magazine. He looked up when the door opened and nodded pleasantly. She managed a smile and a 'hi' in return. Her heart was racing so fast she thought she might pass out. She swallowed and found she had no saliva. Get it together, she commanded herself. She put on a neutral expression. After all, she was supposed to be some kind of actor. So act.

When the young man came into the office from the garage, wiping his hands on an oily rag, she told him about the scratch on her car. Then, she said quickly, before he could offer to check it out, "I-- I'd like Mac to take a look at it, if he's not too busy."

"Yeah, sure. Just a sec. I think he's just finishing up. Your car'll be a couple a minutes, Mr. Howard," he said to the elderly man with the magazine.

Over the sudden howl of what she guessed was a machine that tightens lug nuts on a wheel, though it could have been anything, he opened the door and called out his boss's name. The howl ended abruptly, then began again as he closed the door. "Just puttin' the tires back on 'er," he told the man.

Before she was ready, the man she knew as Marcus Leeland came through the same door as his employee had entered, a Tim Horton's coffee in his hand. She felt as if she'd just stepped into an elevator and dropped twenty floors.

There was a brief flicker of surprise in his eyes when he looked at her. That was all. Had she not been watching so intently, she would have missed it. He was a far better actor than she.

His smile, as he handed the man his keys, revealed square white teeth. Veneers, she thought. The receding hairline in his high school photo had disappeared beneath a thick head of dark blond hair. He was in his mid-fifties, over six feet, a good-looking man, but for the evil he exuded. The coldness in those grey eyes. Or was it just because she knew the darkness that lie behind them? Behind the smile.

The man had paid his bill and left. Marcus Leeland turned his full attention on her.

"That your car out there, Ma'am?" he asked, gesturing through the window. "The blue Cavalier?" He spoke softly, with an intimacy that made her skin crawl.

"Yes. It's just a scratch on the bumper."

He drained his coffee, crushed the cup in his hand and was about to toss it in the green trash barrel by the door, when he changed his mind and shoved it into his jacket pocket, confirming everything for her. His expression didn't change. "Just a scratch, huh."

He wasn't about to let her get hold of anything with his DNA on it.

He was enjoying himself. She'd just upped the ante on the game. A game at which he was the expert.

"Well, let's go take a look at 'er, then."

He walked too close behind her, deliberately close, so that she could feel his warm breath on the back of her neck. Smell the dark, sour heat and paint-smell of him and thought she might be sick to her stomach. Breathing through her nose, forcing herself to stay calm, she raised her head just a little higher in a show of bravado, but she knew he wasn't fooled. Only amused.

"That scratch has been there awhile," he drawled, when they were on the sidewalk, those eyes peering straight into her soul. "Year, maybe."

"I uh, my mother was sick. It happened in the hospital parking lot. I just never got around to..." She was rambling. She gave a helpless shrug, stopped talking.

"Sorry about your mother," he said. He quoted her a reasonable price and asked if she'd like them to do the work now. "Won't take more 'n half an hour."

Sorry about your mother. Not, I hope she's feeling better. He knows she didn't get better, that she died of cancer. He read it in the paper. He knows I live alone. Of course he does. He'd been to my house. Planned to burn it down, with me and Molly in it.

"No, it's okay. I really just wanted to get a couple of estimates." "Uh, huh. Sure, no problem."

She saw the trace of a smile come into those cold eyes that were the color of rotting ice. When she drove away, she saw him in her rearview mirror, still standing on the sidewalk, hands in his pockets, watching after her.

Chapter Forty-One

Naomi didn't allow herself to take a full breath until she was half a mile from the dark, frightening aura of Marcus Leeland. Glancing at herself in the rearview mirror, into eyes that looked shocked, skin pale as ash. Her gaze flicked nervously past her own reflection to check behind her, only too aware that he might have followed her from the body shop. But there was no one behind her.

He knows I know who he is, now. He knows I'm onto him. I've entered his game.

He'll make his move now. Soon. Tonight? She breathed deeply, let it out. It did little to calm her nerves, which didn't begin to settle down until she pulled into Lisa's drive. Barely in the door, she blurted, "I've seen him, Lisa. I've seen the man who murdered Mary Rose."

"Naomi, honey, you're shaking and you're white as a sheet. Sit down, sit down, let me pour you a nice hot cup of tea."

Molly looked at her, then went back to the saucer of whatever Lisa had given her, apparently not missing her all that much.

Once Lisa was seated across from her, Naomi told her what happened, only keeping the name to herself. It was best if Lisa never heard it; never had that name rattling around in her brain. Even coming here she worried that she might be putting her in danger, although she knew he hadn't followed her. She was very careful about that. She must be diligent every second. She was reasonably sure he had followed her out to Debbie Banks' house without her knowledge, but it wouldn't happen again.

"Naomi, how can you...?"

"I had only to look into his eyes to know it was him."

"You say he's a garage mechanic?"

"Auto body work. Over on the west side."

"What makes you so sure it's him?"

Naomi explained about the photo in the school yearbook, about Edna having dated him. "There's not a question in my mind it's him." She took a sip of tea, set the cup back down on the saucer, careful to hold it steady. "God, I always knew Edna hated me, ever since I was a little kid I knew, I just could never figure out why."

"That's not hard. You're a reminder of what her old boyfriend did to a young girl," Lisa offered. "She showed some pretty lousy judgment back then."

"That's part of it. But I think it's more complicated than that. I took her place with mom, at least that's how she saw it. I think she also resented Mary Rose, as crazy as that sounds. I doubt she even knows it, and if she did she'd never admit it."

"Resented her! Why on earth...?"

"Because Marcus wanted her. Because Edna wasn't enough for him. I think my Uncle Harold has been paying the price of Edna's rage for years. And so have I."

"If that's true, Naomi, then she's a very sick woman." "Yeah. I know. Maybe I'm wrong. I hope I'm wrong." "Have you been to the police?"

"No. I'd be wasting my time. But like I said, Lisa, I have a plan." Impulsively, wanting to share with someone she could trust, she laid it out for her. The look of horror on Lisa's face told her she'd made a serious error.

"Clever. In theory, Naomi. But to lure this man into your home, using yourself as bait, is pure insanity." Lisa was almost hyperventilating.

I shouldn't have told her, Naomi thought. It was wrong to worry her. But no taking it back now.

"Calm down, Lisa," she said gently. "It'll work, Lisa. I know it will."

"Honey, you don't know any such thing. You only hope it will work. It's a crazy idea. Call the police, Naomi. You have enough now. The police will pick him up."

"They won't. I don't have any proof. I have only the pendant which Edna insists she found on a beach, and I can't prove anything different. It's all circumstantial."

After a hesitation, Lisa said with an air of desperation, "You can try to get a sample of his

DNA."

"I thought of that, but he's very smart. He was drinking a coffee when I walked in and had been about to toss the empty cup in garbage, but then he thought better of it and crumpled the cup in his hand and shoved it in his pocket. Looked straight at me when he did it. Almost smirked."

Lisa's color drained, and her hand went to her mouth. "Oh, Lord, Naomi, it really is him, isn't it? You've tracked him down. I can't believe it. After all these years. You've found him."

"Yes. I found him. You didn't believe me?"

Naomi took another sip of her tea, felt a calm spread through her. It would be over soon. He would pay for what he did.

"It just seems ... so incredible. All these years. You must know I can't let you go back to that house alone now, don't you? I can't let you sit around waiting for a killer to show up. I feel guilty enough about Mary Rose, this would kill me."

She felt her plan suddenly threatened. "I shouldn't have told you."

"But you did. Thank God. If you don't call the police right now, and tell them everything you know, I will."

"Lisa, please don't say that. I know you mean well, but..."

"No, what you plan isn't going to happen. Unless you have the police watching your house, ready to grab him if he shows, you can forget it, honey. That's the deal."

"I can't make that deal. He'll know he's being watched. He's clever. He'll sniff them out like the dog he is. Mary Rose has led me to him, Lisa. She means me to bring him down. She's been with me every step of the way."

With more argument back and forth that lasted a good half hour, Naomi finally got Lisa's promise not to call the police. Though it wasn't easy and she didn't give it happily.

The truth be known, Naomi half agreed with her. She felt

anything but brave. Leeland had left his vile imprint on her and she couldn't wait to take a shower, not that there was any chance of washing it off. She felt clammy inside her clothes.

She didn't dare let herself think too long about what she had set in motion. It was like being on a runaway train; you could only hang on and hope to survive the crash. Or you got to jump off before it sailed over a cliff, the way it worked in those old serials she saw at the movies when she was a kid.

But she wasn't ready to jump just yet. She still had a little time. She needed all her wits about her. Lisa made more tea. They talked. She told Lisa she also suspected Marcus of killing Norman Banks because he was a threat. "I think he killed Marie Davis, too, and maybe others."

"Marie Davis was a prostitute. Mary Rose was a schoolgirl."

"I know. But she was vulnerable, Lisa. And that's what connects her to Mary Rose." "Mary Rose was a child," she argued. "She knew nothing of men."

"That's true, of course. But we don't know about this girl's life; we don't know what might

have taken her on that path."

"I guess you're right." Lisa sat silent for awhile. She looked miserable and afraid.

Hating that she was making Lisa so unhappy, wanting to cheer her up," she said, "Did I tell you I found the perfect frame for Mary Rose's poem. I hung it in my room."

"Good," Lisa said, standing up suddenly as though she

couldn't bear to sit there any longer. Couldn't bear to think. "You should eat. What can I make...?"

"Nothing. I couldn't eat." "Well, I don't wonder."

It would be over soon. No more looking over her shoulder. She didn't want to feel afraid anymore. She wanted him out of her life, out of everyone's life. She wanted him behind bars. And she meant to make it happen.

She stayed until after eight, then Lisa walked her out to the car. When they got there, Lisa handed her a cell phone. "One of the kids left this behind. It's all charged up. In case you hear something well, you could be in the bathroom, or anywhere. You can call 911. I'm in there too." She gave her a quick tutorial. Naomi thanked her and dropped the slim silver phone into her purse.

It was near dusk, the air warm and soft and fragrant, and beneath it the ever-present but faint briny, metallic smell of the bay. The cobalt sky was strewn with stars and a pale moon floated among them.

Similar to the night Mary Rose was left on the side of a road to die. Hard to believe something so awful could happen on such a night as this one. But it could. It had.

Lisa deposited Molly's carrier on the back seat, then turned and put her arms around

Naomi.

"Are you sure you won't change your mind? Spend the night? Deal with this tomorrow. Or next week."

"I'll take a rain check. Okay?" She gave herself over to the soft comfort of Lisa's embrace before moving away and getting into the driver's seat. Forcing a smile, she said, "I'm grateful for your friendship, Lisa. Just keep a good thought. I'll be okay. Thanks for the phone."

Driving out of the yard, gravel crunching under her tires, she could see Lisa in her rear-view mirror, watching her. She looked to be ringing her hands. I would be too if they weren't on the wheel, she thought.

* * *

Lisa stood in the yard watching Naomi drive away, everything in her screaming at her to run out into the street and call her back, beg her not to go. But she didn't, knowing it would do no good. She could only hug herself and pray that Naomi would be safe. As she watched the car drive away, the glowing red taillights growing smaller and fainter as it moved through the darkness, and finally disappeared as the car turned left onto the main road. God be with you, Naomi.

It was Mary Rose leaving her yard all over again, except she'd been on foot. Lisa envisioned the pendant, the crescent moon as it lay in her hand, felt its warm smoothness. She remembered how pretty and exotic it had looked against Mary Rose's flawless, light coppery skin. She remembered exactly how it looked. Like it was yesterday. They had painted each other's nails. I painted hers with a clear polish because she didn't like the pinky-red I chose for mine. I dabbed a little of my mother's Eau de Cologne on our inner wrists, where you take your

pulse. All those smells are mixed together in my memory.

It seemed to Lisa that Naomi was right, that Mary Rose had set this course, had willed it into being, perhaps even as she lay dying. Or maybe only after she passed on could her spirit then have the power to reach out to this child of her loins. If that was so, then surely she would protect that child, who has grown into a lovely and passionate young woman intent on avenging her death. Or am I being too fanciful. Too optimistic.

What she knew for sure was that on another June night such as this, Lisa had stood on other steps, calling 'See you tomorrow' to her school friend, who had turned and waved, then walked on into the night as the strains of Donny Osmond's Puppy Love drifted out to her through the screen door.

She hadn't been in the least afraid for her friend, had had no premonition whatever of the evil that would befall her within that hour. I fully expected to see her in school the next day, just as I was sure we would be friends forever.

Mary Rose said she was going to be a writer and publish short stories and poems about her people one day. Lisa had no doubt whatever that she would. All things seemed possible back then. But not what happened. No, not what happened.

Feeling that same sense of helplessness she'd felt looking down on Mary Rose's still pale form in the hospital bed, Lisa went back inside, a knot of dread in her stomach and a prayer for Naomi's safety on her lips.

Behind her, the screen door banged shut, a different door than the one from so long ago, but it held a warning now.

To hell with this bull crap, she thought suddenly. I have to do something. I have to call somebody. I promised her I wouldn't call the police, and I'd be betraying her if I did, but I didn't say I wouldn't call anyone. She searched her brain and the only person she could think of who might be helpful was Eric Grant, the writer. She had written him a note of congratulations when his book came out and he'd taken the time to write her a gracious note in return, thanking her for her support. She was sure he'd included his email address.

She found it in the chocolate box where she had also kept Mary Rose's poem for all those years. Yes, his email address was there. He was the one who wrote up Naomi's story for the paper. So didn't he bear a certain responsibility for its outcome? Her logic didn't sit easy, but she could think of nothing else to do. She plugged in the new laptop and brought up her Outlook Express. She had emailing down pretty good now, thanks to the course at the library. She'd phone if she had a home number, but she didn't, and the newspaper offices would be closed by now anyway.

She typed up her note typing URGENT- NAOMI WATERS in the subject so he wouldn't, not recognizing her name, automatically delete it. She clicked on send.

Chapter Forty-Two

There was little traffic on the drive home. The streets were strangely silent, almost eerie, like dark streets in a scary movie. Of course that was her over-active imagination. The streets were no different than on any other night. At least that's what she told herself. But despite her resolve to outwit Marcus Leeland, she couldn't quite shake the feeling that she was driving to her doom. A coldness had nested in the hollow of her stomach.

She was half a block from her house when she noticed a dark car parked on the opposite side of her street, causing her heart to speed up. She'd passed it too quickly to make out if there was anyone in the driver's seat.

And then she was turning up her long driveway.

The night-light lit up the front lawn, throwing far reaches into deep shadow. She parked and turned the engine off, and sat in the silence with the doors locked for a good minute, listening to the faint ticking noises of the car cooling off. Even with the night-light, the house seemed darker and more isolated.

Had that been him in the parked car? A shiver moved through her. Was he watching the house? Waiting for me to come home? Then again, it could just be a neighbor's car. It could be anyone's.

Is he in the house now, waiting? She'd wedged the chair

beneath the back door knob, but that wouldn't stop him. He'd find another way in.

Had she, like Mary Rose, stayed too long at Lisa's?

Molly gave a soft meow from the back seat and Naomi let out the long breath she'd been holding as she fished with thick clumsy fingers through the keys on her key ring for the one to the front door.

"Okay, Molly," she said in a bare whisper. "Let's get on with it."

She unlocked the car door and got out. Despite the warm temperature, the fist of cold in her stomach spread throughout her body. A light wind had come up and she could hear the soft rustle of leaves, saw their shadows moving over the driveway. She drew her jacket more tightly about her, suddenly wishing she was still back at Lisa's, sitting in her cozy kitchen, sipping tea, safe, talking about matters of the heart. Or anything else that didn't include Marcus Leeland.

The yard was full of shadows, deep thick pools that could hide a person. Not turning her back on them, she retrieved the heavy flashlight from the glove compartment and put it in her purse, prepared to swing it at his head if need be. Then she reached into the back seat and lifted out the carrier. Her keys were in the same hand. She hadn't taken into account how awkward it would be toting both the now-heavy purse and the carrier.

The door closed with a clunk that seemed amplified in the night air.

Molly had gone suddenly quiet and Naomi could feel her watchfulness, her fear of drawing attention to them from whatever danger was out there, waiting.

It's you who's freaking her out, she told herself. Clearly, Molly was picking up on her fear. She tried to make her body relax, but it was not possible.

She hurried up the short path, glancing around her as she did, half-expecting him to jump out at her. Nothing happened. She walked up the three stone steps to her front door, then set the carrier down on the landing just long enough to unlock the door. Grabbing it up again, she slipped inside the house.

She hesitated in the hallway just long enough to listen, to feel, to smell to become attuned to the very air before locking the door behind her. She was pretty certain the house was empty.

She believed she would have sensed him in here, otherwise.

Locking the door, she leaned her back against it, closed her eyes. Her clothes felt sweaty against her skin and her heart was knocking against her chest wall as if it wanted to get out.

She let Molly out of the carrier and watched her warily make her way out to the kitchen. She followed. The chair was still in place under the doorknob. Then she made herself a cup of herbal tea to calm her nerves.

Tea in hand, she sat down on the living room sofa and checked the batteries in the remote, even though they were new. She'd put them in herself. She pointed it at the office door and clicked play. At once, she heard herself reading inside the studio, a muffled sound as it would be if she were in there in person, with the doors closed. A remote that went through walls. She could operate her gear from anywhere in the house. Once, no one would have imagined such a thing, but technology just kept advancing and today this wasn't all that big a deal.

'It seemed like a fun little gadget', her mother had told her when she gave it to her, never imagining what she would end up using it for. No more than Naomi herself had.

Everything appeared to be working as it was supposed to.

But would he buy it? Wouldn't he be expecting her to try something after today? Not this, though. Not this. No, don't start second-guessing yourself. It will work.

She thumbed the off button, sat the remote beside her on the sofa. Everything was ready. Sitting in the silence, she sipped her tea and soon grew calm. She could do this. It will work, she told herself again.

But what if he doesn't come tonight? Or tomorrow night? How long could she wait before she started to lose it? She didn't know. He'll come when you're least expecting it, she thought. So you want to make it easy for him. She went out to the kitchen and removed the chair from under the doorknob.

She pictured the gas can outside the door, and knew if he had his way, she would not die easy. She had looked into his face today and saw evil there. He would not take well to her baiting him. As she sat there in front of the blank TV screen, she found herself jumping at every sound, real and imagined, threatening her newfound calm.

She needed a distraction, and it couldn't be the TV.

She left the sofa and got her copy of Eric Grant's memoir, "Freakhead", out of the bookcase, turned the lamp low, and opened the book to the first page. Before beginning the first chapter, she turned to his photo on the back cover. He was standing in a doorway, hair blowing in a breeze, grinning at the camera. Clean-shaven, casual in faded jeans and a checked shirt. Not quite handsome, but something very sexy about him. Very sweet. The smile. The way he stood there in the doorway, looking vulnerable, and at the same time just a tad arrogant. She turned back to the first page, and read: 'I spent much of my childhood trying not to make anyone mad at me'.

She was on the third page when she heard the creak of the back door opening, and the faint ring of chimes, suddenly stifled by what she knew was a hand closing around them.

Every instinct screamed at her to race for the front door and run like hell as far away from this house and from him and she could get. But you can only be terrified for so long. Your mind craves release, as Naomi's did now. It was fight or flight, and Naomi chose fight. Like an actor on stage suddenly remembering her lines, in almost a single motion, she grabbed the remote, pointed it at the studio door, hit the red play button at the top, and darted behind the sofa.

She had memorized the position of the play button in the dark, but with the room cast in dim lamplight, she had no problem seeing everything clearly. Please, please, work.

* * *

Lisa e-mailed her children, surfed the net, and in between kept checking her mailbox for a reply from Eric Grant. Overcome with worry over Naomi's safety, imagination running away with her, she dialed the cell phone number. But the phone just rang and rang.

* * *

Crouched down low behind the sofa, her heart drummed so hard in her ears she was sure he must hear it, even over the sound of her own voice issuing from the studio. Her own ears were trained on his footsteps, slow and measured, crossing the kitchen floor. She heard the floor squeak where it always did when you stepped on that particular spot by the table. The voice behind the studio door drew him closer.

She was startled at the suddenly ringing of a phone in the kitchen, a different ring from her house phone and she realized it was the cell phone Lisa gave her. The footsteps went silent. The phone kept ringing, a muffled sound.

Naomi did not move. She did not breathe. The phone was in her purse on the kitchen table. She'd forgotten it. A good thing, considering. It finally stopped ringing and seconds later the house phone rang. It rang four times and stopped.

The footsteps resumed in the ensuing silence, became muted as he stepped onto the living room carpet. She stilled the need to exhale the breath that rushed up from her lungs, let it out slowly, silently through her nostrils. Only when she was reasonably certain his attention would be on the studio door, did she dare a peek around the corner of the sofa.

Good. His back was to her. He was staring at the studio door, head tilted to one side, listening, as she'd prayed he would be.

He wore a long, black trench coat, dark clothes to evade watchful eyes, to meld in with the night. But she could see him clearly in the lamplight. He filled the room with his presence, this man who had raped and beaten a school girl and left her to die by the side of the road. Marcus Leeland. Standing not four feet away from her. She could smell him; the faint hint of turpentine, cigarettes and something raw and terrifying that defied naming.

He was the boy whose photo she'd looked at in the yearbook. He had grown into this twisted version of a man. Or maybe the beast was already in him, waiting to surface.

The darkness of his soul showed in his face; she'd seen it as she stood next to him in the auto body shop today. But maybe she only saw it because she knew about the monster that lived behind the mask. Others would see him differently, perceive him differently. But then there were those who saw him as she did, who knew first-hand what he was and had chosen not to come forward for their own reasons. As Norman Banks had not come forward. And when he did, he had died for his brief show of courage.

Now, as she watched him reach into his coat pocket and bring out a length of cord, wind either end once around each of his black-gloved hands, her reflections fled. Between his hands, the cord was taut. She saw the tension in his neck muscles. He was standing very still, intent on the rise and fall of her voice behind the closed door. Hunkered down behind the sofa, she continued to watch him, her heart thudding against her chest wall.

Like staring into an abyss. She had read somewhere that when you looked into the abyss, the abyss also looked into you.

As if she had spoken her thoughts aloud, he turned suddenly, and Naomi withdrew her head like a turtle drawing back into its shell, ducking down, trying to make herself one with the floor, blood roaring in her ears, breath trapped in her throat. Had he seen her?

She closed her hand over the handle of the butcher's knife she'd placed here earlier. Plan 'B' so to speak.

Chapter Forty-Three

For the past three hours, Eldon Carpenter had sat in his car dutifully watching Naomi Waters' house, a favor to his good friend, Frank Llewellyn. Elizabeth Avenue was dark, lit dimly by sparsely placed streetlights, and a few lights from rooms in houses set back off the road. There was lots of grass and trees; it was a nice street named for the Queen of England. Not as grand as it used to be though, according to his dad when he was alive.

Now and then one more light would blink out in one of the houses, as whoever lived there packed it in for the night. Earlier the sky was bright with stars, but it had clouded over, the stars winking out like the lights in the houses along the street. A dreary night, quiet -- quieter than Eldon liked. It was the best part of his job as a bouncer: noise, music, people. Like a big family. Occasionally, one of the family went awry, and Eldon took care of it. He rarely had to get rough to make himself understood.

Surveillance was not something Eldon particularly enjoyed, but he had promised Frank, and it wouldn't have occurred to him to say no. In fact, he was grateful for a chance to do whatever he could to repay Frank for all he had done for him. But for Frank, I'd be rotting in jail right now, he told himself, so never mind if his eyes were burning for hunting out shadows darker than the night, and that his back hurt from sitting, (no one knew about his chronic back problems, bad for his image) he was glad to do it. But he hadn't seen anyone hanging around, just the lady herself pulling into the drive a while ago. If he needed to be more accurate, under an hour, give or take.

As Eldon readjusted his position behind the wheel to ease the ache and stiffness in his lower back, he started at a knock on the window. Jerking his head around, he blinked into a bright beam of light. Then the light moved and he saw the cop behind it, looking in at him. He took the glare off his face and trained it over the interior of the car, right hand close to his revolver, but not on it. Eldon pressed the window button and the window slid open. The hand was on the gun now.

"Yes, officer?"

The cop was young, almost baby-faced, but he had wary eyes. Eldon sensed he'd be real quick with that gun. A hot dog. Or maybe he was just nervous. Eldon sometimes forgot how intimidating his size and hit-man look could be.

"Can I see your license and registration, please?"

Eldon produced them. "Any problem, sir?" he asked in his most obliging tone of voice. The cop wasn't charmed. "We got a call from a neighbor that you've been parked down

here for the last couple of hours. Someone suspicious, they said. Big guy! Scary. You scary, big fella?" He aimed the light down on the registration.

"No, sir." Eldon swallowed. He felt a trickle of sweat run down his side. "So what you are doing here? You waitin' for someone?

"No, sir. Just keeping an eye on a house for a friend. His niece lives there and he's worried about her. Says someone's stalking her."

"That wouldn't be you, huh."

"Me? Oh, no sir. Just helpin' out a friend." He wanted to give Frank's name, but Frank told him this had to be kept quiet, so he couldn't tell the cop who his friend was.

"You a private dick?"

"No. Just like I said, a friend." The brass buttons on the dark uniform gleamed in at him like bared teeth.

"You just sit tight..." He shone the beam of the flashlight on the registration again...

Eldon. I'll be right back."

Eldon knew he was going to check out the car, see if it was stolen. Just being questioned by a cop was enough to make his mouth dry, make him sweat, even though he hadn't done anything illegal, or even thought of it. The cop returned a minute later, handed him back his registration and license. The tension had gone out of him, but his expression didn't change. "You're scarier than you let on, Eldon. I hear you killed a guy in a bar brawl some years back."

"Self-defense, sir. I got off."

"Yeah. So I heard. Well, you move along now. Can't park here, makes people nervous." Eldon didn't argue.

* * *

Any other time, Eric Grant would have been at his computer, hooked up to the internet, and clicked on Lisa's email right away. But tonight, his regular workday over, he was working on his novel-in-progress, sitting up in the bed, fully dressed, typing on his notepad, which was not much bigger than a good sized book, and which he used solely for his novel. In the background, B.B. King played killing blues on his Gibson Guitar, Lucille. Sharing his talent. Living out his dream.

Writing novels had been Eric's dream since he was a kid. But bills had to be paid, and novels didn't necessarily get published, and if they did, didn't earn enough to pay the rent. He liked being a reporter, and he thought he was pretty good at it, but it wasn't his passion.

His articles on the middle-east were brought out in book form, and had garnered some attention. Made it possible to get the memoir published, and now that that was out of his system, he was back to reporter-at-large, Joe Harron, his alter-ego. He had a track record now. That should mean something. At least get the novel a serious read.

He knew the business of reporting like John Grisham knew law. And Tess Gerritsen knew medicine. There was no doubt in his mind it was his ability to escape into imaginary worlds, his own and those of others, whose books he devoured, that helped him survive those years in Greyland's.

Later, he would curse himself for missing Lisa Boyce's email, but the laptop was in his den, turned off.

He would wonder later why he hadn't sensed that Naomi's life was in immediate danger, considering how often he thought of her in the run of a day. Unless you wanted to count the fact that his mind couldn't focus on Joe's exploits tonight. Reporter Joe Harron wasn't talking to him. He clicked on save and exited the program, closed the cover. He'd take a walk and come back to it.

Chapter Forty-Four

Naomi's cheek was pressed against the fringed edge of rug behind the sofa, so that she could feel its every knot and weave digging into her flesh. Even through the olive-green fabric and construction material of the sofa, she could feel the full force of those cold, merciless eyes on her.

Eyes Mary Rose had looked into at much closer range, his face being the last one on earth that she saw. The thought sent a surge of fury through her, refocusing her mind to the task at hand. He had not seen her. Thank God. She remained still and hidden. What was he doing?

Please, Lord, be with me. Just a few more minutes?

The sofa stood on six inches of Queen Anne curved legs, enough space to allow her to see his feet, and know when they moved. She'd always liked these sofa-legs because she could get underneath with the vacuum cleaner. There were clearly better reasons she would not have thought of before tonight. He can't see you through the sofa, she told herself. But she still waited to be proven wrong. Her panic was crediting him with supernatural powers he didn't have. Yet he seemed invincible, something you couldn't stop, a supernatural entity.

A soft voice spoke inside her mind. *He's not, 'Ntus. He's not.*

The voice calmed her. Her own voice continued to read from

behind the studio door. From the vantage point behind the sofa, she could see a good wedge of the lower part of

the living room oak-stained baseboard, soft-green leaf-patterned wallpaper. The legs of the telephone table, all cast in faint lamp light. She could see his feet, see that he was wearing dark gym shoes. They were pointing away from her, toward the studio.

In some small compartment of her brain, a silly, baseless thought had lodged that because she was his biological child, he wouldn't, in the final moment, be able to bring himself to hurt her. Or maybe it had just been a subconscious hope she wasn't even aware of. Whatever, she was wrong. Dead wrong. One end of the cord he held was briefly revealed to her, then drawn up into his hands. She could feel his anticipation of the moment when he would tighten the cord around her neck until he choked the life from her. She envisioned her dead self, eyes bulging, tongue protruding as she lay dead on the floor of her tiny recording studio.

Not if I can help it.

She heard the knob on the studio door turn, the door open. Though she knew he had entered the computer room, his stealth was such that she did not hear his footfall.

Her terror was replaced by steely resolve. She grew quiet within herself.

Not yet. Not yet. Wait. Alert as a greyhound awaiting the gunshot, every nerve and muscle in her body taut as a guy-wire. As soon as that inner door opens and he sees I'm not in there, that it's a recording he's listening to...

She crept out from behind the sofa, staying well down, trying not to breathe, ready to spring forward. She could see him now, see the black-gloved hand turning the knob on the inner door, saw the door open a mere crack. NOW!

The symbolic gunshot fired, and before the door could open further and expose her ruse, Naomi dove for the office door, shut it and slammed the bolt home, locking him in, striking her elbow on the door frame in the process, but barely feeling the pain.

With the soundproof door open, her voice, reading from one of the books she'd narrated, had lost its muffled quality and now its clarity competed with her harsh breathing, the blood thundering in her ears as she stood in almost disbelief that her plan had actually worked.

But for her voice, there was no other sound coming from inside the studio. She picked up

the remote and pressed the off button. She stopped telling her story. Like placing a period at the end of a sentence.

The silence complete, Naomi got slowly to her feet. He knows I've tricked him and he's trying to figure out how that happened. What to do. She could hear him breathing in there, or maybe it was herself she was hearing. Why was she standing here? Galvanized to action, she rushed to the phone and dialed 911.

In the same instant she heard a loud thud against the door that made her jump inside her skin. In a fury, he had thrown himself bodily at the door. She said a silent prayer of thanks when the old oak door held solid and tried not to let her knees give way.

She was on the phone with the 911 operator when she was interrupted by an explosion of glass. She stopped in mid-sentence and turned in the direction of the explosion. Realizing what had happened, her stomach sank. Oh, hell.

The nasal-sounding woman on the phone assured her that a car was on the way. Sounding puzzled, she said, "You say you've got him locked in a room?"

"Not anymore," she replied. "I'm pretty sure he just jumped out the window." If someone had told her anyone could have gone through those heavy wood shutters, she would not have believed them.

Naomi hurried to the living room window, stretching the telephone cord to its full length and moved the curtain aside; for a brief instant she

saw him in silhouette, crouching like an animal, dark against a lighter sky, a thing that had, in her imagination, the ability to change into either man or beast.

And then he disappeared from view.

* * *

The distance from the window to the ground was a good ten feet and Marcus Leeland landed with a hard jolt to his entire body. Pain exploded in his ankle like a flash fire. He hesitated a moment, then scurried crab-like around the side of the building and on behind the house, back the way he had come. His ankle throbbed, and he was bleeding from numerous cuts on his hands and face. Shards of glass and splinters had embedded themselves in his flesh. The one just under his left eye stung like hell, but there was no time now to stop and pull it out. Scrambling through the overgrown field, stumbling over bush and rocks and other debris, he made for his van which was parked in a well of dark shadow at the end of the street.

He cursed her as he ran, his breath labored and raspy. The field seemed to stretch a mile before him. The dark coat he wore slowed him down more, like he was dragging it through deep water. But he knew there was stuff in his pockets, receipts, maybe with his name, so he couldn't slough the coat off like so much snake skin, he thought, totally missing the irony of his own simile.

He covered only half the field, and sounded like a horse with heaves. His lungs were on fire. He could hear the distant wail of police sirens, and picked up speed, mindless of the stitch in his side. This goddamn running was not like weight-training. He was in no shape for running. She'll pay for this, he told himself as the sirens grew louder. She'll just be so damn sorry she thought she could outsmart Mac Leeland.

But she did outsmart him, dammit. She did. And knowing this enraged him all the more. The sirens were silent now. The cops were at her house. She would give them his name. But it was only her word against his. Mistaken identity. He continued to run, gasping, panting,

groaning with the stabbing pain in his ankle, as his thoughts chased themselves like rats on a treadmill. With everything that was hurting, it was the sliver of glass under his eye that made his stop long enough to draw it out. Blood flowed down his cheek; he wiped at it with the back of his hand. His heart pounded with exertion.

At the sight of a black and white slowly cruising by, his anger turned to icy fear and he shrank against the side of a building. They drove on past, their lights missing him. His heart pulsed in his throat.

They would be circling the block, cruising every street he might have taken in his getaway.

Suddenly hearing footsteps running across the field toward him, he took off. He thought about the whore he had killed. He'd made sure he didn't leave any DNA behind, he wasn't a fool.

No. She wasn't his problem. The half-breed was his fucking problem.

Chapter Forty-Five

The siren was cut off mid-wail amidst the squeal of brakes. Within minutes two more cruisers pulled up behind the first one, all parked at odd angles out on the street, policeman pouring out with guns drawn like cops in a TV crime show. Naomi ran down to meet them, fully aware now of the throbbing of her elbow where she'd knocked it against the door frame.

"He jumped out the studio window." She gestured to the smashed window, the shutters that hung broken and splintered against the house. A tall, mustached policeman aimed his flashlight where she was pointing. "I saw him go around the back," she said, "I'm almost sure he took off across the back field."

Second later, flashlights in hand, half a dozen cops took off in pursuit. "We'll get him, Ma'am," the mustached policeman said. "You go on back inside now and lock your doors. Detective Henderson will stay with you." With that, he took off in a run after the others.

A stocky red-head with a sympathetic smile came forward and shook her hand. "Hi, Naomi. I'm Karen Henderson. We talked on the phone. 911 gave us a brief rundown on how he happened to be locked in your room, but she was a little rattled in her explanation, to put it mildly. You can fill me in a little more inside."

"What happened, Miss Waters?" an elderly voice called out from at the back of a gathering crowd. "Are you all right?

Naomi turned, and spotted the petite woman wearing a coat over her robe. A neighbor who knew her name. She looked vaguely familiar. "I'm fine, thanks," Naomi said. "An intruder. He broke into my house."

"Don't worry, Miss Waters," a man called to her. "The cops'll get 'em." Mr. Burgess, she remembered. A retired bookkeeper.

Good caring people. The concern she heard in their voices made her feel cared for. Not everyone was here out of morbid curiosity. She'd lived here all her life, and only now did it occur to her that she knew very few of her neighbors. A few names came to mind, but she knew little about them. Mom knew them all. They'd sent food and flowers and come to her funeral. Most, if not all, had read Naomi's story in the paper.

Detective Henderson was putting on a pot of coffee. She seemed comfortable in the kitchen, even one not her own. Naomi went to the window and opened it a crack, watched the circles of light darting across the field like giant fireflies, away from her. It was too dark to see what was happening, but she could hear the excited shouts of men as they closed in on their quarry. And she heard when they took him down. The shouts grew louder, threatening. Then quieted.

"Standing in an open window isn't the best idea in the world," Detective Henderson said behind her. The coffee had started to perk, filling the kitchen with its normal, comforting aroma. "But it sounds like they've got their man, so you're probably safe."

Breathing a sigh of relief, Naomi closed the window. Tears

spilled down her face. They had him. Thank you. Her purse was still sitting on the kitchen table, with Lisa's phone inside. She stuffed the purse in a cabinet, behind a box of bran flakes, for something to do. She was shaking, trying not to.

Both women went into the living room to await the detective's knock on the door. While they waited, Detective Henderson told her that a police cruiser had been a block away when she made the 911 call, which was why they were so quick getting here.

Even from here, Naomi could still hear the excited murmur of the crowd outside.

Looking out the front window, she glimpsed the cuffed man being put into the back of the cruiser. Marcus Leeland was a big man and looked even bigger from here. He must have discarded the trench coat.

The dome lights pulsed rhythmically, splashing the crowd and the street in bloody color before it pulled away.

Even though she'd been expecting the knock at the door, she jumped when she heard it. "Police. Detective Mott." Calm now, no urgency in his voice.

Officer Henderson opened the door to him. His face was flushed with the recent excitement. "You're safe now, Miss Waters, the detective said, "He won't be bothering you or anyone else for awhile."

Relieved beyond measure, she thanked the officers profusely. She was still thanking them when a wave of weakness swept over her, turning her legs to water. "I'm sorry," she said, sagging into a chair by the fireplace. "I'm feeling a little dizzy."

"Here, this'll help," Detective Henderson said seconds later, handing her a steaming mug of coffee. "You've had quite an ordeal."

She gave one to Detective Mott, and sipped her own as the two began to ask more questions. Detective Glen Mott took notes.

Naomi explained her plan to them, showed them how it had worked. They went into the studio, looked at the broken window, Detective Henderson grinning. "Like a rat in a trap," she laughed.

The two women returned to the living room, leaving the lead detective still checking things out.

"Damn dangerous, what you did, Naomi, but ballsy, I gotta admit, "Detective Henderson said. "Very cool." She laughed.

From the studio, Glen Mott called out that she was lucky; she should have let the police handle it.

"I tried," she called back. "No one would take me seriously." That wasn't entirely true. Sergeant Nelson had believed her.

The redhead nodded. "You want to phone someone to come and stay with you tonight?" "No, I'll be fine now."

Detective Mott called out, "You'll need to board up this window until you can get it repaired. "Hey, we've got some blood here, on the sill. I'll call forensics to collect a sample. Can't hurt to have hard evidence."

Better than saliva off a coffee cup, she thought. It didn't matter. Her plan had worked. Maybe not exactly according to plan, but well enough. Marcus Leeland was in custody. It was over. The tears had dried, and she'd stopped trembling. Detective Mott was right; she'd been lucky. It could have turned out a lot differently.

Standing in the open doorway, she watched as the last cruiser pulled away, taking the detectives with them. No pulsing lights now, no squeal of tires.

The crowd had pretty much dispersed. The excitement, the threat, was over. She'd tacked cardboard over the broken window, and re-bolted the door; it would do until tomorrow.

Tomorrow. The neighbors would talk about this over breakfast, at work. They would read about a killer's capture in the paper, watch it on TV. Eric Grant might even write a follow up story. His piece in the Tribune had begun all this; why not?

She stood in the doorway for another few seconds. The last of the stragglers had gone, leaving the street dark and silent. Naomi went inside and locked the door. Now that she was

alone, she sank down on the sofa and dissolved into a fresh bucket of tears.

When she was cried out, she went into the kitchen and drained the last of the coffee Karen Henderson had made into her cup and heated it up in the microwave. Not much chance she'd be sleeping tonight. She thought about phoning Lisa with the good news, but decided it could wait until morning. She wondered if Debbie Banks was back home. It would be a small bit of closure for her. And maybe for Marie Davis' family, too. She hoped so.

Naomi turned around and saw a skittish Molly standing near the door leading into the kitchen, hackles slightly raised, wary. "It's over, Molly. He's behind bars."

Naomi scooped her up in her arms and stroked her soft, silky fur until she settled down. But she didn't purr and her ears twitched nervously, the end of her tail flicking back and forth. It had been a traumatic night for both of them.

As if to punctuate the thought, the phone rang, and Molly sprang from her arms, landing the full length of the floor, leaving a deep scratch on the back of her hand in the process. Beads of blood bubbled up as Naomi picked up the receiver, the scratch just now beginning to sting in earnest. She blew on it. "Hello."

Molly's nerves were as raw as her own. Reporters already? she thought. But it was Frank calling her. "Naomi, I just heard. Are you okay?" She was glad to hear from him. But rather than feeling jubilant, she felt only relief.

"I am now. Now that they've got him in custody."

"That's why I'm calling. They don't have him. There's been a terrible mistake."

She heard her own nervous laugh. "No, no you're wrong, Frank. I saw them take him away in handcuffs. He..."

"That wasn't Leeland."

She felt the blood drain from her body, as if someone had actually attached a hose to her and siphoned it out. "What?" she whispered.

"I'm sorry. I was worried about you and I hired a friend of mine to keep an eye on the house."

The dark blue car she passed, parked across the street flashed in her mind. She'd thought it might be Leeland.

"He saw the guy come crashing through your window and took off after him through the back lot."

"You hired someone?" she said stupidly, as the full implication of what he was telling her began to sink in.

"He a bouncer and sometime bodyguard, name of Eldon Carpenter. Good guy. I knew you'd resent the interference, but Lili would never forgive me if I let anything happen to you. I'd never forgive myself. Naomi..."

"How do you know this, Frank? That the man they caught is this Eldon Carpenter?" Her mind was spinning. How could this be? Please let Frank be wrong.

"He just phoned me from the jail. I'm on my way there now to get him released. I wanted to call you first. Lock your doors, honey. He's still out there."

Chapter Forty-Six

A numbing coldness spread through her as if she'd just been plunged into ice water. Stunned, she could only stand there unable to think clearly. Then, as the full impact of his words hit, she dropped the receiver into the cradle and bolted for the kitchen to wedge the chair back under the doorknob as she'd done in those first days.

But it was too late. She hadn't quite reached the door when she saw the knob turn.

Chapter Forty-Seven

Lisa sat up late, drinking coffee and thinking about Naomi, and wondering why she'd not heard from Eric Grant. And then she turned on the local news and saw that a man had broken into a house on Elizabeth Avenue and was in police custody.

Marcus Leeland, she thought. Thank God. Naomi's plan had worked. She smiled to herself, teary with relief. She wanted to call her but she was probably sleeping by now, exhausted. She'd call in the morning.

* * *

Retired Sergeant Graham Nelson was listening to his police-band radio when the call came in about an intruder at 233 Elizabeth Avenue. Apparently, the resident of the home had him trapped in one of the rooms and he jumped out of the window, but they ran him down. There were a few chuckles amidst the crackling, broken up by static. They'd nailed the son-of-a-bitch and that was what really mattered. He could stop worrying about Naomi Waters.

He was watching CNN when the phone rang. It was Eric Grant, looking for details and Graham's were sparse, except that it was pretty clear they'd got the guy. Eric had dropped by earlier to see him. Graham was always glad to see the reporter, he was good company, and it was clear he was pretty gone on Naomi Waters, despite having seen her only a couple of times.

"I got an email from Lisa Boyce," he said, "formerly Lisa Cameron…"

"The school friend Mary Rose was visiting that night…" Graham filled in. "Yeah, she's pretty worried about Naomi. I could call her; her phone number is in the book," Eric said, "But it's pretty late. Especially considering the crisis is over. I replied to her email."

They talked a few minutes longer then bid each other a good night. But something didn't quite sit right with the retired policeman. For nearly thirty years the guy evades capture, and suddenly it's all wrapped up, tied with a bow? Well, okay, it happened from time to time. But it was rare. Rarer than rare.

"God Nelse, you still up," Angie said, crossing from the bedroom to the bathroom, which was off the hallway. She wore striped pajamas and a ponytail and looked twelve. And she was telling him what time to go to bed.

Chapter Forty-Eight

Terror-stricken, Naomi watched as the door slowly opened. A cool draft brushed her ankles, freezing her in place, drowning her in panic. He's here. Her legs had liquefied and she knew if she tried to run, she would fall.

And then he was standing in her doorway, filling it, his face bloodied and contorted with controlled rage. His smile was the smile of a demon. "Hello, little girl."

He does have supernatural powers, she thought. I was wrong to doubt it. Otherwise, how could be he here now? Why wasn't he in jail?

It was a good plan. It worked; I locked him in. But he was here now. He's an evil entity no one can stop. No, no, Naomi, the voice in her head argued. He's clever, is all. He's had years of practice.

Savoring her terror, her shock at seeing him, he made no move toward her.

Stay calm. Think. The stairs were behind her. Her knees would not betray her. She needed to get him talking. Get him off-guard. Maybe there was a chance.

"The cops know who you are, Marcus. They know you killed Mary Rose." In spite of her constricted vocal chords, her voice was surprisingly even, strong.

"Marcus," he said with a smirk. "No one calls me that

anymore. My mother was in some dumb Shakespeare play in school and liked the name, so she saddled me with it. You can call me Mac. For as long as you're going to be around. No, they don't know I killed Mary Rose. They only know what you told them. And if you're not here..."

"They know you killed Marie Davis, too. And your old friend, Norman Banks. You slit his throat. What kind of a man...?"

He took a step toward her, cutting off her words. She backed up. She didn't stumble. Almost.

"They got nothin'," he sneered, wiping his mouth with the back of his hand, smearing more blood across his face. Broken glass gleamed in his hair, and his hands were bleeding. She could smell the sourness off him, the blood.

"You're the only one giving me trouble, Missy. The only one who can tie me to anything. But that's just about to end."

He took another step, and the floor creaked the way it always did when you stepped on that spot. The sound acted as a spur to Naomi and she whirled round and raced toward the stairs; he lunged after her. His hand caught the back of her shirt, and for one heart-stopping second she was sure he was going to pull her backwards, but she managed to grab hold of the railing and yank herself free of him. She flew up the stairs, taking them two at a time.

Behind her, he yelled, "It won't do you any good to run. You can't get away."

She could hear his footsteps on the stairs behind her, soft and terrifying. But there was a hesitation in his step thump...drop...

thump…drop; he was limping. Enough to slow him down. Otherwise, he'd have had her. He must have done himself some injury when he jumped out that window, aside from the cuts and bruises.

She was on the landing now, heart racing, her hand slippery on the rail. Behind her, his step was faltering, pained, his own breathing harsh. Like something dead brought back to life, impossible to stop. Coming after her. Not satisfied until she was beneath the ground too. She looked over her shoulder, unable not to.

"You know you brought this on yourself, don't you," he called up to her. "I gave you a chance to save yourself, but you couldn't leave it alone. Think you're pretty clever, don't you,

showing up at my work. Laughing at me. Playing your games. Baiting me. Well, here I am, little girl, your catch of the day."

Spittle had formed at the corner of his mouth and his laugh was a mad sound that raised the hairs on the back of her neck. As she ran toward her room, his words followed after her.

"You should never have been born. You were a mistake. My mistake because I didn't make sure the bitch was dead. And now you have to disappear forever."

Before ducking into her bedroom, she took a last look behind her, just long enough to see his enormous shadow climbing the staircase wall, and then she was inside her room, slamming and bolting her door. But she knew it wouldn't keep him out, not for long. She sprinted across the room to the dresser. She would use it to bar the door. But could she move it by herself? It was antique, a heavy old thing, but she'd always loved it. Her mother used to help her to move it when it came time for a thorough cleaning, or to paint the walls. But adrenalin, born of terror coursed through her body, giving her strength to do what she needed to do.

She quickly took everything from the top of the dresser and she set them on the floor. She jerked the dresser out from the wall, first one side and then the other. Inch by inch. Behind her, the doorknob rattled violently in its casing, travelled along her nerve endings.

Having pushed the dresser a good foot out from the wall, now she around ran to the other side, pushing and straining with everything in her. It moved. Then moved again. At last it was out far enough so that she could get behind it. Putting all her weight into it, she shoved as hard as she could, praying the dresser would keep moving, at the same time terrified it would topple over, crash to the floor and break into pieces.

He was pounding so hard on the door it appeared in her mind to bulge in its casing, causing the very walls in the room to vibrate. She took her hands from the dresser and clamped them over her ears to shut out the madness.

The doorknob blurred through her tears as it twisted back and forth, rattle wildly, with the mindless rage of some kind of poltergeist.

She was doing it again. Crediting him with supernatural powers, when in reality he was just a man, albeit a sick, vile man. She swiped at her tears with her shirt cuff, pushed again at the mountainous dresser in front of her. Finally, it moved almost smoothly across the hardwood floor. Keeping her feet solidly under her, she willed the thing to keep going. At one point, when she was nearly at the door, it simply stopped, and all her straining and grunting couldn't jar it another inch. Her arms and shoulders ached with the effort of pushing. There must be a bump in the floor, she thought, and went back to moving it little by little, first on one side, then the other. It worked. Once more, the dresser began to slide across the floor.

Ignoring the throbbing ache in her arms and shoulders, and the insane pounding on the door, using every ounce of muscle and will she possessed, she gave a final push. Finally, bathed in a lather of perspiration, breathless, mouth and throat dry as sandpaper, she had barricaded the door.

She heard him give a frustrated thump against it as if he knew, could see through the door, and Naomi took a couple of backward steps on trembling legs and sagged down on the bed. She could see herself in the vanity mirror. Her hair had come out of its coil and lay like a warm, wet washcloth on the nape of her neck. Her shirt was glued to her body. Through dry lips, she called out, "I'm phoning the police."

He laughed. "I've been in your room, remember? Remember poor kitty?" he mocked. "You don't have a phone in there. And we both heard your cell phone ringing. It was in your purse, in the kitchen. You don't have it. Good try."

"Just plug this into any electrical outlet," Lisa had said. "It'll stay charged. Keep it close to you."

She envisioned her purse with the cell phone inside, stuffed behind the cereal in the cupboard. How could she have been so stupid? But she hadn't thought she would need the phone. She'd believed they had him.

"Naomi," he said through the door, his voice soft now, confident, "you can't get away. I have to give you credit, though, that was a pretty good trick making me think you were in there recording one of those books. But that was your one shot, and it didn't quite work, did it?"

The bastard loved the sound of his own voice. She didn't answer.

There was silence from the other side of the door. Then, "You need to open the door. I won't hurt you, I promise. I just want to talk... you'll at least talk to me, won't you? After all, I am your father."

"No, you're not," she said coldly. "Sperm doesn't make you a father."

He laughed. "Yeah, you're right. You're a smart girl, I can't fool you with that kind of slippery talk, can I? So you can see that I have no choice but to kill you. I could just burn the house down, but you've put the cops onto me now and the fire engines would be here at the first puff of smoke. I've already thought of that so I drove the van up close to the back door. I'll just take your body somewhere and bury it. You are a freak accident; you know that, don't you? It's only a fluke that you're on the planet."

"Go to hell," she called through the door. The words came of their own volition, out of rage at all the pain this man had perpetrated. "That's where you belong. The police know by now that they have the wrong person. They'll be back, you bastard."

"Oh, aren't you a little terror. Like your mom. She was a scrapper, too you know. Oh, yeah, fought me good. Hands clawin' and feet kickin'. Screamed like a bloody banshee. Ah, didn't do her any good though. Just like it won't do you any good. You can't escape. Oh, I suppose you could jump out your window, maybe just break a few bones. Or maybe your neck." He laughed again, a chilling, mad sound.

His cruel words describing Mary Rose's last moments on earth had brought tears to her eyes, anger flooding through her veins.

"Open the door, now, Missy. Talk to Daddy."

At his chilling voice, filled with his madness, her courage was momentarily shaken. He was the devil incarnate. How could she fight him?

He was rattling the door again. Banging on it, every thump of his fist more terrifying then the last. She could feel the rage growing in him like a giant forest fire, threatening to devour her and everything in its path. He cursed her through the door, curses so vile, Naomi's flesh crawled and she looked to the photo of Thomas on her night table, for help. Thomas had been there for her so many times throughout her young life, or at least so she had believed. But perhaps it was that belief that had given him the magic.

Leeland was right about one thing; there was nowhere to go

but out the window. And she probably would break her neck.

It had gone totally silent again on his side of the door. She wondered if he was still out there. What he was up to?

The answer came at once as she heard Molly's stress-filled cries outside the door. Her heart sank. Oh, Molly. I should have left you at Lisa's; she had wanted me too, but I didn't want to take further advantage of her kindness.

"I have your furry friend," he said calmly, like he was talking about the weather. "I'm going to count to five. I'm going to count to five. I'm done playing with you. If you haven't opened the door by then I will surgically remove one of kitty's pretty green eyes."

Horror speared her heart and she was off the bed. She knew he wouldn't hesitate to carry out his threat. On the contrary, he would take pleasure in it. She fought back tears of frustration and helplessness. She'd brought this about and she wasn't going to start bawling like a kid. She simply was not. She needed to do something. Oh, Molly. I'm so sorry.

"One."

"Please don't hurt her," she pleaded. Silence.

"Two."

She glanced desperately at Thomas' photo. *What can I do? Help me?* She swallowed against the dryness in her mouth. "Please."

"It's up to you," he said softly through the door. "You just have to open the door. "She had managed to stop her tears, and now if she could just quiet the screams in her head because it was impossible to think over them.

"Four."

She put her face against the door. "All right. I'll open it. I have to move the dresser away first. It's heavy." She moved one corner of it so he could hear the scraping on the floor. She prayed he would believe her.

He didn't reply. Molly gave a plaintive meow through the door.

I have to do something. Surprise him somehow. He's confident now, sure I'll open the door. Again her eyes sought Thomas' in the photo. As if he had spoken, she suddenly knew what might work. It was a chance. Her eyes darted around the room, settled on the stool by the vanity.

"Four-and-a-half," Leeland said through the door. "Last warning."

On the second syllable in the word, warning, she picked up the vanity stool with both hands, and putting every ounce of force she had behind the effort, she hurled it through the window. At the explosion of glass, Molly let out a startled yowl from behind the door, and her captor yelped and cursed. Incredible relief flowed through her. She's got away. She clawed him and got away. She was crying without knowing it, wiped her eyes with the back of her hand.

Good for you, Molly. You are one smart cat. Some of the pressure rolled off her and she grew hopeful again. They'd both been given a reprieve.

With the tiny shards of glass still tinkling to the floor following the shattering of the window, the silence seemed even more profound. The soft air came in the window, gently lifting the lacy curtains as if with an invisible hand. She prayed one of her neighbors had heard the crash and called for help. Please let someone have insomnia.

Drawn to her house earlier by the commotion and wailing sirens, maybe one of her neighbors was still up, still too excited at the change in the night's routine, to sleep. Yet it seemed unlikely. The police led us all to believe they had their man, and the threat was over. We could all sleep safely.

But she had heard something. For a brief instant, over Molly's howls, she was sure she'd heard the squeal of brakes out on the street. But that didn't mean they wouldn't just keep going.

There was no sound outside her door now. Would he believe she had actually jumped? She waited, eyes glued to the door. The night air was soothing at her back, unsticking her shirt from her body.

A bone-chilling whomp against the door made her heart jump in response, her throat close. Obviously, he didn't buy that she had jumped out the window. She'd barely taken a breath

when once again he threw himself against the door again, hard this time if possible, actually splintering the panel in the door, as if Satan himself were his ally, lending him superhuman strength. He was hurt, he was wounded, and yet he kept on. My God, she thought, this old oak door has endured for over 100 years.

Desperate, she plastered herself against the dresser, trying to hold it in place, as if she could, every aching muscle taut and straining. The third body-slam tore the screws out of the bolt, cracking the wood around it, sending her backwards into the room. Each time he rammed the door, the dresser moved away from it, just a little more.

Naomi scanned the room for a weapon, something she could use to defend herself. Panic was making it hard to think. She zeroed in on the monkey totem, on the floor where she'd set it. She'd bought it at a yard sale a couple of summers ago.

Another body-slam, and more splintering of wood.

Naomi crossed the floor and grabbed up the totem like it was a baseball bat and she was Mickey Mantle. One hand closed around the head of the top monkey, See No Evil, who had his hands over his eyes, while the left hand closed over Hear No Evil. Speak No Evil was free to witness.

Carved from teak, one of the hardest of woods, so the man who sold it to her had assured her, it had a satisfying heft in her hands. The square, heavy base had the best chance of doing damage, she thought, stepping quietly to the side of the door so she'd be behind it when it opened. The totem gripped in moist hands, she did just what Mickey Mantle would do she wiped the dampness from her hands onto her pants, and took a better hold.

She wasn't a violent person. Could she do this? You'd better, she told herself. You'd better aim it well and bring it across his head just as hard as you can. As if your life depended on it. Because it does.

The dresser moved again, and this time his huge, bloodied

hand with its hairy wrist wormed its way through the splintered wood. As if the hand and wrist were a deadly snake seeking her out, Naomi struck swiftly with the totem, bringing it across his wrist. The crack of the wood against wrist bone was sickeningly loud, the howl accompanying it equally so, louder even than Molly's, and somehow enormously satisfying.

He snapped his hand back, cursed her. Feeling proud of herself, fearless, she raised the totem again. Come on, you son-of-bitch. Stick it through again. Stick you damn head through, why don't you?

It was at that moment that she heard what sounded like a gunshot out in the hallway, followed by another, louder wail of pain. Then Leeland's pleas, "Hey, man, take it easy, don't..."

"Get down," a vaguely familiar voice bellowed. "Down on the floor now and put your hands behind your back, or the next bullet will go right between your eyes."

"Sure, sure. Don't shoot, okay? Don't shoot." Naomi peered through the crack in the door.

She lowered her totem cautiously, peered through the hole again to be sure that what she had seen and heard were real, and not a figment of her imagination. Some wishful thinking on her part. But no, Sergeant Nelson was still standing in her hallway, looking more beautiful than Clint Eastwood, a gun trained on the killer. She dropped the totem to push one side of the dresser away from the broken door enough so that it swung open.

Marcus Leeland was belly-down on the hall floor. His face

turned toward her, she could see the tell-tale four claw marks from Molly, deep and nasty, on his face. His hands were cuffed behind his back. Sergeant Nelson was relating the situation over his cell phone, then he snapped it closed.

"You okay?" he asked her, not taking his eyes from his prisoner.

"She came farther out into the hallway. Saw the blood seeping from Leeland's thigh where he'd taken a bullet. "Y-- yeah, I'm fine. How did you...?"

"I'll tell you all about it later."

For the second time that night, Naomi heard police sirens screaming through the streets of River's End.

Chapter Forty-Nine

After the police led Marcus Leeland away in handcuffs, Sergeant Nelson sat with Naomi in her kitchen and explained over herbal tea how he knew the police had taken down the wrong man.

"Well, I didn't know, actually," he said in answer to her question, "it was a hunch mainly. Something just didn't add up. You don't get a guy who's been eluding police for more than two decades, that easily. Not in my experience anyway. It was possible, but my gut said something was off, so I figured I'd just take a drive by your place.

"Thank God, you did," she said, feeling surprisingly calm, considering. "What a coincidence that you just happened…"

"Not such a coincidence," he interrupted. "I've actually driven past your house quite often, lately. Can't sleep anyway. I don't do retirement well. I'm thinking I might get into the private investigator business. Anyway, as luck would have it, I was within yards of your house when that footstool came sailing through the window and damn near through my windshield. I didn't know what it was then, of course, till I got out of the car."

"I thought I'd heard the squeal of brakes. I'm so glad I missed your windshield."

"That makes two of us," he grinned. "By the time I got up those stairs, Leeland seemed to be getting the worst of it. I think if he'd gotten through that door, you would have brained him with that thing in your hand. What was it, anyway?"

"A totem. The three wise monkeys." "A totem? Hmmph. I like the irony."

She laughed. "Not the native Indian kind. Of Chinese origin, actually. I looked it up one time. Many scholars believe they were carved as a visual representation of the religious principle, "If we do not hear, see, or speak of evil, we ourselves shall be spared all evil."

"Sounds like burying your head in the sand to me. Anyway, my first bit of excitement in a while. Like I said, I've been going stir crazy with nothing to do but lie around and listen to my heart beat, so I should be thanking you. And by the way, don't give me all the credit. Young fellow works at the paper, name of Eric Grant was pretty concerned about you, kept in touch with me. Matter of fact, he called me tonight after getting an urgent email from Lisa Boyce. He wasn't getting any cooperation at the station, so he phoned me at home. We've sort of become buddies," he grinned. "He's about the only one around who doesn't treat me like a sick old man. I'm grateful for his company."

At the mention of Eric's name, Naomi felt a flush to her cheeks. "Eric Grant called you?"

"Sure did. It was his dogged persistence that made me take a renewed interest in your case. Even though we both knew it couldn't be in any official capacity. Much to Angela's consternation," he laughed. "I love her to pieces, but it'll be great to move back into my own place. I'm too old to be bossed around by my kid sister."

"Well, she's obviously taking good care of you because you look great."

"Yeah, I owe her. My life probably. You're a persistent woman, yourself, Naomi. Leeland didn't stand a chance with you on the case. Both your moms would be proud of you."

"Thanks, that's really sweet of you to say, Sergeant Nelson."
"It's only the truth. And call me Graham."

He was a good man, and a wonderful policeman, retired or not. She was glad he hadn't given up on her.

"I think you'll make a great private investigator, Graham. Do the doctors think you're well enough? I mean, you look good but..."

"I'm doing okay. Better than I probably should. You're a pretty sharp detective yourself, maybe you'll join me."

He was the second one to suggest it. "I don't think so," she smiled. She was flattered, but not remotely interested. She just wanted her life back.

Pale light filtered through the slats in the living room shades when he rose to leave, telling her his sister would be calling the cops on him. "Try and get some sleep," he said.

At the door, Naomi hugged him and could feel the slimness of his frame through his clothes. The paunch was gone, and his color was good. She had a feeling he was going to be just fine. Better than fine, she'd venture. She walked him to the door and on opening it, saw the footstool near the telephone pole, smashed to bits, held together by material, legs askew.

"I'll always be grateful to whatever force made you drive by my house tonight."

"Like I said, I've been cruising your neighborhood at all hours on pretty much a regular basis. But who knows? Other elements might have been at work. Since the heart attack, I've been rethinking a lot of things lately."

"Oh? Like what?"

"I have my own version of the 'white light' theory. Remind me to tell you about it sometime. Good night, Naomi."

"Good night, Sergeant."

Chapter Fifty

Naomi was more than prepared to go to trial to make sure Marcus Leeland went to prison, but it had proved unnecessary. Frank phoned and told her Leeland had pleaded guilty to the abduction and rape of Mary Rose. They would never have nailed him for Norman Banks' murder, or Marie Davis' so you are directly responsible for getting this killer off the streets. He knew it was over. You can put a period to this whole thing now. You have closure."

Closure is an odd word. Because there wasn't really any closure for something like this. How could there be? Marcus Leeland's victims had died violently at his hands, leaving others to grieve the loss. But Naomi did feel a sense of relief and satisfaction knowing he would be in jail until he was a very old man, and would probably die in there. Mary Rose was finally getting the justice she deserved, and Leeland wouldn't be hurting anyone else.

She'd been right about Charlotte; she didn't hear from her again. As far as Edna was concerned, Naomi was satisfied to let her live with her own conscience. She no longer has the power to hurt me, to make me feel badly about myself. It was all the same to her if she never saw Edna again, and she knew Edna felt the same way. But she refused to let her past dictate her future. She was looking forward to a new chapter in her life. She still could hardly believe the phone call today. She was bursting with her exciting news and anxious for her guests to arrive.

The lasagna was just about done, the salad tossed and the table set. She could smell the good smell coming up from downstairs. Her guests would be here soon. She had thought with the weather so nice that a backyard barbecue might be fun, but somehow the occasion of a new beginning seemed to call for something a little more formal.

Besides, she'd promised Lisa that lasagna dinner.

She liked her reflection in the mirror. She'd splurged on a new mint-green, silk shirtdress, and Prada sandals with slim ankle straps. She lost a bit too much weight over the past weeks but it did the dress justice. The color brought out the green of her eyes.

She did a little twirl, and the skirt flowed around her legs like water. With her hair falling to her shoulders, brushed to a sheen, she almost didn't recognize herself. She couldn't remember the last time she'd dressed up. She brushed on a little blush to enhance her cheekbones, a sweep of mascara, a touch of cranberry mist to her lips. A dab of perfume behind her ears.

She fastened the pendant around her neck. The talisman meant to keep Mary Rose safe. It failed, but it had followed a killer through the years to his eventual capture. Evil can seem more powerful than good sometimes. But she refused to believe that. Evil destroys. Good builds.

The pendant went nicely with the dress, and with her hair loose. Like it belonged.

The doorbell rang downstairs and she gave herself a final

check in the mirror, as nervous as a teenager on her first date. Then she hurried from the room, hesitated in the bedroom doorway and looked back at Thomas' photo on the night table. At the young man with his kind face, who looked so young. And who was no longer even in the world. Crazy or not, she had bonded with him, a young man in a photo. His smile told her she looked very nice in the new dress, and that he was proud of her. She gazed at him a moment longer, smiled and said, "Thanks, Daddy," and quietly closed the door.

She couldn't deny the electricity that swept through her when she opened the door to Eric Grant, rendering her suddenly shy. He looked so handsome in a blue, open-necked shirt and light grey slacks and jacket, holding a lovely bouquet of wildflowers and a bottle of wine. He smelled wonderful too, musky with just a hint of lime. Not bad for a Viking, she mused.

"What's so funny?" he asked, smiling at her, handing her his offerings.

"I'm just happy you're here." Looking into his eyes, she knew that he was more than a little glad to see her, too.

"You look even more gorgeous than I remember," he told her. "And I didn't think that was possible."

She practically floated through the evening. Her lasagna had never turned out better, and the Caesar salad with thick slices of garlic bread completed the meal. Except for the insanely good chocolate mousse with real whipped cream, which Lisa had insisted on bringing. She looked lovely in a blue linen dress and pearls. She was positively glowing and it was easy to see why. Graham Nelson couldn't seem to take his eyes off her, nor she him. The irony wasn't lost on Naomi. Love was in the air.

The summer bouquet of flowers made a lovely centerpiece on the white linen tablecloth. Her mother's silverware glittered, and the glasses of red wine glowed ruby red in the reflected candlelight. Classical music floated softly from the sound system. The evening was all she'd hoped it would be, and more. Not so bad for a novice, she thought, admiring both the table and the people seated around it, laughing and talking, and eating.

Frank had brought a friend, a nice woman he'd met recently, a retired teacher, petite and a bit of a chatterbox. So different from her mother, at least on the surface. Mom would have been pleased for Frank that he'd met someone he found companionable. Maybe the loneliness had got too much after he'd had to put Sam to sleep.

The conversation flowed as easily as the wine, and had turned to Eric's writing. Lisa was praising his book to the table at large. Laura, Frank's friend added her own rave review, along with some insightful comments on his handling of the material, revealing the teacher she had been for over thirty years. Eric was sweet and modest in his response, but obviously pleased, as he thanked them for their kind words.

Every so often she would look across at him, and he'd be looking at her, a grin playing at the corners of his very nice mouth, desire in his blue eyes that stirred her own blood. That certain shyness that came across in his photo on the back cover of his book was there too.

She'd read the book finally, and could only add her praise to Lisa's. She had been moved by his depth and sensitivity. Though he'd lived through a hellish childhood, never once did she detect any note of self-pity coming off those pages, yet his pain was palpable, even through the humor he used to mask it.

Graham made a joke and Lisa laughed, maybe a little more boisterously than the joke warranted. Naomi caught Eric's eye and he gave her a knowing smile.

Lisa noticed the exchange and blushed. "So what book are you narrating presently, honey?" she asked, turning the attention away from herself and giving Naomi the in, she was hoping for to share her good news.

"I won't be narrating novels for awhile," she said. "Earlier today, I got a call from the university offering me a job. Well, it's more than a job, really, at least to me."

"Well, don't keep us in suspense," Graham (whom she still thought of as Sergeant Nelson) smiled, as he dabbed the corners of his mouth with a napkin. "You teaching a course?"

"No. Researchers plan to create a volume of Mi'kmaq stories that will be made available to the public, and benefit future generations. "Enid Bernard, a Mi'kmaq teacher," she said, unable to keep the excitement from her voice, "has joined up with other researchers and over the next several years, they plan to record conversations with those fluent in the Mi'kmaq language. The interviews with elders will focus on what past life was like for First

Nations' peoples. Some stories are handed down, some presently lived. Legends will be recorded, even recipes and old methods of healing. Anyway, I've been asked to narrate those stories in English."

There were enthusiastic congratulations around the table. Frank raised his glass in a toast, and the others followed. "To the future," he said. "To the future," they all said and clinked glasses together and drank the wine.

"You're the perfect one to do this," Lisa said, beaming at her. "I'm so thrilled for you. They're lucky to have you."

"Thanks. But I'm the lucky one. To be a part of this project." Naomi had never wanted anything more. It felt like her destiny. In fact, this whole night, this very moment, felt destined. She was eager to embrace her roots, to make them a part of her, to become complete. Of course there was another side of her too, the side that was related to the Leelands. She couldn't ignore that reality. But she had no interest in exploring it. As far as Naomi was concerned, Marcus Leeland had chosen the life he lived. At some point there was a first time for him to make a decision over good and evil, and he chose evil. And then he chose it again. And again. More and more he became what he did, and like an eclipse of the sun, the darker part of him soon blocked out the light, until only the darkness remained.

Edna had been questioned by the police, but she held to her lie that she found the pendant on the beach. She could not admit to having once dated Marcus Leeland and said as much right to Frank's face, even knowing he knew the truth. Whatever happened back then, it would remain her secret. But secrets can eat at your soul, and have a way of unearthing themselves eventually.

Naomi preferred to live in the light. She had much to be thankful for.

Sitting here at what had been her mother's dining table, now hers, so many emotions swept through her it was hard to pin one down. She wished her mother were here to share in her happiness, to meet her friends, to meet Eric. But who's to say she wasn't?

She could imagine children sitting around this table one day. A real family. Her family.

She no longer felt the pressing urgency of Mary Rose's presence, and knew there would be no more disturbing dreams. Mary Rose could rest now.

And so can I, she thought. So can I.

"Would anyone like more wine?" she asked around the table.

The End

About the Author

As well as penning Award-winning suspense novels including Chill Waters, Nowhere To Hide and Listen to the Shadows, Joan Hall Hovey's articles and short stories have appeared in such diverse publications as The Reader, Atlantic Advocate, The Toronto Star, Mystery Scene, True Confessions, Home Life magazine, Seek and various other magazines and newspapers. Her short story, "Dark Reunion" was selected for the Anthology, Investigating Women, published by Simon & Pierre. Joan lives in New Brunswick, Canada with her husband Mel and dog, Scamp.

From the Publisher

Thank you for purchasing and reading this Books We Love novel. We hope you have enjoyed your reading experience. *Best Regards and Happy Reading, Jamie and Jude*

Books We Love and Books We Love Spice

http://bookswelove.com

http://spicewelove.com